SLEEP SWEET
A STEAMY MILITARY ROMANCE

ERICA EASTON

Copyright © 2026 by Erica Easton
All rights reserved.

Visit my website at www.ericaeaston.com
Developmental Editor and Proofreader: Rachel Rowlands
Editor and Formatter: Jovana Shirley, Unforeseen Editing
(www.unforseenediting.com)
Cover Design by Andy Payne
Published by Hot Pants Romance, LLC

No part of this book may be reproduced or transmitted in any form or by any means, electronic or mechanical, including photocopying, recording, or by any information storage and retrieval system without the written permission of the author, except for the use of brief quotations in a book review.

Additionally, please note that no part of this book may be used or reproduced in any form or by any means for the purpose of training artificial intelligence systems or technology.
Thank you for complying with copyright laws.

This book is a work of fiction. Names, characters, places, and incidents either are products of the author's imagination or are used fictitiously. Any resemblance to actual persons, living or dead, events, or locales is entirely coincidental.

ISBN-13: 979-8-9930931-0-9

*For all the good girls searching for their anchor.
Stop looking and let it find you.
It should help keep you steady, but never tie you down.
Unless you like being tied down, that is ...*

Playlist

"There She Goes"—The La's
"Intuition"—Jewel
"what do you need"—Hailey Knox
"angel"—Camylio
"Powers"—Lostcrowboy
"Sailor Song"—Gigi Perez
"Yoü and I"—Lady Gaga
"run for the hills"—Tate McRae
"Available for Me"—Hailey Knox
"Mr. Sandman"—SYML
"Austin (Boots Stop Workin')"—Dasha
"Always Something There to Remind Me (2018 Remaster)"—Naked Eyes
"Jessie's Girl"—Rick Springfield
"Gateway Drug"—Daniel Seavey
"I Wanna Know"—NOTD, featuring Bea Miller
"You're Somebody Else"—Flora Cash
"Figure You Out"—VOILÀ
"Crash into Me"—Dave Matthews Band
"Ultraviolet"—Freya Ridings
"Guest Room"—Echos
"Please"—OMIDO & Ex Habit
"Distance"—Boys of Fall
"Who Will Save Your Soul"—Jewel
"Tummy Hurts"—Reneé Rapp
"Right for Us"—VOILÀ
"Control"—Natalie Taylor
"Walk This World with Me"—The Home Team
"Little Did I Know"—Julia Michaels
"You Were Meant for Me"—Jewel

Author's Note

SLEEP SWEET IS INTENDED FOR readers 18+. It contains mature themes, profanity, and sexually explicit content. This story also includes, but is not limited to, subjects of addiction, mental health, post-traumatic stress disorder, obsession, intimacy, abuse of power, and morally gray behavior.

Additionally, there are brief mentions of childhood neglect.

Please use this knowledge to ensure this story is the right one for you.

Prologue

Elle

"THERE ARE SEVERAL THINGS I am about to tell you, and I need you to listen to them very carefully."

"Okay, you're scaring me," I admitted.

I wasn't afraid of him, but of what I might learn from him. Gentle giants often harbored dangerous secrets behind their facades.

"I want you to know that Recruit Jenkins is safe. He wasn't injured in any way, and you do not need to worry about his well-being. He's fine. Unfortunately, that doesn't change the fact that you aren't allowed to see him."

The words, meant to help me, further salted my fresh wound. Why couldn't I see him? My heart pounded as anticipation pricked my flesh from the inside out. The uniformed man who sat beside me at his desk wasn't touching me, but his statement still burned my skin. His right leg inched closer to mine, leaving our knees less than a foot apart.

"It speaks volumes of your character and dedication that you came today. Those traits can't be faked. You should be incredibly proud to possess them," he said.

My shoulders dropped as I attempted to piece together his verbal puzzle; nothing fit where it should have.

"What I'm about to show you is government property. There are extreme consequences for both of us if you speak a word of this to anyone." His warning came wrapped in a threatening tone.

This is it, I thought.

The information I'd kill for.

"I've weighed the pros and cons of sharing this with you, but I feel strongly that you deserve to see it with your own eyes. I would want to see it with mine if I were in your position. I'm asking for your verbal agreement. You must promise to keep this discussion—and the evidence in this office—a secret. Speak of it with no one, aside from me. Do you agree?" The quiver in his voice betrayed him.

"Yes, yes, I'll keep my mouth shut. Just tell me already!" I nodded, knowing it looked more like a pathetic beg. I'd give my last breath to find out what had happened, so agreeing to keep things between us was the easiest choice I'd made all day.

"One more thing, Elle." He paused.

I braced for the impact, knowing that whatever came next had the potential to destroy me. Destroy us.

"What you are about to witness is going to hurt you. It didn't hurt him, but it will hurt you." His palm met my knee before he continued, "One day, you will look back on this moment and realize it was one of the best of your life. Integrity is built, not born. You will get through this in time, I promise you."

"Enough! Fucking show me already." I was tired of the endless detours getting in the way.

I was ready to know.

I deserved the truth.

A solemn, silent nod indicated he'd received both my agreement and annoyance. He'd briefed me on what was to come, even if I had no idea what he was warning me about. The time for caution was over and done. I watched intently as he clicked his mouse a few times and closed all the open programs on his computer, aside from one central window. He clicked the mute button first, followed by a puny triangle that brought the video to life. One day, perhaps I'd be thankful for the security footage that would forever tether my soul to his.

March 31, 2012, was not that day.

ONE

Elle

January 2010
Two Years before He Left

COASTAL PENSACOLA COLLEGE WASN'T PART of the Ivy League or the most competitive school on the East Coast. It was, however, one of the most picturesque campuses in Florida—at least, I'd always thought so, having grown up practically next door. The institution was a beachside melting pot of locals, military-bound students, and out-of-state prospects who would pay big money to attend a school centered between the Naval Air Station and the Alabama border.

Citywide Mardi Gras celebrations, the Blue Angels, and seafood pulled straight from the Gulf were a few of the things I loved most about growing up in Pensacola. A hop and a skip from New Orleans, the graffiti-kissed cityscape also got more seasonal variation than expected from the Sunshine State, which was a huge benefit for people wanting the coastal lifestyle without the hot-as-balls year-round heat.

Perhaps the biggest draw of all though was the city being home to multiple military bases, overflowing with an endless variety of handsome, professional men in uniform. At least, that was what the influx of young female prospects from across the country must've thought as they hovered around the recruiting booth set up on the campus's main lawn the day I met Jesse Jenkins.

The day he crashed into me and I fell.

My morning walk to class began the way it always did, with one exception.

One of the two uniformed men manning the booth asked the sea of faces, "Excuse me, have you given any thought to joining the Navy after graduation?"

It was somewhere between a command and a shout, landing on everyone and no one specific at the same time. The quieter serviceman, standing several heads higher than his counterpart, was the main attraction, garnering interest from students at an impressive rate. It wasn't hard to see why. Prickles of potential fell down my spine. The guy was a total smokeshow.

The perfectly groomed, much larger man said very little. His presence said it all for him. *Join the Navy and fuck a big, strong guy like me*, and, *If you join the Navy, women will flock to you like they're doing to me right now*, were the messages being sprinkled into the growing crowd by his silence. He appeared several years older than the students clogging up the pathway, yet not old enough to be a professor's age. Experienced and far less stressed-acting than the louder, more jittery of the two. His solemn stance and crossed arms showcased respect and a deep understanding of the seriousness behind the decision the recruiters presented.

My pace slowed as I drifted closer to the action, noticing the billowing gaze that surged over the sea of females and latched on to me. I had no intention of joining the Navy, but something about the changing energy of my commute to class drew me in like a silent current. Was the energetic crowd exciting me or the man whose gaze cut right through it? A humble smile crossed my face.

The intimidating man kept his eyes locked on mine from an impressive distance while his face and body stayed perfectly still. Sturdy.

It was the brand of stare that a woman could feel lingering on her, even without looking.

The face of my watch told me I had thirty more minutes until my exam in Addictions and Their Impacts on Psychological Health, which meant if I continued at my current enthusiastic speed, I would be almost twenty minutes early. Did the type A in me enjoy being punctual? Yes. Did I want to be the outcast who showed up too early for an exam even though I'd studied for hours the night before? No, thanks. I had time to kill. Why not let a little curiosity kill it for me?

The chill that made its home in the January air wrapped me in a rare brand of comfort when I slowed, like I was meant to be in the exact place I stood. The exact place on the uneven sidewalk, in front of the recruiting booth, where my curiosity was shattered by a body thrusting into my back from behind. The force knocked me off-balance into a muddied spot on the grass, dampening the knees of my leggings. Dozens of students and visitors turned to stare at me, along with the notebooks and textbooks that had fallen from my arms.

"Holy shit, are you okay?" a male voice shouted from the ground beside me.

I didn't need to look up to know who it belonged to.

Jesse Jenkins.

I grabbed my right shoulder, ensuring it was still attached. The pain radiating down my arm from the impact of someone's body colliding with mine was impressive. My determination to avoid public tears in front of my peers was even stronger until his eyes captured mine.

They were bluer than blue. They were deeper.

Darker.

And so haunting that I chose to focus on the pain instead of getting lost in a trance.

What the hell is up with me? I had to be ovulating. It was the only explanation for my unusual level of attraction to testosterone.

"Yeah. I ... *ughhh* ... I'm fine, I guess," I responded tartly. The whirlwind of thoughts pummeling me rode a nervous gulp down my throat.

A few moments passed while I processed what had just occurred, semi-wishing the voice at my side belonged to the impressive recruiter man who'd stolen my attention moments earlier. I looked around for him, allowing the frantic movement to distract me from my embarrassment, but he was no longer behind the booth. Nowhere to be seen.

My new collision buddy helped gather my belongings, which were strewn around us, and grabbed my hand, helping me to my feet.

"*Ouchhh*," I groaned, plucking grass from my sleeve. The pain softened, but still lingered when his grip on my hand loosened.

We'd never formally met, but I already knew him. Everyone did. His energy was ... consuming. Sure, I was a sophomore and had no classes with upperclassmen like Jesse, but he was at every single party I'd ever had the guts to attend. The keg-stand king, the guy who was a blast to spend time with before ever knowing him because he brought the booze, the dirty jokes, and the far-reaching sex appeal.

He always looked comfortable on campus and was rarely alone—a real socialite. The band geeks, the jocks, the Greek life gods and goddesses—he effortlessly pulled them into his tent like a ringleader.

The moment his ocean eyes crashed into mine, it was clear.

No one was immune to his impact.

Not even someone as serious about swearing off conventionally hot men and staying focused on their education as I was.

"My bad ... I should have been paying attention to my surroundings, but something else caught my eye," he admitted, grinning in a way I would consider more provocative than genuine. Sunlight reflected from his perfectly aligned teeth.

"Clearly."

"I'm paying attention now—that's for sure." He took me in from head to toe, almost studying me, like he wanted to stay there for a while. "I'm Jesse."

He smiled again, his dimples sinking deeper than the first time. God, there was no denying how hot he was. My stare ran wild around his symmetrical face, sharp jawline, and tousled blond hair that had no business landing so imperfectly across his eyebrows.

"I know who you are." It was the only response I could think of. I steadied myself and collected my bearings, brushing dirt from my pants, no-longer-white Converses, and a sweatshirt that sported our school's logo—the cresting wave. Thankfully, I'd taken the time to do my makeup that morning. A simple look—including some concealer, mascara, and a glossy, lip-lined pout—padded my confidence.

"Do you now?" His tone and smirk suggested that he was used to people knowing him before he ever spoke a word to them. "Well, I bet you didn't know I'm about to sign my life away to the government so, in exchange, they'll pay for my last two years of college."

Damn, he had me there.

"And I'd be lying if I said I didn't want you to join me." His charm and right arm stretched toward me, lightly skimming my hand, before a deep voice startled us both.

A very deep voice.

That could only belong to a very specific man.

"You Jesse Jenkins?" The no-longer-silent-but-still-deadly recruiter reappeared with a clipboard in hand.

Seemingly searching for Jesse, he approached me instead. Did he think I was Jesse? Because I could pretend to be Jesse for a moment if that was who he was looking for.

Closer to him than I was before, I noticed that the eyes staring into mine were the most incredible shade of green. Like ivy, their vines strangled my pupils. I wanted them to live there. Only they were uprooted by Jesse's response.

"She's not Jesse. I am," the real Jesse pronounced. His posture remained relaxed before he approached the embodiment of authority towering over us both.

I ran a hand through my pin-straight blonde hair, gathering myself like a disheveled piece of meat between two toasty slices of bread. *Yep, definitely ovulating.*

"Great. I've been waiting for you. If you're ready to sign and finalize the details of your agreement, as we touched on in our emails, you can follow me. I'm Austin Carterson, the recruiter you've been in contact with," he said.

I paused, hesitant to intrude on such a massive moment in Jesse's life when we'd only just met.

"Today's my last day in Pensacola. I'm shipping out tomorrow for my new duty station. If you want to contract under the grant program we discussed, we'll need to finalize the paperwork before then. I hate to put pressure on you like this, but it's the reality."

"No worries, man. It's cool. I'm ready," Jesse replied, unruffled.

How could he be so calm? Did he fully understand what he was getting into?

"Can my new friend here come with us?" Jesse's head dipped toward me, his expression hopeful.

Shocked by his request, I looked at him with a face that said, *Are you sure about this?* and then upward to gauge Mr. Carterson's reaction. Surely, he wouldn't welcome an outlier at such an important contractual meeting. There had to be regulations against that, *right?*

"That's your call. She's welcome to join us if you'd like some moral support. A friend can sometimes add the softness a man may need to cushion him before making a big life decision." Austin emphasized the word *friend*.

It was strange.

Great. Not only would I be late for my exam or completely miss it, but there was also no way I could *not* help Jesse through such a significant moment in his life. I was getting a degree in psychology, which, by unspoken law, prevented me from avoiding a rare, emotionally charged situation like the one I'd found myself in. Although I usually liked my men like I liked my education—free—I couldn't miss such an appealing learning opportunity.

Gosh, I couldn't wait to tell my roommate, Ruthie, about my morning. My best friend would be so pumped that I was talking to *the* Jesse Jenkins in the flesh.

"Christ, he's a real fucking panty-dropper," she said anytime we saw him.

She'd even admitted to flicking her bean to a mental image of him once while she was drunk.

I had given her hell for it.

And I always would. Forever.

Jesse's smug expression panned my way as he confirmed what I'd already known. "I'd love to have you with me while I do this. I can't think of a more personal first date than this."

A date? His cockiness simmered my attraction to him. Presumptuous much? Still, I nodded in agreement, my answer silent yet sturdy.

"You can both follow me then," Mr. Carterson commanded.

Two

Austin

I HELD THE DOOR OPEN as Jesse and the dream girl entered the brick-faced campus building. One gust of air from the glass door was all it took to blow her honey-blonde hair out of her face, revealing eyes so light brown that the only thing holding their irises together was the golden ring encircling them. Their innocence was the sole factor keeping my professionalism intact because, my God, she was gorgeous.

A spark of heat lit something within me that had lain dormant for far too long when I realized, on the lawn, that *she* might have been the Jesse I'd been talking to through email about joining the service. Disappointment quickly extinguished that flame the moment I realized that name belonged to the all-American-looking prick who'd rammed into her like she was invisible.

How the hell could she be invisible to anyone? Especially someone like him, who had a real chance at making her his? Maybe ramming into her from behind was his pathetic attempt at one day *ramming into her from behind*. I didn't know her name, but I wished it started with the letter *M* and ended with an *I-N-E*.

Instead, it felt like her name started with an *H* and ended with an *I-S*.

"As I mentioned, I ship out tomorrow for my new duty station, so excuse the chaos," I reiterated, making eye contact with the overflowing cardboard box of office belongings and other scattered items I hoped weren't overly noticeable.

The only possession I truly cared about in the box was the pewter-framed photo set on top—the one of my grandparents on their wedding day. I'd displayed it in every office I worked in since I'd pulled it off the wall in their house, where it lived for over fifty years. It was one of the things that kept me grounded whenever the need arose. Whenever I wished the most remarkable people I knew—the ones who had raised me in place of my shitty birth parents—were still alive.

Embarrassed to show off the sparse, makeshift cubicle I worked from on campus-event days, I walked Jesse and someone I would love to impress right into it. My new office would be much more suitable for someone of my rank. Someone who had already dedicated eight years of his life to serving his country.

I sat. Jesse sat. But she stood frozen. The pair hadn't shared a word or touched since entering the building, meaning they weren't comfortable together. Were they even friends? Or was their collision their meet-cute? I sincerely fucking hoped not. Jesse's casual use of the term *first date* proved how unprepared he was for what was to come.

"Please, have a seat and join us, Ms. ..." I hinted, motioning toward the remaining tired chair that had seen more ass in its day than I had in my lifetime. If I had the time, I could turn that old piece of oak into something worth displaying. Helping anything become the best it could be was something I loved doing.

Her petite-up-top, curvy-down-below frame settled into the chair gracefully before she responded with an angelic, "My name is Elle."

What a name. Different without being weird. Her voice matched her dainty, manicured hands. She placed a gray backpack and a stack of books on the carpet beside her. Based on their thickness and the various mental health titles decorating their spines, she was a studious little thing, perhaps a psychology major. My uniform pants tightened as I continued inspecting her. Intelligent women got my blood pumping.

Everything about her—from her relaxed makeup to the overstuffed backpack—told me she took her education seriously. I cleared my throat in response to the heat the thought lifted to my face. Thankfully, it was loud enough to ward off the almost blush I was conditioned to rarely let through. What was it about her that made it so difficult for me to stay focused? Better yet, what wasn't it about her?

"Thank you for being here today, Elle. I'm sure it means a lot to Jesse here," I said. A glance in his direction was all the attention I gave the young man I was almost jealous of. Not because of his looks, but because of his accessibility to her. "It's nice to meet both of you," I continued.

Jesse's leg bobbed against the underside of the modest desk we'd gathered around. Elle didn't appear to detect it, but he couldn't hide it from me. He was nervous, fidgety even.

For very different reasons than I was.

He was also less experienced at hiding it from a trained eye. I'd had an early childhood filled with reasons to suppress my emotions. Had he?

"I know we hashed out the details via email, but would you mind walking me through everything one last time?" Jesse asked, cooly voicing the reassurance he needed—a trend common among young students about to sign away years of their lives.

He slickly ran his hand through his hair like my response wouldn't matter. We both knew better.

"Of course," I assured him.

Elle now had a notebook and a pencil in her lap. What did she need them for? I'd never been more curious. Her feet bounced lightly on the carpet, vibrating her body. My mind couldn't sit still either, latching on to every subtle movement she produced.

Recapturing my focus on the reason for our meeting, I continued, "The Navy has a limited number of grants it offers to local students who have two years or less remaining in their degree programs. If you sign a four-year agreement today, they'll agree to pay for the remainder of your college courses and on-campus housing until you graduate. Once you graduate, you'll immediately be shipped to the Waulumbee Shoreside Training Center in Illinois for a twelve-week boot camp stay. After completion, you'll continue rate-specific training depending on your job placement." The rehearsed words flowed robotically, like they'd done hundreds of times before. "At the end of your four years serving, you can either reenlist or get out and wipe your hands clean of the Navy." I finished my spiel with a smile, waiting for Jesse to process his reality.

A dry swallow fell down his throat.

What would that noise sound like, coming from her throat instead? *Down, boy.*

"If I sign, is there anything I'd need to do to prepare or remain in good standing before then?" Jesse broke my fantasy, his concern transparent.

"You'll need to be cleared through medical to ensure you meet the health requirements for entry. You'll also have regular checkups at the local hospital to make certain no new medical issues arise. Anything the Navy determines as detrimental would result in immediate termination of the agreement," I clarified.

Jesse nodded in understanding. Elle listened intently, tucking a few strands of her hair behind her ear.

"You'll also be required to meet the same physical entrance requirements as other recruits, but you look like you'll have no issue with that."

"I'd hope not. With the amount of physical activity I partake in, I should set the damn entrance requirements." The tone of his voice told me he was proud to be a womanizer. It told me all that I needed to know about the boy.

The smaller, more athletic guys, like Jesse, could pass physical fitness tests with flying colors. In my opinion, the entry standards had become too easy. My height, muscle, and bulk had slowed me down back when I joined. It was challenging, training to get my run times where they needed to be. I hadn't been the fastest, but I didn't need to be because I prided myself on being among the strongest. Stronger than Jesse could ever hope to be, regardless of what he considered to be *physical activity*, which, if my gut was correct, was something that lasted no more than three minutes.

"So, if I sign today, when exactly would I ship out for boot camp?" Jesse leaned forward and placed both elbows on my desk.

Elle's eyes narrowed, her gaze zeroing in on my mouth. Was she that interested in what I had to say? A deep exhale preceded my response.

"Based on the course review sent in by your academic advisor, you're set to graduate in December 2011. That means you would be headed north in January 2012," I confirmed.

"Two more years of freedom? Everything paid for? I can handle that." He chuckled before leaning back.

Poor Elle's complexion lightened. Her breathing froze. Her legs stilled. It was obvious she grasped the power of Jesse's decision far more than he seemed to be doing.

Once an agreement was signed, there was no wiggle room for getting out of it, except in cases of medical necessity. I assumed Jesse's need to pay for the rest of his time at CPC was stronger than his hesitation to join the Navy, much like the other students lucky enough to snag a grant. Opportunities like the one I'd presented to him weren't offered often. He'd be crazy not to take it.

But he'd be crazier not to take it seriously.

"You're good at this, bro, a real straight shooter. I have all the information I need. Let's do it …" Jesse's empty stare ran past me, like he was only pausing to convince Elle and me that he was finalizing the decision in his head.

Surely, it had been on his mind since our first email. I hoped so anyway, for his sake.

Once he signed his agreement and the Band-Aid was ripped off, maybe the weight of his future would hit him. Until then though, he'd probably continue down the path of the three p's—parties, pussy, and pretending to give a fuck about anyone but himself.

Grabbing the paperwork and a weighted US Navy–engraved pen, I slid Jesse's future toward him and witnessed him flip through the stack too briefly and make the same choice I'd made almost a decade earlier. I didn't have traumatic flashbacks from that time in my life though. Joining the Navy had changed my life for the better. It'd made me. Maybe it would make him too. Or break him.

Appearing relieved, Elle took notes as if she were attending a signing meeting of her own design. She occasionally glanced between Jesse and me for the next few minutes in a back-and-forth pattern I didn't like.

Look at me, I thought.

Only me.

Was the same riptide that had drawn me to her drawing her to me too?

I was also dying to know what in the world she was writing down. Was she *studying* us? Our differences? After all, Jesse Jenkins and I were very different. I was bigger.

Older.

Wiser.

Better.

At least, I wanted that to be the conclusion she drew in her notebook. But I'd never know because she slammed it shut the second she caught me trying my damnedest to sneak a peek. Quickly, I looked away from her private notes like I'd just been caught cheating on a test. The thrill got my blood pumping. She got my blood pumping.

What the hell was in her notebook?

And why couldn't I stop looking at her?

My job as a recruiter was to read people, and suddenly, I wanted nothing more than to read every last page of her. Unfortunately, my loyalty to the Navy had prevented me from reading books like her in the past—something that would only continue as I prepared for the most significant advancement of my career. The one that would begin on my seven a.m. flight the next day.

Elle's face flushed. Several lonely blades of grass remained stuck in her hair. They lost my attention when her top two teeth centered on her lower lip and sank with a slow concentration that completely broke mine. She looked into my eyes when she bit down, ignoring the fuckboy beside her. She knew exactly what she was doing before she turned away.

I wished Jesse weren't here with us.

I wished the Navy didn't own me.

I wished things were different and I could ask her out for a coffee like an ordinary civilian could—like Jesse could.

But things weren't different. And the wants I had for my life, the ones I'd worked so hard to stash away as I continued to put my career first, would forever follow me.

The swirling sound of ink meeting paper was distinct, the promise of a brighter future just beyond the moment of no return. Jesse had signed his agreement. He was one of us now. Funny how I wished I were sitting in his place.

"Well, do we pop a bottle of champagne or something? This seems like too big of a moment for silence," Elle said sweetly.

Her cheerful interjection was a gift to both Jesse and me. Seeing her playfully nudge his arm was not.

"I agree that we need to celebrate, but sadly, I don't supply the champagne." I grinned, breaking the dangerous path my gaze was on before rising to my feet.

Elle and Jesse rose too. Seeing her stand before me stole the usual celebratory statement from my lungs. It was the first time in my career that I hadn't congratulated someone the moment they signed. *Weird.* Although I knew exactly why ...

"Congratulations, Jesse. It takes determination to make this decision. This is a journey well worth embarking on. I wish you the best."

I extended my hand to shake his. His delay in returning the gesture told me he didn't respect the chain of command.

He would.

"Thanks, man. Appreciate you," Jesse spewed, turning to face the beautiful woman gracing us with her presence.

He would have to alter his language when speaking to his future superiors, but I chose not to comment so Elle didn't think I was an asshole. I couldn't let her first and last impression of me be a negative one. But what did it matter?

I'd never see her again.

"And thank you, Elle. I'm glad you were here with me today. I'm sure this wasn't how you saw your day going, but I think our little run-in was meant to be. Don't you?" Jesse added.

I cringed, begging my face not to showcase my disappointment.

"I'm just glad you weren't alone during such a heavy moment," Elle said softly. Another comforting Jesse shoulder touch followed her words.

I could picture the two of them getting cozy, and the idea seasoned my thoughts with envy. *Lucky prick.*

"Heavy? Sure, maybe a little. But now that it's done, I feel free as a bird."

Jesse's pupils dilated like a hungry shark's, water meeting black blood. The devious grin I had watched grip his face before he ran into Elle on the lawn returned. The one that said, *I want her and only her.* His fingers nearly landed on her lower back as their bodies shifted in unison to leave my office, but he was smart enough to wait for an actual touch. A delicacy like Elle would require finesse—something Jesse lacked.

The girl I craved more *almost* moments with turned to face me one last time. "It was nice to meet you," she sighed.

A quick smile and wave were all I got. I'd have a hard time forgetting them.

Forgetting her.

"It was nice meeting you too. I'm glad you came." I was beyond glad. Ecstatic was more like it.

Returning to my chair, I gathered Jesse's agreement and busied my hands. My eyes were busy too.

Watching her walk away.

I overheard Jesse's shrinking voice ask, "You want to grab dinner tonight so I can get to know you as more than just the girl I pummeled into the grass by accident?"

God, what a terrible line.

They vanished from my line of sight, but I didn't need to see or hear either of them to know her answer.

Three

Elle

Two Years Later

Midnight waves flowed around my heels as they hid in the sand. My dirty-blonde hair was extra dirty, sprawled out over endless seashells and sand. No part of my naked body was spared by the moonlight or the uncomfortable temperatures Pensacola Beach offered in winter.

What a terrible place for a date night.

Freezing seawater repeatedly drenched me, salting my pores. The needle-like sensation hammering my skin was unavoidable. Jesse had me pinned on my back, attempting to take me one last time before he left for boot camp. Unfortunately, the elements enveloping us made it feel more like Navy Seal water torture and less like the passionate sex on the beach I had hoped for.

"Fuck yes, that feels so *gooood*," I lied, making sure my moans hit the sweet spot between my boyfriend's ear and collarbone.

I never wanted him to feel like he wasn't good enough. He was a great guy. I focused on ensuring he got what he needed when we were together. However, partner satisfaction was something we viewed differently.

Very differently.

I saw it as a means of connection. A way to say, *I love you, and I feel good when you feel good.*

He came every time we had sex. I made sure of it. But he didn't often check to make sure I had gotten mine—making my orgasms extremely easy to fake.

And so I did.

"Come for me, Elle," Jesse whispered in my ear.

On cue, my rehearsed moans ended quicker than they had begun.

His irises still reminded me of the cerulean sea when he looked down at me, sweeping my worries into the ocean and returning hope in their place. Even in the dark, I lost myself in their endlessness.

Jesse's body was my sole source of warmth, preventing me from becoming hypothermic in the thick, salty breeze. I continued pretending to love every second of his beach-date idea, even as shivers screamed at me to wrap things up and put some clothes on.

Our night had to be perfect.

It would be our last for a while.

His breathy voice usually soothed my soul, but I was too distracted by my thoughts, telling me it would be months before I heard it again.

Don't get me wrong; the head of his swollen cock felt great, ducking in and out of me. Still, I knew his quick, short-lived strokes would get him off before I ever had the chance.

The pressure building on my clit elevated as Jesse's hips shifted to one side, allowing his impressive dick to reach a different spot inside of me. I wanted to close my eyes and relax into an actual orgasm. But this was a movie I'd seen before, and unfortunately, I knew the ending was me not being able to get off. It didn't matter that our sex life wasn't like the movies though. It was still enjoyable. And it was ours.

Sure, we had things to work on, but what couple didn't? He was still my world, and I was proud of him.

I kept my eyes open and focused on memorizing our last night together.

The details of his face.

The relationship we'd built in our two years together.

Unfortunately, the sandpaper-like sensation scraping my back and shoulders with every jolt forward was a major distraction. Jesse's arms snaked around my body and pulled me into him, crushing my chest under his weight. He was a pure heartthrob from head to toe. And my heart throbbed in return, as I knew he was mine.

"Kiss me," I begged.

My wispy words drifted into his mouth. It lowered to meet mine.

The pressure between our lips intensified while Jesse hungrily pumped one last stroke inside me. A stream of heat ignited my core.

"Mmmm," he growled with a satisfaction that high-fived the good girl in me.

I loved praise. Feeling like I'd rocked Jesse's world brought me as much pleasure as the few times he'd *almost* been able to get me off.

I raised my hands to meet his cheeks. My shivering fingertips ran through the thick, outgrown blond hair I knew the Navy would take clippers to the second he reported for boot camp. I wasn't ready for it to be our last night together. But it wasn't goodbye forever.

It was only goodbye for now.

When I sat up, Jesse's cum spilled out of me, some of it sinking into the sand.

He slipped his jeans back up and over his muscular thighs while I looked around, frantically searching for the oversize gray sweatshirt I'd thrown on before we left my apartment. The waves found it before I did.

Hesitant, I had no choice but to force the dampened material over my head and thread my shivering, sand-coated hands through the armholes. Jesse quickly followed suit with his hoodie. His tremors told me he agreed that the weather was not ideal for our seaside rendezvous.

"I know this wasn't the best idea I've ever had, but I'm still glad I suggested it. You're like my own personal mermaid. Good God, look at you," he confessed.

Reaching around me, he pulled me toward him for what I assumed was a silent apology for turning his girlfriend into a gritty, sopping, nipples-so-hard-that-they-could-cut-diamonds mess. His sweetness was one of my favorite things about him.

His delectable body was another.

"I'm glad you suggested it too."

My too-quick response and barely formed smile snagged my boyfriend's attention. He knew the reason for my somberness over the last few days. The wall of anxiety I'd built between us left me to face the music of what we both knew—that the morning was inevitable.

We'd known it since the day we'd met. I just never realized how fast it would rear its ugly head. A few more hours would instantly put nine hundred forty-seven miles of separation between us.

"Boot camp is only twelve weeks, babe. It's nothing," Jesse said coolly. He grabbed my right fist, pulling it to his lips before speaking into my knuckles like they were a microphone. "You can move in with me once I finish training and settle in, in a few months. Even if we get an apartment off base. Wherever I end up, we'll make this work for both of us."

His confident expression was full of hope.

Hope that I'd blindly agree to his request.

"I'm pretty sure that's not how it works. If you like the idea of me being a *wifey-wife* so much, maybe you should put a ring on it," I half joked, flashing my numb left hand like a last-place trophy.

We weren't ready to get married. We both knew that.

I was still a year away from finishing my graduate program, not including the time it could take me to land a job. Besides, I needed a real commitment from Jesse before uprooting my life and moving to who knew where. Our two-year relationship was important to me, but I needed reassurance that *my* dreams meant as much to him as his dreams meant to me.

Because that was the only way I would consider leaving Pensacola and following him around the world for the next four years.

"Look, you know you mean everything to me, babe. Not only do I love you, but I'm in love with you." The moonlight added radiance to his already-perfect skin, which gave every word he sent my way an extra glow. "You're my best friend. Do you really need a ring to believe that?"

My tense shoulders eased at the rationale coating his point. His words told me he loved me. However, his hesitation to include my career whenever we discussed a future together left me second-guessing. It wasn't about a ring. It was about the words I craved.

"Can't you just … I don't know … finish your last year near me? I'm sure they have counseling programs everywhere," he rattled.

My hands retreated into my lap.

"You know I can't do that. You know how hard I've worked to get accepted into this program. It's the only one in the country that focuses so heavily on post-traumatic stress disorder and addiction studies. Being so close to the air station, it's where I need to be if I want the edge military hospitals look for when hiring new grads," I professed.

Jesse had heard my plea before; his eye roll proved it.

He'd experienced my excitement firsthand when I told him why I chose to stay at CPC for their specific concentrations. If there was anything I prided myself on as a first-generation college student, it was my follow-through. And nothing could stop me from completing the counseling program I was so close to finishing.

My countless connections made with professors and peers throughout my undergrad years were extremely valuable. Severing that network prematurely could severely limit my career opportunities. How could he think that was the right decision for my future?

Airmail would be the only form of communication allowed during boot camp, so I planned to write to Jesse as much as possible, attend his graduation ceremony, keep in touch with his parents and brother, and do anything else needed to fertilize our relationship while he was away.

As if he was unsatisfied, Jesse's eyebrows furrowed in the middle of his forehead as I continued to justify those things. He wasn't sold on my idea of our future.

"I understand." Jesse exhaled. "I just ... I want to be with you, and I hate the idea of being away from you for so long and missing out on such a big part of each other's lives for any length of time." Caressing my shoulder, he continued, "Let's get through the next twelve weeks and figure out the rest when you come up for graduation."

Unsure where our conversation could go from that point, I stayed silent. Anxiety rattled around my head. I wasn't a fan of not knowing how our lives would come together after boot camp, but I tried my best to remember that things had a way of working themselves out.

"Promise me you'll come for graduation?" Jesse asked. He needed to hear it again.

"Of course I will. I wouldn't miss it. Plus, I can't wait to see you in uniform. *Ughhh*, it's going to be so hot ..."

"Jesus, I'm going to be so pent up by the time you see me; you'll need crutches when I'm through with you. They say the first post–

boot camp fuck is the best of your life. Possibly the quickest, but also the best."

I chuckled, nodding in agreement.

I doubted it would be the best sex of my life. But I hoped for his sake, it would be the best of his.

"I can't imagine not touching your body or hearing your voice for months. It's going to fucking kill me. Hopefully, the infamous saltpeter doesn't completely kill my vibe because I thoroughly plan on writing you the filthiest letters you've ever read. Far spicier than any of your little smut books," he confessed.

"Wait, what the hell is saltpeter?" My curiosity would not let me continue our conversation without knowing.

"The old sailor's myth says they put it in the food they serve recruits to ensure testosterone levels don't get too high. It prevents the guys from getting into brawls and supposedly helps them jerk off less. It's like a dash of high-velocity blue ball, sprinkled right into our scrambled eggs each morning."

What the ...

Jesse's calmness shocked me. I could never.

"Sounds horrifically appetizing," I joked, deflecting from my disturbed grimace.

Even if he didn't show it, Jesse was probably nervous as it was. I didn't need to add to it.

"Speaking of appetizing, I took a mental picture of that pussy so I can dream about it for the next twelve weeks ..."

The velvety voice I had fallen in love with caressed my ears. Jesse couldn't get enough of me, which padded my confidence in us. We could make this work.

We were worth it.

"Wait ... you didn't take a mental picture of my charming personality to keep you company?" My words dripped with sarcasm as I pretended to scoff, bringing a hand to my chest in fake disbelief.

"I'll get that in your letters, I'm sure. What I won't get is that dripping pussy staring at me or that perfect ass bouncing around." Jesse lightly bit down on his closed knuckles like a hungry serpent.

"Oh, shut up." I laughed before shoving playfully at his chest.

Having the perfect male specimen as my boyfriend had taken some getting used to. The attention he got from other girls and the reactions he effortlessly pulled from the people around him used to bother me. I had a feeling that experiencing the absence of his charm and how he looked at me like I was the only one in his world would bother me far more.

"Come on. Let's go back to my place. Only five more hours until I leave for the airport. I want to spend it spooning the sand out of you." He kissed my cheek after saying the words that promised a warm bed and the last time we would sleep in the same one for a while.

The shoreline disappeared behind us as we gathered the half-empty bottle of strawberry wine and our flip-flops. We walked hand in hand back to his pickup truck, which matched the darkened sky.

Like releasing a message in a bottle out to sea, I looked to the moon and willed my thoughts to reach anyone who might be listening to my silent plea. *Keep me calm, keep him safe, keep us together.*

Four

Elle

"ELLE! IT'S HEEEERE!" RUTHIE SCREAMED, jolting my attention away from the assignment I'd been distracting myself with.

I heard our front door slam shut. Studying and doing homework had become my coping mechanism, even more so since Jesse had left two weeks ago. I'd been forced into playing a waiting game by our new circumstances.

And I was losing.

When I stood up from my desk, the limbs that had felt like lead, anchoring me to the ground, suddenly had a new buoyancy. I erupted into the kitchen and desperately tried to rip the envelope from my roommate's hands.

"Don't you dare open that. Give it here!" I squealed, jumping toward the envelope.

She waved it above her head like a cheerleading pom-pom.

I'd already waited far too many days for Jesse's letter. My desperation begged me not to add another second.

When Ruthie—my personal sous chef, best friend since freshman year, and current roommate—was home, the delicious smells of freshly baked sweets, which brought our kitchen to life, usually excited my senses. Today, they only added to the nervousness pummeling my stomach, overwhelming me instead. I was one wrong move away from decorating our kitchen with vomit. Fuck Ruthie's gooey chocolate chip cookies. Fuck the wait. I needed that letter immediately.

Ruthie must have sensed my growing need. The mail in her hand became a white flag of surrender before she handed it to me.

The envelope, addressed to Ms. Elle Madelyn, displayed an official-looking anchor insignia in the top-left corner. The paper capsule, covered in dried watermarks of various silhouettes, was creased and unexpectedly filthy.

I could understand if the mail route traveled through the Everglades, sat in the front row of a roller coaster, and crossed paths with a hurricane. But the shape of the letter made me second-guess its journey from Waulumbee, just north of Chicago, to me. Who gave a fuck though?

It was finally here.

"Read it out loud! Read it out loud!" Ruthie chanted.

She placed her chin on my shoulder and wrapped her arms around my waist, begging to read Jesse's letter along with me. There was no way in hell I would let her. I shared almost everything with Ruthie—she was practically my sister. But my first moment of connection with Jesse since he'd left had to stay between him and me. It was all we had for now.

"Bitch, we talked about this. I need to read this thing in peace. No distractions!" I pleaded. My heart rate rose like the Florida sunrise in my chest, releasing hot rays of nerves down my arms.

Unable to wait any longer, I left Ruthie's embrace, grasped the mail close to my heart, and took off toward my bedroom.

"*Ughhh*. I know. I know. I'll hound you about all the juicy details later. Don't think you're getting off that easy!" she called. Her voice faded when I shut my bedroom door and locked the handle.

Settling onto my bed, I shredded the envelope open like a bitch in heat. My heart pounded.

Jesse's handwriting looked up at me.

Jenkins, Jesse

Division 28

Fuck, babe. I made it! The second I landed, things got intense—quick. The first day of boot camp was hellish. A lot of what they call "hurry up and wait." We went twenty straight hours without sleeping during processing, only to be herded into an assembly line for vaccines. Your worst nightmare, I know. The final jab was injected directly into my bare ass cheek. I wish I were bending you over to shove something in …

Instead, I was bending over for the middle-aged woman I can only describe as your traditional lunch lady. It was a real full-moon fantasy, if you know what I mean.

The first official week of boot is over. Today was tedious. They've been reviewing uniform inspections with us and other essential things we need to know. Our uniforms get inspected from top to bottom often, and some guys here can't figure it out. We had to get dressed and undressed five times in a row. It was a total pain in the dick.

I swear, some of the dudes in my division are like children. They won't shut up or listen to the instructors. Just today, six of them got demerit chits. Demerit chits are bad. If our division gets too many of them, then we won't be able to graduate on time. I can't let that happen.

I can't believe how much I already miss you. It feels like we're on different planets. I need to be back with my mermaid, the one I can still feel wrapped around me on the beach … I knew this would suck, but I didn't think it would feel this dreary so soon.

On another note, the countdown to graduation has begun! Maybe a little premature, but it's less than twelve weeks until I hold you in my arms again—and in my bed. Our DC, or division commander, told us that our graduation date is set for Saturday, March 31, which means you can start making travel arrangements! I wanted to give you plenty of time to plan. I know your course load and work schedule can be challenging to coordinate.

Our reunion will be perfect—I know that much.

If it's too expensive, I gave my parents strict instructions to help you get here. Please don't hesitate to call them and ask for help if you need it. Only three attendee tickets are available per recruit for the ceremony, but because my parents don't agree with my decision to join the Navy, I'm sure you'll be the only one attending. It's okay though. Because you're the only one I need here anyway.

I'll have liberty that weekend, so we can spend a couple of days together before I ship out to A School for more training. I can't wait.

I also can't wait to get a letter from you! The mail system here is laughable. They only collect letters twice a week. But that won't stop me from writing to you more than that, so don't worry. Expect saved-up loads … wink, wink.

There are rumors that instructors screen the incoming mail, so don't send any nudes until I give you the all clear. Yikes, I can't believe I'm even writing that. "Don't send nudes." What the fuck has gotten into me?! If you'd like, please send some regular pictures though. Seeing your face would make my day.

Someone got a singing card with a glitter bomb in it, and we all had to do fifty push-ups. I don't know how the hell Jimmy's grandmother got the address so fast, but I hope they thought the division-wide punishment was worth it. I thought you would laugh at that ... I sure did.

Sleep sweet, Elle.

I miss you already.

Jesse

    Tears clouded my vision, dribbling down my cheeks with each lazy blink. It wasn't a full-on sob, but the relief surging through me, knowing my Jesse was still with me—that his sense of humor and determination were still intact—found its way out.
    I reread the letter twice, feeling closer to my boyfriend with every pass. Words were my love language, and I was thankful that Jesse had no choice but to speak mine back to me. Maybe this kind of communication would help us in the long run.
    I had a return address and could finally write back. I had a boot camp graduation date and could start planning my visit to see him. But mostly, I had renewed optimism that told me I could relax into my new reality because Jesse would be fine during our time apart.
    And so would I.
    My room in the two-bedroom, two-bath apartment Ruthie and I shared off campus comforted me exactly how I'd hoped it would

when I first decorated it the day we moved in. Zen was the theme, and I appreciated the cool tones of periwinkle plastering the walls, the wooden furniture, and the matching coastal wall art that accented it. The color scheme brought me peace.

The same feeling I got from Jesse's first letter.

I grabbed the cold chai latte I'd brought home from work several hours earlier and took a hefty gulp, washing away the lingering tension crowding my throat.

What better way to celebrate hearing from Jesse than calling the people who would be just as excited about the news as I was—my parents?

My mother picked up on the first ring.

"Did you hear from him?!" she squealed at a pitch many would consider unnatural.

Suddenly, I was one of those new moms who noticed that everyone now greeted the baby instead of the person who had just given birth. Straight to the main attraction.

"Well, hello to you too, Mama Goose." I reserved her favorite nickname for the times she needed to be brought back to earth. It was one of those times.

"Sorry, Elle. You already know I love you. But I've been getting anxious here!"

I heard the Jets football game unfolding on television behind my mom's voice, followed by a lively cheer. My father never missed a game. Win or lose, he was their biggest fan.

"Hold on. Let me get Dad and put you on speaker; I know he'll want to hear too!"

My parents never did anything without each other. Not even boy talk with their only daughter.

"Okay, we're both here, sweetie. Tell us everything!" my mom said excitedly.

"Hey, Screwy Lewey," my dad chirped, using the nickname that always made me laugh. He'd bestowed it on me as a nod to my early interest in psychology, and it stuck.

My family was a mixed bag of nuts. Perhaps that was why I loved the field of mental health so much.

When I clicked the speaker button on my cell phone's broken screen, I was transported into the same room as them.

"Hey, guys. You were the first people I called. I just finished reading his letter. Jesse sounds good. Tired but good!" I confessed.

"That's our boy. I knew he could handle it," my dad added.

I'd always appreciated his support, but it never surprised me. We were tight like that.

"Does it seem like they're treating him nicely?" My mother worried about things she shouldn't, including my boyfriend. I knew it was only because she cared so much.

"He said he was a little sleep-deprived, but no real complaints. Oh, and he got a shot in the ass cheek, but otherwise, he sounds like his sweet old self."

"Let me tell you something, darling ... whoever gets to see the cheeks on that boy will experience a shade of blush that Estee Laroux herself couldn't replicate!" Before I could react, my mother laughed.

"Mom!" My head shook from side to side at her directness, but I was used to it.

She always found creative ways to tell me how attractive she thought Jesse was. In a non-creepy, supportive way, of course. I smirked because it was true. He had the ass of a Greek god after all.

You'd better believe I'd memorized those ham hocks. Apparently, Mom had too.

"Kimberrr! That's enough ... I'm sitting right here!" my father growled playfully.

He, too, was used to my mother's shenanigans. The ones that kept our family laughing. The ones that only landed well because of how comfortable my parents were together after thirty years of wedded bliss.

"Seriously though, it felt amazing to hold proof in my hands that he's okay, and now I can write back to him and send my thoughts his way instead of letting them run wild." My lingering excitement beamed through the phone.

"Just don't get too distracted, honey. Jesse's a good guy, and we're so proud of you both for taking this step. But don't let the worries get in the way of your studies. You're almost done, and when you are, you'll have more time to focus on the rest of your priorities." My dad's wise words solidified my conversation with Jesse that night on the beach.

Education came first. The rest would fall into place the way it was meant to. My dad was my go-to consultant on the subject, and I trusted his expertise because it was a testament to his lifetime of experience. While my mother was the sweetness every girl needed growing up, he was the dose of reality that was equally necessary.

"Our daughter is smart, Tony. She can easily balance books and boys—or should I say, men?" My mom believed in my ability to navigate my education *and* love life simultaneously. Because of that, I believed it myself.

"Anyway … I've got to run. I was just out the door for class," I lied, needing to end our conversation before it pulled me down into the rabbit hole of overthinking. I wanted to enjoy the high Jesse's letter had gifted me before the wait for the next one began. "I just wanted to fill you guys in and let you know I'd heard from him. I'll keep both of you posted on my travel plans. I'll be headed to Chicago for a long weekend at the end of March."

"Okay, honey, you have a good class. Give that crazy Ruthie a kiss from us. Would you ask her if she's coming for dinner next weekend when you visit?" my mom asked.

I loved that my parents treated her like a second daughter. Me being an only child, I was sure they loved it as well.

"Of course. I'll ask her and let you know. Love you both!"

"We love you!" they gushed in unison.

The rapid click of our call ending set me free.

My dad would finish watching his football game while my mom cheered beside him. That kind of predictability sounded soothing.

I sat down on my bed and leaned back, sinking into the mattress while I clutched the letter I had never set down.

Suddenly, I was back to a reality of my own.

The one where the wait for words started all over again.

Five

Austin

TWO YEARS HAD PASSED, BUT I never forgot her face.

Her striking brown eyes.

Those full, glazed lips.

That porcelain skin.

The innocence.

I'd tried to forget her, begged my memory to erase her. But she always found me. Why would today be different?

I sat up in my bed, leaving her in my dreams, where she belonged. My slow stretch forced my solid hard-on through the hole in the front of my boxers. Pushing my flannel comforter aside, I let the morning chill wake my skin and deter my blood flow.

The lace curtains my grandmother had hung when she lived here did a terrible job blocking sunlight. I made a mental note to replace them with blackouts the next time I hit the hardware store. The warm rays from the sun and her sweet memory dissipated my grogginess.

Many things had changed since I'd moved back into the house on Haroldeen Lane, where I had grown up. Unfortunately, being able to recall Elle's face wasn't one of those things. It was weird. The more time that passed, the closer I felt to her. Hopelessness disguised as hopefulness.

I had tried to find her through her college's website, searching terms like *Elle* and *undergrad psychology department*, which failed to turn up anything useful. Hell, I even attempted to use my recruiting connections with Coastal Pensacola College to track her down. By the time they returned my call, I was already settled into my new promotion, and it didn't make sense for the institution to shell out a student's information without backing. I'd stopped pressing for information for the sake of my professionalism.

And sanity.

There was no way she was on social media either. Because if she were, my numerous searches for women with her name living in Pensacola would have led me to her.

Did she and Jesse have a happily ever after?

He'd be a fucking fool if they didn't.

The bitter thought left me stomping down the hall, pulling creaks from the planks supporting my feet with every step to the kitchen. The wood was solid, but so was I. It surprised me how well the floors my grandfather had laid so many years ago held up.

I shared his love of wood as a medium. Splitting firewood, carving, whittling—if it could be repurposed or transformed, he had done it. And when my young hands were around, he had taught them how.

I'd tried my best to maintain the house since moving back into it, painting when needed and polishing its natural surfaces. I incessantly mowed the grass surrounding the house on my days off duty and maintained the shit ton of landscaping to the best of my ability.

Still, the emptiness echoing in the halls made the house feel colder than I remembered, no matter how much effort went into preserving it. I often missed their laughter and love. It was a warmth that only a connection like my grandparents could bring—a connection I hoped I'd be lucky enough to duplicate one day. So far, no such luck.

I switched the light on when I entered the kitchen. An unhealthy amount of hazelnut cream swirled around my cup as I layered it into the coffee that auto brewed every morning at five thirty a.m., leaving just enough time to eat, shower, and dress before I reported to base. I leaned back against the chilled countertop, swallowing a sip of the sweet liquid and giving my lingering boner a minute to chill out because time wouldn't allow me to take care of it before work. I didn't have time for many things because the Navy came first. Always.

That was the life of a chief petty officer.

Twenty minutes later, my stomach was full of breakfast. The weather here was unforgiving in January, meaning I needed a peacoat over my uniform. I grabbed it from the foyer, slung it on, and stepped outside. I smiled, knowing the low temps would wake my class right the fuck up. Intake days were always exciting, and helping boys become men was something I never grew tired of.

At six a.m., I swung open the driver's door and climbed into my 1989 Jeep, ready to enjoy the ten-minute morning commute to base. The emerald beauty was my favorite car, long before my grandfather had willed it to me.

She sprang to life and purred when I cranked her up. The Ol' Green Goddess was a classic. Reliable and fully restored. Complete with glossy caramel leather seats and matching stitching, she embodied a rugged yet classic charm.

I fucking loved her.

My ride to work was peaceful, aside from the part where "Jessie's Girl" by Rick Springfield spilled out of the aftermarket speakers on both sides of the dash. Of course it did—because why wouldn't I need another reminder of Jesse and Elle? The song's uncomfortably relevant lyrics continued pummeling me.

Taunting me deep in my core, where they didn't belong.

"Not again." I shook my head, inhaling her absence.

Elle was long gone, and in the two years since I'd seen her face, I still hadn't learned how to leave her there. Insta-love wasn't real. So, why couldn't I get her out of my goddamn head?

By the time the song ended, my base's main gates greeted me. A light coating of frost glistened from their tall steel beams. I waited several minutes before approaching the front of the line of cars headed through the security checkpoint. I lowered my window before coming to a full stop.

"Good morning, Chief. Identification, please?" the armed guard asked.

I obeyed with a nod and handed it over.

Romano knew me—we'd worked together for two years. Still, he needed to scan my ID before letting me pass through the gate. Security was the top priority on any military base. We all took it seriously.

"Good morning, Romano. How are those twins doing? And Jenny? Is she recovering all right?"

Romano was an exhausted new father. I knew that not just because he'd told me, but because the bags supporting his barely open, bloodshot eyes had doubled in size since I'd seen him the week prior. Jesus, those things were gnarly.

"The girls are great. Thanks for asking. Have a nice day now. Enjoy the newbies." He chuckled.

An authoritative *beeeep* left his handheld scanner. He returned my ID to me, triggering the arm of the entrance barrier to lift.

"Oh, you know I will." A smirk lit up my face before I pulled forward through the checkpoint and toward the sizable bend in the road, leading straight to my assigned building. The sound of gravel crunching under my off-road tires accompanied me.

My lingering grin spread wider because I knew precisely what those newbies had in store—twelve weeks of Chief Austin Carterson as their instructor.

Six

Elle

"THINK SEXY, ELLE! GIVE ME a look that says, *You can look, Daddy Jesse, but you can't toooouch.*" Ruthie giggled. She clutched her instant camera like a professional photographer.

So many things were happening in my bedroom that I could barely focus on the task at hand. Operation Make Jesse Jizz His Pants was underway.

Jewel's "Intuition" played throughout the room. My favorite voice on the planet comforted me while I posed on my bed. Attempted to anyway.

Sitting up on my bare knees and back on my heels, I used the insides of my arms to squeeze my tits together and force my cleavage higher. The white tank top stretching across my chest barely supported my large C cups, allowing small, hardened nipples to peek right through.

I was freshly showered, so my hair was dripping wet. Damp spots pooled and slid down the front of the thin fabric, clinging to my body like elastic wrap.

"I'm too embarrassed! Stop looking at me!" I demanded.

I was shy, but not usually in front of Ruthie. Shit, we'd gotten topless spray tans together and skinny-dipped numerous times. The photo session should have been shameless.

"First of all, how can I stop looking when I'm the one taking the picture?"

Point taken.

She continued, adjusting her standing position by the foot of my bed, "Second, you're fucking hot, babe. The glistening skin, that girl-next-door smile—you're every man's wet dream! Maybe even mine because *dayum*!"

Embarrassment tangled with the peachy blush I'd stroked onto my cheekbones, giving me a little extra flush. I was never the confident one of our duo. Ruthie's praise made my heart thump as if I were.

"Can I just close my eyes and visualize him for a second? Maybe it will help loosen me up." My eyes shut before she could respond. I found Jesse's face in my mind.

A strange thing had happened after Jesse left. Whenever I envisioned his profile, the ocean eyes I loved so much had an overtone to them. They looked mossier than I remembered, as if seaweed had overtaken their once-clear pools. Before I reopened mine, I made a mental note to stare at his picture later and refresh my clouded memory because I never wanted to lose those eyes.

"Or perhaps our dear friend Mr. Tequila can assist?" Ruthie grabbed one of the two shots of liquid lust she'd purposefully staged on my footboard for the occasion and brought the short glass to my lips.

Hesitation advised me not to swallow her overpoured shot the night before my six a.m. shift at the coffee shop. My best friend's desperate puppy-dog expression urged me to do it for Jesse. He'd asked me to include a few photos with my letters. Letting him down wasn't an option.

An overstuffed envelope judged me from my desk across the room. If we ever got the damn picture, I planned on sending it out with my fat stack of letters the next morning. Imagining my boyfriend opening a week's worth of my words, accompanied by images I knew would drive him wild, made me giddy. As much as I craved Jesse's words and missed his face, I was sure he needed mine even more.

Seemingly disappointed with my hesitation, Ruthie downed my shot like a drunk, unfazed sailor, barely batting an eyelash at the taste before reaching for the other glass and offering it to me again.

Fuck it.

I accepted her challenge and followed suit. Pursing my lips at the tequila that warmed my esophagus as it sloshed down my throat, I replied, "Did it smudge my lipstick?"

"You look perfect. Now stop overthinking this and look at the camera like you look at Jesse when he's about to get you off!" The excitement in her voice rose, and the twinkle in my eyes fell. "What's wrong?" Ruthie couldn't conceal her wary expression.

"It's nothing …" I trailed off.

"Liar." Ruthie put her instant camera on the mattress and lowered herself onto the edge of the bed, leveling our eye contact.

She knew me too well.

"I feel bad admitting this … but I feel like Jesse's better at making me come when he's gone than when he's here. Like it's easier for me to think about him and pretend he's touching me than when he's *actually* touching me," I confessed.

Since he'd been gone, I'd made myself come more times than he had in the last few months combined.

"What about the IUD? Didn't it help?" Ruthie had high hopes for the recent introduction of birth control into our relationship. Higher than she should have.

"It helped *him* get off faster. He loves not having to use protection. But now I don't even stand a chance with how quickly he can blow his load …"

Ruthie's laughter erupted and sliced the tension like a blade.

Little bitch.

"Oh, Jesse … Mr. Perfect needs to step up his game if he expects you to marry his ass." Her eyebrow rose, complementing her little dig.

"That's the thing. He asked me to finish my grad program wherever he gets stationed, but he doesn't make real promises. Without a ring or a place to land my career when I graduate, I'm not sure I'm ready to uproot my life. I mean, does he even care about my future? My career? Or just his?" Frustration brought my hands to my eyes.

"Shit, babe, I didn't know you were sitting with all this. I knew you guys had some bedroom issues, but I never took Jesse as the commitment-phobe, make-his-girl-chase-him type. *Attached at the hip* is an understatement for y'all. He's obsessed with you."

"If he wasn't fully committed, he wouldn't be writing to me, right?" I asked. The worry softening my voice bubbled from the question. "His letter was freaking perfect. It was sweet and loving, funny even. He makes me laugh and smile, and he even set up a romantic night on the beach before he left. College guys don't do those things unless they're in love. We fit; there are just some loose pieces we're trying to pop into place ..." I justified.

Was I justifying us to Ruthie or myself? Anxiety and alcohol curdled in my stomach.

"Is he helping you fit them together? Or are you the only one thinking of how to do that without giving up on *your* dreams?"

A single tear fell from the corner of my eye. I swatted at it to save the makeup we'd just worked so hard to perfect. No relationship was free of obstacles, and our time apart was not the right time to work on things.

My boyfriend—the man I loved—needed my support.

"All I can say is, no man is worth wasting twenty-five-dollar mascara on. Enjoy the pen-pal moment while it lasts, drive him crazy in your letters, and when you fly up for graduation, I'm sure the absence will help him realize how lucky he is to have you. If he's your person, things will work out."

"Yeah ... yeah, you're right. I'm sure they will," I agreed, hoping he already knew.

"Now, sit back and let me snap the perfect shot of my sizzling hot best friend. We need Jesse's eyes to pop out of his head when he gets this."

After taking a moment to reinflate my confidence, I rearranged the still-soaked ends of my hair. Jesse liked it in front of my shoulders.

Focusing on the camera's lens staring back at me, I flashed a glare and a smile that I prayed screamed, *I'm yours*. It was innocent and alluring, to the best of my ability.

Before it fell from Ruthie's camera, I snagged the pic and shook it, allowing the air that revealed the image to tell me it was the quintessential shot for my man.

"Oh, hell yeah, it's perfect! I'm a damn photographer!" My best friend glanced at it and agreed before taking a bow.

Tequila-powered, I walked to my desk and placed the photo inside the envelope that cradled three pages of my thoughts and commitment. Leaving myself with no time to change my mind, I licked the sticky strip closed, sealed the mail, and placed it in my backpack for send-off.

The mailbox would be my first stop on my way to work tomorrow morning.

There was no way I was letting Jesse forget how lucky he was.

Seven

Elle

THE RESTROOM STALL AT DRIPTINI'S—Pensacola's first boozy coffee shop—was the only place I could hide long enough to read Jesse's letters during my shifts.

On my way out this morning, I'd found three waiting for me in the mailbox, which I checked as if I were addicted to the white metal box. Thankfully, it was affixed to the front door of our apartment. Meaning I didn't have to go far to get my fix.

I studied human behavior and, more specifically, addiction. That meant my need for the reassurance his letters delivered was evident to me. Slightly concerning, truthfully. I didn't *enjoy* relying on another person for emotional regulation, but the nature of long-distance relationships guaranteed it. The miles between us were only temporary. My self-reliance would return—I was sure of it.

My fourth shift of the week, slinging caffeine, was catching up to me. I knew because when I grabbed the string of my uniform apron to prevent it from falling into the toilet as I sat, I completely missed it.

Even though I worked the caffeine-infused coffee morning shifts instead of the alcohol-infused afternoon ones, they still stole my time away from what I craved most—writing to and reading letters from Jesse.

I exhaled, clearing the autopilot headspace I reserved for work, and moved into supportive-girlfriend mode—at least briefly, before my boss came looking for me.

Excitement fueled my fingertips as they tore across the top of the first envelope, inviting Jesse's words into the half of my heart that was still with me.

Jenkins, Jesse

Division 28

Elle,

I still haven't gotten a letter from you yet, but I know there's a delay because you couldn't send anything until my first letter with the return address reached you. Only a few of the other guys have received letters so far. I sure hope you haven't forgotten about me already. Could you ever?! The answer is NO!

Today was literal hell. We were screamed at for oversleeping and ordered to scrub the toilets with a toothbrush. The toilets in our division are lined up in a row, and let me tell you, each one got the scrub of its life.

Someone found a bag of potato chips taped to the underside of one of the toilet seats—I think to save it as a midnight snack. I can't decide if that's brilliant or disgusting. It was sealed after all ... but I don't think I could eat a snack that my bunkmates' bare asses had been next to.

People do crazy things to satisfy their cravings. What I wouldn't do to satisfy mine ...

Sleep Sweet

Please include some stamps, paper, and envelopes with one of your next letters, if possible. They only give you a certain amount here, and I want to make sure I don't run out—that's no excuse for not writing to you! We occasionally go to the store here on base and get supplies when permitted, but we don't have much money besides what comes in our paychecks. The money from our first few checks is used to buy our uniforms, shoes, socks, and tighty-whities. Yes, we have to wear tighty-fucking-whities. You would laugh at me so hard, but I think I look decent in them. I know your mom would agree!

I wish you could see my buzz cut. Not to toot my own horn, but I think you'd dig it. However, I don't think you would dig how pale and clammy my skin has become, how busted my knuckles are, or how chapped my lips look from the blistering cold weather here. I feel like I'm in bloody Siberia.

I had a medical exam yesterday and found out that I'm going to have to get both of my lower wisdom teeth removed. I'm freaking out about it! I'm sure whatever letter you get after that experience will be one for the books. You know I'm a total pussy when it comes to dental shit.

I'll be proud of myself when this is over and my career begins, but it all still feels like a big shock.

Please know that I love you. I can't lie—I'm freaked out by how different life is here, but I love you.

Do you think this was a mistake though? Joining the Navy against my parents' wishes? How else did they expect me to pay for my last semesters of college? I'd rather spend four years scrubbing toilets than start my life drowning in debt. Yes, it sucks, being away from you, but at least you have Ruthie to keep you busy, and there's so much keeping me busy here that I hardly have time to care about what anyone thinks of the choice I made.

Sidenote: I can't stop thinking about our night on the beach. I didn't have much extra time to write today. Expect my words to have a little extra "spice" when I do.

I hope I get a letter from you soon. I can't wait.

Sleep sweet.

Jesse

    He'd better get my letters soon. I didn't want him to start thinking something was wrong. I reassured myself that I'd mailed at least five out in the last few weeks. They'd get there when they got there.
    Stamps were expensive and the only thing I spent spare money on. I stashed the rest of my paychecks for my upcoming travel expenses. The whole ordeal would cost me an arm and a leg, but it didn't matter. He was worth the extra shifts. And I certainly wasn't taking him up on his offer to ask his parents for help. They had chosen not to support their own son's decision. Why the hell would they support me?

Half of the smile that snuck across my face was because Jesse sounded like himself. The other half was because getting myself off to a dirty letter sounded ... intriguing.

Perhaps he can make me come after all ... I thought, my shoulders shrugging at the potential for sexual growth within our words.

Sliding the letter I'd just inhaled under the stack, I moved on to the second, thankful our time together wasn't over yet.

Jenkins, Jesse

Division 28

Elle,

I just opened MULTIPLE letters from you, and I can't tell you how happy I am right now!

First off, that picture of you. Goddamn, it made my fucking day. You're so hot. That tank top is barely holding on—kind of like me when I saw it.

I promise you, babe, when you come up for graduation weekend, it's going down. I hope you're ready because I'm coming for you ...

Can I make a request though? Will you bring that red lingerie you wore for me over Christmas break? I can't stop thinking about it. That image is single-handedly fueling my desire to graduate. I love it when you wear sexy getups just for me. It makes me feel like a man.

On another much less horny note, I'm happy to hear classes and work are going well for you. But I could have guessed that. If I know my girl, she's passing her time without me by rewatching *Twilight* for the millionth time and jamming out to Jewel. I know you've always had a thing for that sparkly son of a bitch. But does Edward really have shit on me? Because Bella definitely can't compete with you. Rosalie maybe...

Kidding!

This letter will be a quick one. We're supposed to study lessons from class today, but I'm sneakily writing to you instead. All I want to do is talk to you. You're my escape from this testosterone-packed prison. They separate the men and women here like they're allergic to each other. I wanted you to know that.

Also, my wisdom teeth removal is scheduled for three days from now. I'm stressed about it. I'll keep you posted, babe.

Sleep sweet.

Jesse

    So many words to focus on.
    Knowing I only had a few more minutes of peace before returning to the register, I quickly sifted to the final letter in the pile, promising to reread them all later with the attention they deserved.

Sleep Sweet

Jenkins, Jesse

Division 28

Elle,

The good news is that they allow four days of rest and recovery in bed after any medical procedure. That's the most I've been allowed since arriving, and I fully plan on using every second to my advantage! This means I now have more time to write to you!

Bad news ... I'm so swollen—way worse than that time I got stung on the chin by that yellow jacket. And I can only drink smoothies and milkshakes.

Isn't that a plus, you might ask?

NO, it isn't because the food here is literal trash, and I'm thinking they really might put saltpeter in it. I haven't popped one lousy boner since I got here, and that's not like me. Usually, all it takes is me thinking about you, and my dick is standing at attention, but, no, thinking of you now is pure torture with no release in sight. These thoughts in my head need an outlet ...

Let's just say I miss you and leave it at that.

What has your release been since I left? Do you touch yourself when you think of me, Elle? Maybe you can use your psychology major insight to help me get hard from your next letter. I'm so desperate that it hurts. SEND HELP!

Anyway, I'm hitting the hay. I have a busy day of resting in bed ahead of me. I've never been so excited in my life to do absolutely nothing. It's a welcome break from the demanding schedule here. I swear, these big bad instructors have something to prove.

Sleep sweet.

Jesse

My boyfriend's touch remained trapped in the pages resting in my hands. I finished the third one quicker than the rest, meaning the wait for another started all over again.

Talk about whiplash.

I wished his words could touch me, whisper in my ear what I yearned to hear, and kiss my bare shoulder in a way that said, *I love you and will never let something as insignificant as distance impact our future together.*

But they couldn't because none of the letters had mentioned our future together.

Was he staying surface level on purpose? After all, he was going through a massive change and needed to stay focused. I understood that.

I retreated from the restroom stall, tucked my paper trail into the back pocket of my jeans, and approached the sink, surrounded by trendy checkered wallpaper and tasteful graffiti. The girl in the gold-rimmed mirror staring back at me looked drained. Her usual optimistic expression was missing.

So was her man.

I hoped the cold water I splashed against my face would counteract the extra time I'd put into everything except myself lately.

It barely made a difference.

His letters told me he believed in us. His dedication to writing them told me he missed me.

But seeing that dedication in action on March 31 was the only thing that could pull me out of my head and into his arms.

Eight

Austin

Valentine's Day 2012

CUPID WAS THE PERFECT LITTLE arrow-slinging son of a bitch to remind me of my loneliness. I knew the day would come—my grandparents' wedding anniversary. They hadn't celebrated it on earth for nearly a decade, but I always thought about them when Valentine's Day came around.

"One day, Austin, I hope you find a woman like mine," Grandpa gushed, *whittling away at a fractured piece of driftwood he'd collected before the sun rose.*

I couldn't tell what he was carving, but there was no question who he was carving it for.

The faded ink scrolled across the underside of his wrist, reading My Justine, *proved it.*

After my grandparents, Justine and Joel Carterson, had officially adopted me at age two, we spent our summers in Blue Hill, Maine, winterizing their fishing cabin before the extreme temperatures froze every pipe for the season.

Grandpa taught me how to be a man, and I loved it because my birth parents had taught me nothing, aside from how to beg for the things I needed in life, like affection.

"What makes her different from all the others?" I asked, *our small paddleboat drifting farther from the dock.*

"Ha! Become a bit crass in your teenage years, Austin?"

I noticed the way his voice cracked as he got older. Years of antiseizure medications had a way of playing games with his vocal cords. His time was borrowed, but he still had no problem sharing it with those he loved.

"I'm only speaking from my own experience. And so far, it hasn't been the best," I said, referring to my only ex-girlfriend, Gwen.

She had broken up with me when she found out I was adopted. More specifically, who I was adopted from. Her family wouldn't let her date me anymore. But why? Was my birth parents' reputation really that bad around town?

"All I can tell you is this ... one of your biggest goals in life should be to find a love that needs little explanation. It's classic when you need tenderness, and it's unbreakable when you need strength. It will last forever because you treat it as such. It's everything. That's what my Justine and I found, and all these years later, I'm still as in love with her as the first time I saw her."

"Sounds easier said than done." I took a big gulp of my sweet iced tea. Grandma never let us leave the dock without it.

"You see how we're slowly bobbing toward the open sea, and neither of us is even looking at an oar?" He pointed away from the coastline, drawing my attention to the vastness of the mirror-like ocean supporting our boat.

I nodded.

"The tides will move us from point A to point B if we don't fight them," Grandpa said, looking at me for a moment longer than necessary.

"The tides go in and out every single day. Water moves. What does that tell me?" I sighed, challenging him.

"If we both paddled as hard as we could to return to shore right now, it would exhaust us, take every ounce of our manpower. But if we're patient and wait for them to pull us back to the dock, we can enjoy the ride and make it back in time for lobster bisque."

I rolled my eyes. Gramps could draw connections between just about anything. All I heard was lobster bisque ...

"Trust me, boy. I was your age once. The waves will find you, and you'll know when they do ..." he reiterated, ignoring the pronounced grumble that left my stomach at his mention of fresh bisque.

"Will the ropes find me, too, and tie me to the chair, like Dad used to?" I stiffened, recounting the moments still infecting my early memories. I repeated them aloud sometimes, only to ensure I remembered the kind of person I didn't want to be.

"No. But those can be untied and repurposed for something more useful. Like this ..." He repositioned the pocketknife's handle and handed me his

creation—a delicate driftwood anchor. Grandpa reached for the manila rope hanging over the stern and cut a thin strand—the perfect size to thread through the hole at the top so Grandma Justine could hang her new sentiment.

Two hours later, I sat at the kitchen table, which was topped with a fresh pitcher of iced tea and a bowl of fresh lobster bisque, alongside my grandparents.

Their weathered hands never untangled as they shared more with each other than just a touch and more with me than just a meal.

I stirred the shrinking sugar cubes around my iced tea as the memories sat with me in my office. I wished they'd dissolve just as fast because they distracted me from deciding what to teach the newbies.

Knot-tying techniques, radar detection, and drill formations were all options. They needed to master an endless list of skills before graduating from the program. If they didn't understand even one concept, the blame landed back in my lap.

Since they'd already been here for weeks, the basics were out of the way. The important shit could begin. I gathered my clipboard and lesson of choice for the day and stood, readying myself for my two p.m. instruction. Helping young men prepare to hold meaningful jobs in the Navy never got old.

"Chief Carterson …" Romano's head peeked around my office door. His stiff nod told me our conversation would be all business.

"Sir." I responded with words and eye contact, ensuring he had my full attention.

"I've been asked to request a security review on all surveillance cameras in the instructional buildings. Direct orders from the captain. He said it was urgent."

"Of course. I'll get on it immediately and report back to him. You'll have to cover my instruction today; I was headed that way in five," I suggested.

Canceling class was not an option. I had only six weeks to teach a large amount of material. Romano was a team player. No doubt he'd help me out.

"No problem. I love playing substitute teacher." A short-lived smile crossed his face, lightening the thickened suspense that had blown in with his request.

An order from the captain meant that something crucial had happened and needed to be investigated immediately.

"He said to pay attention to building six—something about suspicious activity and wanting to be sure the janitorial staff is only accessing their assigned divisions during working hours," he added.

Part of my job was ensuring the safety of the recruits in my division. Direct access to the dozens of security cameras sprinkled around every building on base was the best way to do that.

"Here, take this." I handed him my clipboard. "Classroom C. I planned to focus on formations today, but feel free to switch things up. Give 'em the Romano special." I winked.

"Roger that. Take your time. After their instruction, I'll release the guys to the chow hall and report back." Romano turned and exited my office, pulling the door closed behind him.

I sank deeper into my desk chair and circled to face the computer monitor, holding the answers the captain asked me to find.

"Let's see who's trying to pull a fast one on Chief Carterson."

Nine

Elle

FEBRUARY 14, 2012, WAS THE date etched across the top of the chalkboard fastened to the wall in my best friend's classroom, reminding me that I was solo on Valentine's Day.

"We have a *very* special guest today, class," Ruthie announced to her middle schoolers.

My own beautiful, black-haired Ms. Frizzle had only been teaching for one year. In that time, however, she'd flourished into her version of the eccentric teacher with a modern touch. Her students were lucky to have her.

She'd begged me to come in and talk to her final class period of the day for career week, likely only because she wanted to grab drinks with me afterward. I had taken it as a compliment, knowing a bestie night would do us both some good.

"Hello, everyone. It's exciting to be here today. I'm Elle, but you can call me the *emotion whisperer*!" I chirped, fanning my hands like an overly enthusiastic birthday party magician.

Heat immediately engulfed my face. My attempt at grabbing her class's attention fell so hard that even Ruthie's look of empathy couldn't cushion the blow. Good thing half of her students were asleep.

Reddened blotches of embarrassment peppered my chest as I pushed through. "I'm in my final year of the mental health counseling program at CPC, and I want to share a bit about why I chose to pursue counseling as a career."

"Sebastian, wake up!" Ruthie tapped her long burgundy fingernails on a student's desk, directly beside his head, which lay still against the small surface.

How could that be comfortable?

The boy shot upright and coughed. He adjusted his chest toward the whiteboard I stood next to.

"Like Ms. Ruthie here, one of my biggest aspirations is to teach people. I like to think of a counselor as a teacher, but for behaviors and emotions," I added, pointing to their beloved teacher, whose expression was growing increasingly frantic by the minute. It was fun seeing her in her work element—a huge departure from the Ruthie I knew and loved.

"My dad says counselors and therapists are quacks," another student barked.

His comment pulled a few laughs from the sea of bored pupils, but not enough to sting me. The term was one I'd heard before.

"Well, tell your dad he can come talk to me in the parent pickup line if he'd like some clarification," my best friend sassed. She flipped her hair over one shoulder before softly smirking at the redheaded boy sitting next to Sebastian.

You tell him, Ruths.

"As I was saying, there are many concentrations to pick from in the mental health field. I, for one, chose to focus on helping people with addictions. I show them how to cope with their circumstances in healthy ways. How to heal and how to give power to things that can help them live their lives to the fullest."

"Have you ever been addicted to anything? How can you teach others how to navigate those things if you haven't?" a blonde girl sitting in the back row asked.

She reminded me of myself—asking too many questions before she was ready to learn the answers.

I've been addicted to Jesse's words, the quest for real orgasms, Jewel's angelic voice, studying to escape the anxieties of everyday life ... I thought.

"That's a great question," I replied through my intrusive thoughts. "My clients and I form an understanding, and I love helping them better themselves regardless of their situations. Although I haven't personally struggled with addiction, I've worked with a lot of people who have. And they've taught me things about life that school never could."

"Like what?!" Ruthie probed, helping my discussion progress since the awake half of her students were doodling or texting under their desks during my failed attempt to educate them.

Tough crowd.

"Like how sometimes, the only reason people become addicted to something is because it's easy to access or it makes them feel good for a short moment. It's comfortable. But comfort isn't always the thing to strive for. Uncomfortable, out-of-reach things often give the better outcome, even if they're harder to get to. Even if those things seem so far out of reach that you can't even imagine them." More than just the words left my lips. Heavy realization accompanied them.

Were Jesse and I only holding on because it was comfortable for us? Because my personality, affection, and accessibility were easy for him to latch on to, and vice versa? Was I addicted to our past yet afraid of our future? One where I'd be forced to support his career and scatter mine in whatever direction the Navy took us? My train of thought sped south at a rate that was sure to spiral out.

Ruthie's interruption was my North Star.

"Speaking of addictions, if I see one more of you little heathens on your cell phone, I will be canceling the pizza party next week," she warned. Her threat snapped every single student out of their trance. "Now that I have your full attention, can we please thank our guest speaker for her time today?"

"Thank youuuu," they called in unison.

"You're all very welcome. And remember, each one of you has the power to choose a job that will fuel you one day. Try to pick one that will make a difference," I urged.

Suddenly, a bell rang, dismissing the class from their seats. I walked over to Ruthie and sat my clearly-not-meant-to-be-a-middle-school-teacher ass on the edge of her desk.

"How the hell do you do that every day?"

"As much as these kids drive me up the wall every now and again … every single one has my heart. I like showing them they've got someone tough in their corner because some of them don't get that at home." Ruthie's pride overflowed from her sentiment.

She was meant to be a teacher.

I was meant to be a counselor.

Jesse was meant to be in the Navy.

But were Jesse and I meant to be those things *together*?

"Let's get out of here. Driptini's starts serving booze at four, and I would kill for an espresso martini right now." Ruthie swatted several fallen curls out of her face. Her faded makeup gripped her skin for dear life.

She was tired, but she was never too tired for a good cocktail or gossip session. Now I could understand why.

"Shit, me too. No dick for over a month is keeping me from thinking straight," I joked. But it wasn't a joke. It was my reality.

"Girl, I can't say I feel too bad for you. Since graduating and starting this teaching job, I haven't been on one date. Not one! If I can forgo dick for almost a year, you can certainly handle going without for a few months. I wish I had a sexy sailor sending me love letters, you lucky duck."

God, she made me laugh. My teeth met the air through a wide smile I couldn't slow.

"You're right," I agreed, vowing to leave my self-thrown pity party behind in her classroom. "I still couldn't do this without your support though, so thank you …"

"No, thank *you* for giving us an excuse to spend more girl time together. Besides, it's freaking Valentine's Day! Let's get going. I need a full rundown of what you and Jesse have been writing about in your letters. I want every sexy detail so I can live vicariously through you. Has he mentioned any lonely friends in boot camp? I'd love to be someone's new pen pal …" she rambled on, as if convincing herself she'd just spouted the best idea of all time.

Thirty minutes later, we pulled into Driptini's as raindrops drizzled down the windows of Ruthie's convertible.

Maybe my place of employment was helpful for something other than discounted lattes and saving up for a flight to see Jesse after all. Like girls' night.

And overthinking just about everything.

Ten

Elle

Dear Jesse,

Where do I begin? It's Tuesday night, February 28, around six p.m., and I'm spent. I picked up a few extra shifts this week when class allowed. Emma still comes in and asks about you. She might be your ex, but how you're doing in boot camp is none of her business. I hope you don't mind, but I let her know it.

Besides, I'm only a few hundred dollars away from booking my flight and our hotel for the weekend. I refuse to let anything dampen my excitement. I can't wait!

I researched some hotels near the base and read a few online blogs about how far ahead I needed to book. It seems like the earlier, the better because they all fill up quickly for graduation weekend. Don't worry about that though. I'll figure everything out. You have important Navy things to worry about now! I'm proud of you, and I'm proud of us for sticking together through it all. I can't wait to see where this journey takes you. I also can't wait to see you in that uniform because I know it'll wreck me.

Classes have been more exciting than ever! Not ... I swear, Professor Oramae IS trying to kill us with how much homework she gives. Little does she know, I find it therapeutic ...

As our time apart grows, I struggle with staying focused. My thoughts always lead back to you, and when I write to you, it's like we're sitting together on my bed like we used to. Once I put the pen down, you vanish again—my personal ghost.

Another month or so, and you'll be back in my arms. I can't imagine the feeling. Thankfully, I won't have to imagine it much longer!

Also, Ruthie says hi. It's more like, "Ask your boyfriend if he's got any hot bunkmates who need a pen pal." But you get the idea.

She's been my lifeline since you left and asked me to tell you that the next time you're in town, she promises to make you that strawberry pastry you like. I don't want to make you feel bad because I know the food sucks there, but ... it was so damn good last time she made it, right?!

Little things like strawberry pastries make me think of you. Everything makes me think of you. That's how I know that even though hundreds of miles separate us, we'll be just fine when we get to the other side of our distance. March 31 is right around the corner. It can't come fast enough.

I'm headed out to grab dinner with my parents, but I wanted to ask if you had any picture requests. Is there anything special you want to see me in? I want to make sure you have what you need. Wink, wink.

Also, as you can see, I shoved more stamps and paper into this envelope. I hope it's enough to keep your letters coming. Not sure I could live without them.

I love you, and I miss you! I'll write to you again tomorrow.

Love always,

Elle

Eleven

Elle

Dear Jesse,

It's been exactly two weeks since I've gotten a letter from you, and I'm trying not to freak out, but I totally am. My anxiety is through the fucking roof right now. I'm telling myself there's a logical explanation. For future shits and giggles, here are my guesses for the delay:

A) You ran out of stamps because you're such a great guy and you shared the ones I'd sent you with the other guys.

B) You got so hot and horny, thinking about me, that you spontaneously combusted and disappeared into thin air.

C) You're hurt. (Trying hard not to think about this one.)

D) Your whole division got in trouble, and you're stuck dealing with the consequences.

E) You're extremely busy learning all the ~~top-secret~~ Navy things they teach you in boot camp and simply haven't had time to write as often as you did before.

I booked my flight and our hotel room for graduation weekend last week. I fly in on March 30 and stay until Monday, April 2. It will be a quick trip, but I'm sure it will be worth every penny. Have you heard where they're sending you for A School yet? I bet you're as curious about where you're headed after graduation as I am.

If, for some reason, your graduation date is delayed, please let me know so I can reschedule. I honestly couldn't afford trip insurance, so I'll need to change things as soon as possible if that's the case. Hopefully, it isn't though because I can't take another second without seeing you and talking to you in person …

I'm sure there's a very valid reason why I haven't heard from you, but PLEASE tell me what that reason is as soon as you can. The radio silence is seriously killing me. I wish

I could call the base or something, but I know I can't.

I don't want you to worry about me though, so when you read this, please know I'll keep sending out letters until I hear back.

Even in the dark, I'll be here, waiting for you. Come back to me soon ...

I love you, Jesse.

Love always,

Elle

Twelve

Elle

Ruthie: Get home now! The mail just came! Two letters for you!!!

Me: Are you serious?! Oh my God, DON'T OPEN THEM!!! I'm leaving class early. Heading to my car now.

Ruthie: I'm serious! As much as I need to know what they say, I'm sprinting out the door for parent-teacher conferences. When I get home, you're MINE. At least text me to let me know he's okay …

Me: If I'm still able to function, I'm yours. I'll text you. Love you.

Ruthie: Love you more. XO

TEN AGONIZING MINUTES AFTER RUTHIE'S text, I arrived home and flung our front door open. Was I about to pee my pants? No. I was about to lose my shit instead.

Three days had passed since I'd sent Jesse my SOS. I needed his letters like I needed air. My lungs sputtered when they came into view.

The letters rested quietly on our kitchen counter. Unopened, they sat next to a sticky note from Ruthie that read, *See, I told you he loved you!*

Frantic, I grabbed the envelopes and took off toward my bedroom. I closed and locked the door behind me, craving solitude through my struggle. Yes, I was alone, but I needed to be more than alone when I ripped them open. In case of bad news, I wished to be surrounded by things that comforted me, like silence and no one around to judge my reaction.

Deep breaths, Elle, I thought.

I pressed play on my laptop, and it resumed the last song. "Who Will Save Your Soul" by Jewel embraced me, like it had countless times before.

Sinking onto the edge of my bed, I braced myself, ready to read his why. Every beat of my stressed-out heart brought me closer to the two neatly typed letters before me.

Jenkins, Jesse

Division 28

Elle,

I want to start with an apology. I know you haven't gotten a letter from me in weeks, and I can't imagine the level of panic and worry that has put you through. I'm so sorry about that, babe. It's been hard on me too…

You need to know the situation was out of my control and that, if I can help it, it won't happen again for the rest of my stay here. A male and female recruit were caught having sex in a storage closet, which thoroughly pissed off the instructors and immediately resulted in a "no outgoing mail for weeks" rule. They take coed mingling very

seriously here, which means both impacted divisions faced the consequences. The horndogs were too selfish to refrain from taking actions that would affect the rest of us. Dumbasses.

Reading your letters and not being able to write back to you nearly killed me. I hoped they wouldn't stop coming, and when they never did, it made me realize how dedicated you were to us. It's hard to find that in someone. I always knew you were perfect, but the distance between us has helped me realize that I need you to know you're not just perfect.

You're perfect for me.

I don't care how far apart we are or how much say the Navy will have in my life after boot camp. I only care to reassure you that I'll never take you for granted again. The last few weeks have shown me just how much you deserve. And that's a life full of happiness, fulfillment, and love. A life with someone as honorable and dedicated as you are.

A life with me.

When I see you for graduation, I promise it will be memorable. I can't wait to look you in the eye and hear everything you've wanted to tell me in person. I want to hear how your classes are going and what you think your days after graduation will look like. I want to hear about Ruthie and all the trouble you two have gotten into.

As supportive as you've been, I need to do better at ensuring you have what you need from me to achieve your dreams while I work toward mine. Of course, I hope you can do that near me, but if you can't, I would never let that stop me from being with you.

In other news, I made friends with the mailman here; he's another recruit in my division, and we're tight. He promised to send out my mail three times per week instead of just twice, like the other guys get. Expect more letters than usual going forward! I had to bribe him and promise to pay him a little bonus when we graduate. You're more than worth it.

You might have noticed that this letter is typed too. I got an upgrade! Each month, the three highest-scoring recruits in class are rewarded with a laptop to borrow in their downtime. It doesn't connect to the internet, but it does connect to a printer and enables whoever earns it to write more letters faster. This means I can make up for the last few weeks. It also helps with studying and even has a few games, which are a great incentive. So, lucky me. Your boy finally aced something! If you can't tell, I'm excited because this means I can write more words to you in less time. I plan to pass all my exams with high marks so I can keep access to this thing until I graduate. They'll have to tear it away from me ...

I've got to get back to prepping my uniform for inspection tomorrow. Shoe shining will be the death of me. Get the good night's sleep you've been needing.

You never leave my mind.

I love you.

Sleep sweet.

Jesse

The reassurance, the love, the promise of a future together I had been dying to hear finally found me, like he could sense my need for it. Like he finally meant it.

Relief washed away every bit of the fear I'd been holding on to for weeks. He was safe. *Happy.* And he had annihilated every rogue doubt flooding my brain. The Jesse I had fallen for was back.

Could the second letter top what I'd just read? I couldn't wait to find out. I tossed aside the paper I'd forever cherish, ready for my boyfriend to take me higher.

Jenkins, Jesse

Division 28

My Elle,

Good morning, beautiful. I'm not sure what time it is for you. It's about four a.m. for me. I woke up earlier than everyone else to have a few quiet moments with you. Well, with the laptop. I'm pretending I'm sitting with you though, staring at you... touching you...

I'm so excited that you booked your hotel and flight for graduation weekend! The countdown begins, with only a few weeks left! The moment I see you is going to obliterate me. I almost forget what it's like to hug you and feel your chest pressed against mine. I could never really forget, but with all the anticipation, I think it will feel like the first time I ever held you.

I can't stop thinking about it.

I keep your letters hidden under my mattress so I can reread them whenever I have time. I love getting to know your mind in this new way. It feels classic and romantic, kind of like me. Ha-ha. Okay, that was a bit corny, but I'm trying to keep you laughing in my absence. I can't have you finding someone funnier to spend your time with.

Now that I'm making a steady paycheck, I plan to pay you back for your travel expenses. Let me know how much the trip came to, and I'll take care of it. You deserve to be cared for like you care for others. I want to do more to take care of you, moving forward. You deserve it.

I've got to go. The boys are starting to wake up, and we'll be headed to class soon. I hope you've enjoyed reading this as much as I've enjoyed writing it. I'll see you in my dreams.

```
I love you.

Sleep sweet.

Jesse
```

I love you too, Jesse, I thought.

I loved boot camp as well because whatever they were doing to him in there was opening his eyes to how lucky we were to have each other.

I reread the letters, latching on to every word like they were nature's antidepressants.

Flopping back onto my bed like a carefree schoolgirl, I kicked my feet. I felt like myself for the first time in weeks, knowing Jesse was safe and in love with me.

With a grateful heart and nothing but confidence in us to fuel me until I saw his face, I whispered my quiet mantra. *Keep me calm, keep him safe, keep us together.*

Thirteen

Austin

March 31, 2012
Graduation Day

Ahhh, Holding Division 201. A place where any male recruits who had been injured, whose graduation date had been rolled back for some reason, or who had found themselves in trouble waited for their circumstances to change. If they were physically able, we put them to work, doing tasks such as cleaning or kitchen duty, while the Navy determined the next steps for them.

I called it *limbo on lockdown* because it wasn't restricted enough to mimic prison. Yet it remained fully regulated to ensure seclusion from other divisions and a communication filter with the outside world.

The time—*7:00 a.m.*—flashed from the face of my watch. The room, lined wall to wall with bunks, vibrated with the bustle of a new day as dozens of men dressed for their assigned jobs.

Jenkins hid in the farthest bed from the door I'd just passed through.

A coward in his natural habitat.

And I couldn't wait to throw a bone into his cage—one only I had the key to.

I approached the animal, which I only respected because I had to. His expression grew wary as he quickly rose from his thin mattress.

Was it so he could beg for mercy? He'd find no mercy in me.

"You gotta let me out of here, bro. My girlfriend is coming today! Has anyone even let her know I won't be graduating?" Jesse spat nervously.

His buzz cut had grown out of regulation length weeks ago, but recruits who found themselves in holding had far more significant problems.

Especially him.

"I'm not your bro, Jenkins. What part of this dynamic do you not understand?"

Jesse had balls, calling me bro—I'd give him that. What he *didn't* have was a say in when or how his girlfriend would be notified of his little change of plans. That power remained in my hands.

I'd never been more grateful.

"Look, I know I fucked up, but she flew in from Pensacola. She deserves to know that I'll be stuck here for a while," he begged. A look of pain stretched across his face. It was pathetic. Like him. "Please, just let me see her for five minutes ... I need to talk to her!"

"But she doesn't deserve to know why?" I reiterated.

He wanted her to know he wouldn't graduate today, but I doubted he wanted her to understand the reason.

Luckily, I had all the proof I needed to convince her. "Interesting that you think *now* is the time to give her what she deserves. Your timing is impeccable." I adjusted the collar of my dress whites, not wanting Jesse's *poor me* expression to soil the uniform I'd spent an hour starching the fuck out of last night. It had to be perfect for her.

"I was waiting to tell her what happened in person. She's a good girl, and I need to explain myself. She doesn't deserve to worry herself to death over the consequences of my actions. Fuck! Please, you have to help me."

His begging did nothing to change my impression of him. Plus, I didn't need him to tell me she didn't deserve that. An enemy could treat her better.

"Explain yourself? How do you explain sneaking around with another woman and screwing her in a storage closet? Maybe you should have thought about your girlfriend when you were busy getting your dick wet," I barked.

Anger tempted my neck with heat. But knowing I would see her in a few short hours iced my growing desire to punch him in his plastic-looking jaw.

"So, no one notified her? You want her to show up today and freak the fuck out in front of everyone? That's real nice, Chief," Jesse scoffed, balling his hands into useless fists.

He could try to use her against me, but his efforts would be wasted. I worked with hundreds of young men. In fact, being promoted to a division commander, teaching recruits in boot camp, was the highlight of my career.

But using Elle's emotions to get what he wanted was the sure sign of a master manipulator. I was too experienced to let it bother me.

"Don't worry. I'll personally see to it that she's notified and given a full briefing on your delay."

The moment the promise escaped my lips, his eyes widened.

Yes, Jesse, today is the day she finds out your truth.

She'd have to wait a bit longer to learn mine.

I grinned. "You'll have a chance to explain yourself to her when you're officially kicked out of the program. Until then, I'll ensure she's cared for exactly how she should be."

"What the fuck is that supposed to mean?" His face shifted slightly to the left, a look of confusion strangling his jawline and tightened mouth. I'd never seen eyes so wide that they looked like they could pop out of the sockets.

"It means, you're a boy and I'm a man." The words slipped off my tongue. I had no control over them. "You've demonstrated that you have no idea how to treat another human being. Thankfully, I know precisely how to do that." My poisonous pitch softened to keep any wandering eyes off us.

The room was large enough that we had our space from the others. Still, attracting more attention to Jesse's situation was the last thing I needed. As far as they knew, we had no connection outside Division 28.

"Can you just tell her … I'm sorry, and I'll call or write to her as soon as I find a way to?" Jesse said, defeated.

Stay professional, Chief, I thought.

I didn't feel bad for him, but I needed to make him feel like my words weren't a full-on assassination of his character, even if I knew they were.

I was still his instructor. I'd also have to attend his Captain's Mast review in a month and give my recommendations for disciplinary action. The captain on base would have the final say in his future in the Navy. I had no choice but to remain in his life until then. Right now though, his fate belonged to me.

"If it makes you feel any better, I notified her you're safe," I admitted. *Here's your bone, Jesse.*

"What?" His level of confusion matched the panic spewing from his reddening face. A veiny right hand flew up to his scalp and ran through his disheveled blond hair. His narrowed eyes showcased the questions that blinded his brain. "When? How?!"

"Don't worry about the whens and the hows. If I were you, I'd spend my newfound free time thinking about how to explain myself *when* the time came. Today isn't that time, but it's coming ... I promise you."

I couldn't stop him from talking to Elle forever. She'd need the closure. Soon, I'd give it to her for him. It would be like a favor, only not as much fun to repay.

Surprisingly, his internal chaos faded. I saw it in the way his stare met the linoleum floor he'd been shining with a toothbrush for weeks. His posture retreated into the shell of the boy he had been when he arrived as a hopeful recruit twelve weeks ago.

His transparent attempts at persuading me to see her today had told me he still cared for her. How easily he had given up told me he never truly loved her. If he did, he'd kick and scream at me to unlock his cage until I obeyed. Instead, he dropped back down on his bunk and wallowed in his defeat.

I took several steps toward the exit, needing to return to my office before the base entered full-on graduation mode. The families would be arriving soon, and I needed a level head before readying the deserving men in my division for the first milestone of their careers.

"Can you just give her this if she shows up today?"

Jesse's fractured plea stopped me in my tracks. My few paces toward the exit bought him enough time to find and bring me a folded piece of loose-leaf paper.

He held it out for me to grab. Jesse wasn't permitted to send mail once he entered the holding division, but he had plenty of free time to write.

Fuck.

"Sure thing," I lied, stealing the lone sheet of paper from his grip.

I returned his hopeful stare with one made of disdain. He had no choice but to trust me to deliver whatever bullshit apology he'd penned for Elle.

A few minutes later, I sat down in my office chair for one final moment of reflection before the graduation chaos began, just after crumpling up and throwing Jesse's pathetic attempt at an apology into the garbage can. I hadn't read it. Hadn't cared to.

Instead of dwelling on it, I switched gears and grabbed the shoebox-size metal tin from the top of my bookshelf, hidden behind my grandparents' wedding photo. I placed the box on my desk and removed the lid to reflect on what was inside.

It was amazing how much it held.

Disbelief slowly shook my head left and then right, my smile illuminated by the box of fate that had brought us together. My favorite photo of her topped the collection of loose letters, pictures, and envelopes I'd found when I cleaned out Jesse's bunk after it was determined that he and a female recruit, Rita Camellino, were the ones triggering the security cameras.

Elle stared up at me from the glossy instant photo with the same innocence I remembered. Had she taken the picture for me specifically? No. However, there was no way it wasn't meant for my eyes because Elle Madelyn had been fucking made for me.

I had known it the first time I saw her.

I had known it when the magnetism in her written words possessed me all over again.

I had known it when hers was the only face I could see when I closed my eyes at night.

And I had known it when Jesse wrote the final chapter of their story, making room for ours to begin.

Soon, I'd have congratulations to spread and my usual graduation-day leadership duties to complete, leaving one final undertaking lingering on my list. The chance I'd waited two whole years for.

Somehow, the tides had drifted Elle back into the safety of my harbor.

Nothing could stop me from making her mine.

Fourteen

Elle

THE SHITTY, WATERED-DOWN ATTEMPT at a latte coated my throat while I choked down a piece of toast from the continental breakfast bar. You'd think a hotel as busy as the one I found myself seated in would have decent breakfast options. Spoiler alert: they didn't.

A strong dose of caffeine and a hearty meal would have been helpful ways to cushion the lingering side effects from yesterday's flight, taxi ride, and evening check-in. Instead, my enthusiastic nerves and rampant Jesse jitters had allowed me only four lousy hours of sleep and a side of anticipatory nausea.

Sitting alone at the table across from mine, a middle-aged man hid everything but his eyes behind his newspaper, glancing at me every time he flipped the page or slurped on his orange juice. Creepy newspaper guy reminded me that I was a young woman, rooming alone at a hotel I'd never stayed at, in a town I'd never been to. Another reason why I couldn't wait for Jesse to stay with me tonight.

The lobby of the Waulumbee Lake Inn was full of characters. Men, women, children, and even the slurpy paper guy shared something with me—a yearning to witness their loved ones graduate boot camp.

Time ticked on as if it were an average day, the clock unaware of how far it was from average for so many. Only three hours remained to shower, get ready, set up our room, and catch the hotel's shuttle to the base. My endless to-do list taunted me.

I pushed my plate aside and stared into space as if it were a painting, pausing to reflect on everything that had brought us to the moment before me …

How Jesse and I had met on the same day he signed his agreement to join the Navy.

The last two years we'd spent building our relationship.

The highs, the worries, and the reasons we had both found in our letters.

The realization that Jesse finally cared as much about my future as he did about his own. And that, together, we were ready to take things to the next level.

A renewed energy surged through my chest, and I smiled wide. Jesse's growth in our time apart had shown me precisely what I needed to see.

The only thing left to do was see it in person.

I returned to my room, forgoing an extra cup of coffee. On my walk back, palpable energy radiated from the people I encountered in the halls—a mutual respect for the time and distance we'd spent away from the people we would soon see. Sure, we were strangers, but the solidarity silently threading us together united us in ways unseen.

The minutes that ticked on felt more like hours. A good thing, seeing as I needed every second to prepare myself and finish setting up the room for Jesse's arrival before the shuttle to base was scheduled to leave.

Did the idea of seeing him for the first time in months excite me the most? Or was it the guarantee of the infamous post–boot camp sex with him that brought a surge of heat to the space between my thighs? Was that how the term *sweatpants* came to be?

The faux rose petals I'd brought from home, sprinkled upon the king-size bed, complemented the bedside table I'd topped with strawberry massage oil, a small vibrator, and the lingerie my boyfriend had requested. The room oozed sexuality.

I imagined Jesse's inevitable protest when it was time for him to leave it, knowing the inviting space would be quite an upgrade from boot-camp living.

Candles would have been a nice touch, but the hotel's strict *no candles* policy warned me against them. Dreamily, I imagined setting off the smoke detectors and evacuating the room, wearing only skimpy lingerie and Jesse's arms wrapped around my waist. A sexy fireman and his clumsy victim, who had accidentally lit their hotel room ablaze, wasn't the vibe I was going for, although it would make an excellent romance novel.

"You and I" kicked off the Get Ready playlist I'd curated on my flight to Chicago, and, boy, did Lady Gaga know how to put a pep in my step. Of course, Jewel, Dave Matthews Band, and the *Twilight* movie soundtrack appeared deeper in the list. The only songs that had made the cut were the ones that grounded me.

Familiar lyrics buzzed loudly around the bathroom for the entire forty-five minutes it took me to shower, shave, and moisturize every bit of hair and skin on my body from the neck down. If *plucked chicken* were a skin type, I'd be a damn plucked chicken.

There wasn't much I enjoyed more than the feeling of a fluffy, freshly bleached towel to wrap up in after a long shower. Hotel linens were my weakness. I couldn't fully enjoy the feeling of the fabric pressed against my skin though because I couldn't concentrate on anything other than Jesse.

Jesse, Jesse, Jesse, Jesse, Jesse …

I wiped a path through the condensation that blanketed the bathroom mirror and stared back at the girl who had gotten me through the last twelve weeks.

That's right, Little Miss Anxiety; we did it. You did it, I thought.

A chuckle filled the steamy air. I was truly proud of myself.

On another note, how the hell could I put my makeup on without looking like Mona from *Cry-Baby* if my hands wouldn't stop shaking? It was funny how the moment I needed my makeup to look its best came with a side of trembling hands and incoordination. Several deep breaths and a two-minute meditation cut through the layers of nerves that smothered me.

Thirty minutes later, cool tones of brown and shimmery mauves caressed my eyelids while thin winged eyeliner and pink-nude lipstick completed my amped-up signature look.

My makeup also complemented the tight white sweater I'd spent fifty bucks on for the special occasion. Splurging on clothes was not my norm, especially lately, but I needed to feel my best. The amount of cleavage peeking out of the neckline, coupled with the soft, figure-hugging material tucked into my skintight jeans, made me feel just that.

Slutty, which I assumed would be the unspoken uniform for many of the other girlfriends attending graduation, wasn't one of my goals. Mine consisted of stealing Jesse's attention, staying true to my classy yet sexy style, *and* staying warm in the northern chill. Would my getup be enough to accomplish all three?

The floor-length mirror fastened to the bathroom door practically screamed, *Yessss*, when I turned around for a second look. My ass looked great, even better, accompanied by the black suede boots stopping just above my knees. My dark jeans smoothly tucked into them like a dream, and the few extra inches of height their heels gifted to my five-and-change-foot frame were a nice touch. They weren't sky-high, but they were still alluring.

Jesse would undoubtedly agree. He'd never seen his Florida girl in a pair of winter boots.

The remainder of our time apart crept by. I used the final seconds to fluff my hair and apply one last spritz of floral perfume to my neck and chest.

"You did it, Elle. You made it, and you look smoking hot. Nothing can bring you down now. Just enjoy it, bitch!" Ruthie's distant voice in my ear inflated my ego, giving me the confidence only she knew I needed.

I vowed to text her on the shuttle ride to base. No doubt she'd be obsessively awaiting an update.

I lifted my small crossbody bag over my shoulder, positioned the strap across my chest, and double-checked that my graduation ticket, wallet, phone, and room key were still there. The two months' worth of overthinking my body refused to shake were also in there, always along for the ride.

One last glance around the room and the *click* of the auto-locking door behind me were the only things that separated me from the most anticipated moment of my life.

It was finally time.

A short elevator ride later, my fast-paced steps were forced to slow as the shuttle bus line appeared in the lobby.

The echoing room was packed full of people I assumed to be parents, siblings, and even young children, ready to be reunited with the Navy's newest graduating class. Every single one had my respect.

Sleep Sweet

The past twelve weeks had left me feeling like I was on an island that only I knew existed. The crowd surrounding me proved there were more islands. None of us had ever been alone.

I inched forward toward the hotel's automatic glass entrance, knowing I was about to witness Jesse in a way I would never forget.

Centering myself, I stopped before boarding the shuttle, looked to the sky, and whispered my mantra one last time. *Keep me calm, keep him safe, keep us together.*

Fifteen

Elle

A MASSIVE STEEL SIGN READING *Welcome to the Waulumbee Shoreside Training Center* greeted us as we sped down a lengthy private road. I grasped the seat belt buckle cutting into my waist in a poor attempt to remain calm and collected. It did nothing to help.

Speakers lining the shuttle's aged cloth interior repeated the same automated message they likely had hundreds of times before. I tilted my head and angled my ear toward one, hoping it would help me catch the crackling robotic words. How could I follow the directions if I couldn't hear them?

"Once we pass through the main gates and come to a complete stop, please exit the shuttle and follow the sidewalks and signs to the auditorium, where further screening will occur. Before entering, you will be asked for your ID and your ticket to the ceremony. If you do not have an approved form of identification and a proper ticket, you will be escorted back to your hotel.

"Please take note of this shuttle number and proceed to the loading area after the ceremony for your return ride. Rides will run every fifteen minutes, starting in two hours, and until five p.m. this evening. Please check your seat and ensure you have all your personal belongings with you. Any belongings left behind will be confiscated for security purposes, as shuttles are promptly checked after every unloading.

"Finally, congratulations are in order for everyone heading to the ceremony. Without your support, we would not have the honor of welcoming so many courageous sailors into the Navy today. Please enjoy the ceremony, and again, we thank you for coming."

I'd been to the Naval Air Station in Pensacola for field trips, but being on a base of this caliber was entirely different. Navy SEALs, Blue Angel pilots, captains, and countless other heroes had all spent time learning within its gates. Chills of respect and pride filled me, knowing I would soon hold a hero of my own.

The formality of the announcement emphasized the security that protected the base's perimeter. Our arrival felt official and authentic. As promised, three people stayed on the shuttle before ever leaving it because they'd forgotten proper identification—a scenario I was sure to avoid.

Getting kicked out before I ever had a chance to see Jesse?

There was no chance I'd let that happen.

Once the shuttle parked, the remaining families stepped out of the vehicle and made their way through multiple security checkpoints, laughing and craning their necks to see further ahead before finally entering the massive, brightly lit auditorium.

Chattering excitedly, hundreds of people of all ages found vacant seats in the rows of bleachers lining one side of the echoing room. Baby coos and inaudible jabbering surfed through the electrifying energy that fueled me as I turned in all directions, memorizing the moment, the feeling nesting deep in my stomach.

Several wide overhead doors remained closed on the opposite side of the room, forming a backdrop.

Is that where the graduates will enter? The thought compelled me to find a seat close to the front row so I wouldn't have to fight through aisles of eager family members after the ceremony. Every second closer to Jesse was crucial. I wouldn't be responsible for putting one more between us.

Minutes, hours? It was impossible to tell how much time had passed between finding my seat and the abrupt arrival of several uniformed officials approaching the staged podium at the head of the auditorium. Pins and colorful ribbon bars filled the breast area of their white-as-snow uniforms, their experience and rank easy to spot, even from yards away.

Their arrival signaled the start of the ceremony I'd clung to for months. My future was about to walk through those doors and show me what he was made of, how we could get through anything, and how it only made us stronger. Pure, unfiltered pride bubbled from my pounding heart. My legs bobbed. Sitting still was unrealistic.

A sudden, sharp echo of horns and percussion instruments quieted the audience surrounding me.

More uniformed service members, holding flags, marched across the floor, forming extremely precise formations that garnered respect from everyone in the room.

Silence had never been so loud.

A moment later, the colors were presented. Beside me, tears rolled down an older man's face as he clutched a ball cap to his chest, the words *Navy Veteran* sewn across it. The sight splattered perspective all over me, reminding me of the sacrifices many had made to protect our country.

"Wow," I whispered to myself.

The gentleman's admiration of the moment left me with a sense of appreciation that was hard to convey but extremely easy to feel, defining *patriotism* in a way that beautifully haunted my previous understanding.

"Good morning, everyone. Thank you all for being here on this incredibly special day. We ask that everyone stay seated until liberty is called." One of the men spoke into the podium's microphone, directing our attention to the stage.

After a brief pause, the second, older gentleman began, "I understand this is a very exciting time for all of you, but these men and women have put their all into the ceremony today, and we request that each of you honors their hard work and gives them your full attention until today's proceedings have concluded." His request should have been a no-brainer, but absence had a way of overpowering common sense.

I forced myself to remain as still as possible, my slick, sweaty hands begging me to wipe them. How was I supposed to remain seated when I desperately needed to pace back and forth and release the intense emotions frantically searching for a way out of my body?

The national anthem began to play, followed by a startling, unexpected rumble that welcomed hundreds of uniformed men and women through the open overhead doors, no longer hiding them.

Their faces were unique, yet their straightforward stares, pressed dress-white uniforms, and perfectly coordinated marches were in sync. Each step forward drew them closer to us. Everyone in my row, including me, struggled to remain silent.

I scanned the formations of male and female sailors, my eyes frantic in their search for Jesse. The group's impressive cohesiveness made it impossible. The swoonworthy locks and athletic body I typically used to identify him were concealed, leaving few unique features to be recognized.

From what I knew about it, boot camp had been designed to strip people of parts of their individuality, uniting them as a single force. The graduates before me all looked eerily similar—physically, in gaze, and in mentality. In a good way though because they also appeared incredibly strong and cohesive. Worthy of absolute respect.

The sight stole my breath.

One of the voices from earlier dropped a vibrant, "Attennnnntion!" from the podium, commanding the graduates to a halt.

Using their stillness to my advantage, I desperately searched for Jesse. How could I not recognize my boyfriend in the crowd?

Sure, most of the men standing before me were similar in age and stature, but Jesse was the only man for me. Picking him out of a lineup shouldn't have been such a challenge, even in a sea of look-alikes.

Knowing Jesse, I'd bet his ego had likely taken a hit during his time away, as all the men and women facing me were attractive in their own unique ways. I made a mental note to ensure he felt like the only man in the world.

He was the only man in mine after all.

The rest of the ceremony was a blur. I focused on finding Jesse instead of the heartfelt, patriotic speech the master of ceremonies gave. Time dragged on agonizingly, like an undeserved punishment.

Twenty minutes of forced stillness later, the magic word *liberty* was called. Cheers, howls, and an intense stampede of family members erupted as the bleachers unloaded like saltshakers without lids.

Fireworks made of tear-laced embraces lit up the auditorium floor. Each step I took closer to the action became more difficult. People flooded every inch of my vision, leaving me disoriented and overstimulated. The level of emotion infecting my body wasn't my friend.

I needed it to end.

My head swiveled, Operation Find Jesse taking longer than I'd hoped.

Inching my way through the thick crowd, I turned around, kissing backs with a uniformed man the same height as Jesse. Buzzed hair, matching Jesse's unmistakable color, poked out from the bottom of his Dixie Cup cover. The familiar scent I'd recognize anywhere infiltrated my nostrils. I admired him from behind.

My man.

Holy fucking fuck pulsed through my veins at the same rate as my heartbeat, pushing my anxieties aside to make way for our long-awaited reunion.

It didn't matter how much deodorant I'd applied or how much perfume rested on my neck; a light glisten of sweat coated every inch of my skin. His stature was impossible to miss, even from behind.

Turn around, Jesse. I'm right here, I thought.

It was time for our moment—*the moment*—which required patience but had character built into its framework. I finally felt good about building a future with him because the words in his letters had cemented their confidence into my heart.

Our new life started the moment I placed my hand on his shoulder.

Sixteen

Elle

"Jesse!"

My fingertips desperately longed for his touch. I grasped the shoulder of his uniform like a life raft to keep the moment from sweeping me away. My smile spread like wildfire, ready to scorch his eyes when he turned around.

The man turned toward me and revealed a snoozing baby in his arms. A young woman stood behind him, offering me a concerned stare. It was coated in empathy.

"Sorry, ma'am, but I'm not Jesse," a deep Southern accent smoothly replied.

Immediately, every blaze was extinguished. His words weren't what I had expected, and neither was his face because, to my surprise, it wasn't fucking Jesse.

What the hell?

"Oh … I'm so sorry. You look just like my boyfriend from behind. I apologize for intruding." I tugged the neckline of my sweater upward to ensure my cleavage wasn't reaching the wrong audience.

Am I a complete moron?

I turned to disappear and find a hiding place for my embarrassment. Heated blotches peppered my skin.

"No need for all that now. We go by last names in boot, which might help me point you in the right direction. Our ceremony today was organized by division. Do you know what division he was in?"

The man's helpful response shocked me because it interrupted the long-awaited reunion he had been sharing with his family. If anyone could understand its significance, it was me.

"I'm Trafalgar, by the way. Jimmy Trafalgar."

"He was in Division 28. Jesse Jenkins. You know him?" I asked, turning back to face him.

My tone was desperate, but so was his downturned grimace when the name reached his ear.

Jimmy definitely knew Jesse.

"I was in 28 also. I knew Jenkins ..." Jimmy glanced back at his wife.

"Knew him?"

"Yeah, he, uh ... he got rolled back and moved to another division after the incident," he said.

Jimmy's eyes never met mine. His crow's-feet tightened, shifting from caring to something unfamiliar.

Something wasn't right.

Jesse never mentioned any incident in his letters, and his division never changed. The return address had clearly indicated Division 28 on every envelope I got from him. Jesse would have told me about whatever "incident" this dude was referring to. *Right?*

"What does *rolled back* mean? And what incident are you talking about?" The questions spewed from my lips, making me sound jealous that Jimmy knew more about Jesse than I seemed to.

I was.

"*Rolled back* means a recruit's graduation date changes for some reason. Depending on the situation, they stay here longer than expected ... sometimes indefinitely. Did an instructor notify you of the delay?" The young father's eyes dropped to the floor.

"Delay? What delay? Oh my God, is he hurt or something? Please, I need to know what's going on here!" I shouted.

No one had notified me of a delay because if they had, I sure as fuck wouldn't have saved every dime I'd stashed away to get here.

"He never mentioned anything to you?"

Silent secrets begged to be freed from his tongue. I could see it. I felt it.

"No. He mentioned a lot in his letters, but never anything about getting rolled back or an incident. I need to know if he's hurt. Is he okay? Please ... I—"

Jimmy's response cut me off. "He's fine, ma'am. He isn't hurt. He got into some trouble a while back, and they separated him from our division. I saw him in the chow hall on occasion. He sat alone and didn't talk to anyone after it happened …"

"After what happened?! I need to know!" My frustration grew like a weed fertilized with liquid fear. Fear that ran down both sides of my forehead.

I looked around.

Was I trapped in an episode of a bad hidden-camera show?

"It's not for me to say. You should hear it from him. I'm sorry, but that's all I know. Bro code and all that."

Jimmy's sharp words shattered the final pillar of my remaining faith.

Screw bro code and screw Jimmy. Why did he get to decide what I deserved to know?

I couldn't find the manners to thank him, nor did I want to.

I turned away from him, using every ounce of my remaining strength to stumble back to the bleachers and take a seat. I gripped the surface, attempting to steady myself as my vision blurred with panic and tears.

Where are you, Jesse? I thought. *What happened here?*

The scene before me played in slow motion as a thousand useless thoughts danced together through my skull. So many questions needed answering. Unfortunately, nothing I already knew could answer them. My attempt to slow my breathing was met with shorter, quicker breaths that left me feeling unstable and lightheaded.

I had been told Jesse was safe, which calmed me enough to function, but where was he now? On base? Could I see him? Why hadn't he mentioned it in his letters? Why did he sit alone in the chow hall and stop talking to the others? That sounded nothing like the outgoing Jesse I loved. Had boot camp broken his spirit? Was it worse than he'd expected it to be? Worse than he let on in his letters?

A new countdown had begun. A countdown to the truth.

Only this time, there was no end date, expectations, or guidelines to rely on for reassurance.

Anger overthrew my overwhelm. How could he do this to me? How could he keep writing to me like we were perfect and allow me to show up, knowing I wouldn't find him?

As if cemented in place, my limbs flushed with hurt that could only be soothed by finding answers. I peered around, knowing I'd have to wait until the chaotic auditorium cleared to start looking for them.

My instinct was to text Ruthie while I waited, but I needed to stop and think before making my next move. How could I process something when I didn't know what I was processing? How could I explain it to my best friend when I couldn't even explain it to myself?

Twenty agonizing minutes of solo spiraling later, the crowd evaporated.

The higher-ups must've blended into the funneled crowd because the only person left on my radar was a janitor. The squeak of his wet mop dragging across the floor was the perfect soundtrack to accompany my shitty situation.

I straightened. Sitting on my ass would get me nowhere. If I wanted answers, I'd have to find them. Or at least someone who could point me in the right direction. I lowered my chin and scanned the space around my seat, ensuring nothing was left behind.

Before I could look up, two reflective dress shoes stepped into my view.

"Jesus," I shouted, jumpy. Their sudden appearance startled me. My face lifted to meet whoever was about to ask why I was still around.

I might as well have looked straight to the ceiling. The base of my skull sank into my upper back—the only way to accommodate the man's height. Thankfully, it wasn't stressed for long.

He quickly knelt before me, meeting me at eye level. Although he was a bigger man, his stance remained nonthreatening, even as it stretched well within my personal space.

"Ms. Elle Madelyn?" His voice was deep.

His right brow angled slightly in question. Evergreen eyes magnetized to mine.

I remembered exactly where I had first seen them.

"Do I know you?" I lied through my teeth. I knew I did.

He was the recruiter who had helped Jesse with his paperwork that fateful day two years ago.

So, this is where his promotion took him. And he remembers my name?

"I believe we both know the answer to that." His grin remained frozen, iced to his sharp, clean-shaven face. His white dress uniform gave him more authority than the depth of his response. He was much more intimidating than I remembered. "I go by Chief

Carterson these days. Can you come with me, please?" He launched his large, clean, callous hand toward me.

"Do you know where Jesse is?" I jumped at the opportunity to ask.

He held rank, based on the collection of pins and stripes fastened to his uniform. Rank was exactly what I needed to find Jesse.

"We can discuss this further in my office. Due to confidentiality, I can't discuss it here," Chief Carterson said. He tilted his head toward the janitor, who sluggishly dragged his supply cart across the floor. Apparently, even one person overhearing us would be a breach. "It isn't far," he urged again.

The formality in his tone intrigued me. He knew more than he could say. I needed to hear it all. It didn't matter that mascara-tinted teardrops stained my sweater or that my composure was completely depleted. Nothing could stop me from learning more.

Five minutes later, I approached a door with a keypad lock at the handle, following the man with the name *Carterson* stitched into the right breast of his uniform.

What's his first name again?

I racked my brain, but it was far too muddied with recent trauma to recall a name I'd first heard so long ago. If I remembered anything about him, it wasn't his name.

It was pretty much everything else.

A *beep-beep-beep-beeeeep* sprang the door open after he entered a green-lit code on the pin pad. Chief Carterson held the door open, inviting me to enter the impressive office before he did.

Accolades lined the walls. The remaining spaces were filled with a bookshelf, filing cabinets, and multiple computer monitors spread across a wide desk. I noticed a framed black-and-white photo of a dapper-looking couple on their wedding day, along with various wood-carved knickknacks that kept the picture company.

The space was professional with plenty of character—much different than the cubicle he worked from on campus.

"Please, take a seat." He ushered me toward the spare chair next to the larger leather one, tucked under his desk, and pulled it out for me.

I obeyed.

"Can you tell me where Jesse is now?"

My patience was thinner than his shallow breaths as he sat in the seat beside mine. A man I barely knew had fetched me from the auditorium and was about to feed me confidential information on Jesse's whereabouts.

What could possibly go wrong?

Seventeen

Elle

THE SOFTNESS THAT CHIEF CARTERSON had used to lure me to his office drained from his face. Something far more haunting was left in its place.

"There are several things I am about to tell you, and I need you to listen to them very carefully."

"Okay, you're scaring me," I admitted.

I wasn't scared of him, but of what I might learn from him. Gentle giants often harbored dangerous words behind their facades.

"I want you to know that Recruit Jenkins is safe. He wasn't injured in any way, and you do not need to worry about his well-being. He's fine. Unfortunately, that doesn't change the fact that you aren't allowed to see him."

The words, meant to help me, only further salted my fresh wound. Why couldn't I see him? My heart pounded as anticipation pricked my skin from the inside out. The uniformed man who sat beside me at his desk wasn't touching me, but his statement still burned my skin. His right leg inched closer to mine, leaving our knees less than a foot apart.

"Is he here? On this base?" I asked. Confusion sprinkled my questions.

"He is. But I'm afraid he's been moved to a separate division, where visitors aren't permitted."

"So, when can I talk to him? Surely, he can't be held against his will without contact with the outside world. This isn't a prison."

"When a recruit fucks up as bad as he did, the Navy can enforce whatever restrictions they see fit."

His F-bomb surprised me.

"What do you mean, he fucked up? What did he do?" I pleaded.

Bypassing my questions, he continued, "I know you've supported Jesse during his time here. You were the only one who showed up today in his honor. The anticipation of seeing friends and family is usually enough of a motivator to keep recruits on track, but. ..." A look of concern crossed his face.

My bottom lip took a beating when I bit down on it, sucking it to distract from the tears pressuring my lower lids to set them free. The last thing I wanted to do was fall apart in front of someone who appeared so strong.

I'd been there for Jesse—I knew I had—so why was it so hard to hear that my attempts hadn't been enough?

"It speaks volumes of your character and dedication that you came today. Those traits can't be faked. You should be extremely proud to possess them," he said.

My shoulders dropped as I attempted to piece together his verbal puzzle; nothing fit where it should have.

"What I'm about to show you is government property. There are extreme consequences for both of us if you speak a word of this to anyone." His warning came wrapped in a threatening tone.

This is it, I thought.

The information I'd kill for.

"I've weighed the pros and cons of sharing this with you, but I feel strongly that you deserve to see it with your own eyes. I would want to see it with mine if I were in your position. I'm asking for your verbal agreement. You must promise to keep this discussion— and the evidence in this office—a secret. Speak of it with no one, aside from me. Do you agree?" The quiver in his voice betrayed him.

"Yes, yes, I'll keep my mouth shut. Just tell me already!" I nodded, knowing it looked more like a pathetic beg. I'd give my last breath to find out what had happened, so agreeing to keep things between us was the easiest choice I'd made all day.

"One more thing, Elle." He paused.

I braced for the impact, knowing that whatever came next had the potential to destroy me. Destroy us.

"What you are about to witness is going to hurt you. It didn't hurt him, but it will hurt you." His palm met my knee before he continued, "One day, you will look back on this moment and realize it was one of the best of your life. Integrity is built, not born. You will get through this in time, I promise you."

"Enough! Fucking show me already." I was tired of the endless detours getting in the way.

I was ready to know.

I deserved the truth.

A solemn, silent nod indicated he'd received both my agreement and annoyance. He'd briefed me on what was to come, even if I had no idea what he was warning me about. The time for caution was over and done. I watched intently as he clicked his mouse a few times and closed all the open programs on his computer, aside from one central window. He clicked the mute button first, followed by a puny triangle that brought the video to life.

Ninety percent of my attention was focused on the screen. The remaining ten percent noticed he'd pinned his to me.

A slightly pixelated, colored image of a young woman sprang to life. She appeared to be hiding in some sort of room. From afar, she looked a bit like me. Boxes piled high surrounded the blonde. She paced in circles and fiddled with her hands. Her lips remained still. Silent.

Like mine.

The small room on the screen had no windows—or at least none I could see. Based on the scattered boxes and indistinguishable supplies, it looked to be a storage closet. The young woman's movements grew erratic and anxious, only stilling when a man entered the room and quickly closed the door behind him.

The man I called mine.

Jesse.

I gasped. My hand flung up, spring-loaded, hovering over my open mouth.

The same hand that used to hold his.

Mere seconds passed before I watched in horror as Jesse removed his dark sweatshirt, threw it aside, and marched toward the young woman as if she were his long-awaited prey. His purposeful movements instantly crumbled us.

Our future.
Our plans.
Our love.
Our trust.

All of it. Ruined in an instant.

Without thinking, I grabbed Chief Carterson's hand, which was still on the mouse. I squeezed it firmly, thanking him for showing me the truth. He hadn't had to. But for some reason, he had.

"Unmute it," I whispered.

"Elle ... I don't think that's a good idea—"

"Do it!" I demanded, this time with little room for rebuttal.

He exhaled, nodded, and clicked unmute, honoring my request whether he agreed with it or not.

Numbness overtook me as my ex-boyfriend wore the skin of a stranger and proceeded to kiss another woman with a hunger only a desperate man could display. His tongue swam around her mouth aggressively.

Possessively.

The Jesse I knew evaporated, leaving a ruthless savage in his place.

"You gonna keep quiet, or do I need to shut your mouth for you, Camellino?" he growled, removing her shirt.

She moaned.

I listened closely as Jesse whispered in her ear the exact phrases that he used to whisper into mine. He licked his way down her neck and chest. Sounds of lust jumped through the computer speakers and into my bloodstream, but there was a big difference between the woman's multiplying moans and the ones I used to give him.

Hers sounded real. Like she was enjoying his savagery.

Fueled by whatever had made Jesse do what I was watching him do, he ran his hands down her body with a vigor he'd kept concealed from me. It was raw and vulnerable and the very thing missing from our sex life.

Jesse spun the woman and crushed her chest against the brick wall, sliding her pants down below her knees from behind. He finger-fucked my replacement and then spit down the crack of her ass, lubricating his target.

I shook, staring in horror as he shimmied off his pants and took her from behind, covering her mouth with the same hand that had once known my body so well. Like a psychic not believing their own visions, I no longer harnessed the power to see a future with him. Instead, there was only darkness.

No way through.

"That's enough!" Chief Carterson snapped, pausing the video.

He abruptly turned my chair so I couldn't see the screen. I faced him instead.

"No, it isn't! I need to see the whole thing so I'll never want to look back. *This* is what he wanted." I pointed at the paused video with a hurricane-strength rage.

My heart could only handle one pass of the video—that much I knew—but it was necessary if I ever wanted to process our separation without whispers of regret. It was funny how two minutes had the potential to unravel two years. Two minutes was all the motherfucker had ever needed anyway.

"I need to know that she's what makes him happy now. Not me. I need to see if he comes inside of her, see if he looks remorseful when they're done. There's so much more this video can tell me."

The admission sliced through my escalating anger. Every ounce of my effort was funneled into trying to stop myself from bursting into tears for a man who didn't deserve them. I could cry later.

"I can tell you anything you want to know about your ex-boyfriend. There is nothing the rest of that video can tell you that I can't."

"Why did you show it to me then, huh? Why not just tell me about it and save me the extra heartache?" I asked.

Chief Carterson sighed, keeping me on edge.

"Because I knew seeing him cheat on you would be the most effective way to soothe that heartache. You deserve more than him, Elle. And I hope you don't waste any time realizing that."

How do you know what I deserve? I thought.

"It's not my job to tell you what you deserve. All I can do is show you what you don't," he added, dropping the shoulders that had shot up with his admission. His minty exhale skimmed my face after the last word left his lips.

"Well, you sure did that …" I assured him.

"If it makes you feel any better, he asked me to show it to you."

"Wait, what?" *Did I hear that correctly?*

"He said he couldn't face you today and asked me to rip the bandage off, so to speak, because he's a coward. I was one of Jesse's instructors in Division 28 and the only person authorized to access the security footage without additional permission. That's why he came to me," he said.

My own boyfriend had had the audacity to cheat on me, keep writing to me, and then ask another man to break the news because he couldn't bear to do it himself.

Wow.

Without hesitation, I leaned forward into Chief Carterson's broad chest and threaded my arms around his waist. We both remained seated while his heavy arms answered my call. I let myself linger in his embrace.

It was all I had.

It didn't matter how strong I thought I was; the tears found me.

His words had entered my veins like they were the most lethal injection ever administered to a death row inmate. Instead of killing me, they only ignited every doubt about Jesse I'd ever had.

"I'm sorry. I just … I can't believe he could do this to me …" I sobbed. My mascara liquefied, smearing the sleeve of the uniform my face rested against.

"Shh, it's okay. Don't apologize. Please just let me get you out of here. I'll take you back to your hotel." Hesitantly, he stroked my head.

I barely knew this man and certainly wasn't making a great second impression. I contemplated my options and immediately scratched off the one that took me back to my hotel. There was no way I could return to that room to witness more of my wasted efforts. The rose petals, the lingerie that shithead had requested—it would push me past my limit.

Leaving the support of Chief Carterson's arms, I composed myself enough to ask, "Do you know of any hotels around here that might have vacancies tonight? The thought of going back to mine makes my skin crawl. I set it up for a romantic night and …" Murkiness reentered my peripheral vision.

"Of course you did."

He shook his head, looking past my face. Could he see the darkness too?

The clench in his sharp jaw pulsed with something that evolved into what I recognized as fury.

"Honestly, the hotels around here get booked months ahead of graduation weekend. You could stay in Chicago, but I wouldn't recommend a young woman like you to take the train into the city or stay there alone."

Yep, I was screwed.

I slumped backward into my seat and searched for the courage to accept my fate for the evening.

Chief Carterson interjected, "I completely understand if you wouldn't be comfortable with this, but my house isn't far from here ... I have a guest room. Would you consider staying with me tonight?"

A slow swallow swam down his throat. It was silent, but tattled on whatever was fueling his proposition.

"Ummm ..." I squinted my eyes and bit my cheek to avoid deciding too quickly.

The offer was incredibly kind, but had it knocked my senses loose? How could I even consider staying the night at his house? He wasn't quite a stranger, but I didn't know much about him either. Staying together felt personal.

Almost intimate.

What I *did* know was that he was a very large, high-ranking Navy chief and that he cared enough about my well-being to show me the video. His hardened hands and face full of experience told me he was several years older than me, too, which proved he'd come this far without being arrested and sentenced to a lengthy prison stay for doing bad shit. He presented himself as an honorable man—a protector. So, yeah, perhaps taking him up on his offer would be a bit personal. But at least it wouldn't be as depressing as going back to my hotel.

Hesitation cradled my lingering pause.

"If you'd prefer to stay there alone, I could drop you off and then come back and sleep on base tonight. I keep a bunk here for overnights, so that wouldn't be a problem. You should feel one hundred percent comfortable."

His empathy was impressive, leaving me with two choices: I could call all the hotels in the area and beg for a room—but even if one was available, I couldn't afford to pay twice—*or* I could let Chief Carterson take me anywhere but here and rely on my senses convincing me he was a decent man.

Clearly, character judgment wasn't my strong suit after what Jesse had pulled off. But I vowed to give actions more weight than words, moving forward. So far, Chief Carterson's told me he was a good guy.

"*Fuck it. Put your knowledge of human behavior to good use for once,*" imaginary Ruthie whispered in my ear.

"We met two years ago, right? I mean, we're practically old friends …" I reassured myself aloud.

"Practically." He chuckled, though his smile was strained. Was he trying not to let it grow too fast? "My friends call me Austin."

That's right. His first name was Austin.

"Okay then, Austin. I'll take you up on the guest room. But only for tonight, until I can make other arrangements, and I'm definitely not kicking you out of your own house. Aside from the inevitable sobbing, you won't even know I'm there." *Awkward.*

My attempt at a joke fell flatter than my nonexistent relationship. There would be tears. I was sure of it. He needed to know he would likely witness their downpour.

"Sadly, sobbing might be sort of a good thing. It'll mean you're that much closer to getting over the asshole that made you cry in the first place."

Using humor to soften a bad blow was a very effective way to defuse a bad situation.

He was good at it.

"Well, I'm glad that's settled," I said, accepting the plan I wasn't fully sold on. It would be better than the hotel, surely. It had to be. "I'm ready to go." I needed many things, but staying in the office that had forever broken my trust in Jesse wasn't one of them.

"You've been through a lot today. I need you to know you can trust me," Austin revealed.

Could he read my mind?

I nodded.

He stood.

I stood.

"I trust you enough to get me the fuck out of here. Can we go now?"

Eighteen

Austin

Did I do the right thing by showing her the video? The incriminating evidence?

Yes, yes, I fucking had because Elle Madelyn was in my Jeep, The Ol' Green Goddess, staring out the passenger-side window and texting on her cell like it was her lifeline. I lost count of how many times I'd imagined the moment. But my imagination had not done her justice because my smoldering little obsession was a hundred times more intoxicating than I remembered. Her caramelized eyes sweetened my original memory of her while the energy we shared still made it harder to breathe.

The adrenaline swimming through my veins as I gripped the steering wheel to keep from drowning in her presence proved it. She was the same girl I'd met two years earlier. Only now, our paths had collided, and I had nowhere to be tomorrow except by her side.

The name *Ruthie* lit up her phone's screen repeatedly. I hid my amusement. Elle struggled to respond quickly enough before more messages came through, garnering a few hardened smiles, soft chuckles, and tears she tried to pocket.

For the most part, Elle was quiet the entire way.

The silence only gave me more reasons to steal glances in her direction.

Ten minutes after leaving the base, we approached the tip of my hidden driveway and turned down the winding, paved path. A thick wooden sign with the words *Haroldeen Lane* and an arrow greeted us.

The sign had been the first thing to welcome me when my grandparents adopted me at two years old. That was my turning point.

Would Elle find her new beginning on Haroldeen Lane too?

She slid her phone into her pocket and slowly craned her head around the vehicle, likely taking notes of her surroundings from every window.

Smart girl.

"The address is 2818 Haroldeen Lane, Waulumbee, Illinois, if you want to share your location with anyone. New places can be disorienting. I want you to feel safe."

She had plenty to worry about. Her own safety shouldn't make the list.

"I don't mean to make it weird, but I started sharing my location with my best friend the second we got in the car. I hope you don't mind," she said. A confidence riddled her admission.

"Of course not. I'm happy to hear it. Is that who's been making you fight that smile?" I asked, already knowing the answer.

"Yeah, that's my roommate, Ruthie. I swear, if I get to Jesse before she does, he'll be the luckiest asshole on the planet. She will literally rip his dick off for what he did."

I like Ruthie already.

"Sounds like a good friend to me," I revealed, pulling my Jeep into its usual gravel parking spot a few paces from the steps leading up to my porch.

My inherited house wasn't huge, but it offered comfort, charm, and me.

All the things that I knew could help Elle after her day from hell.

"Jeesh, you've got quite the spot here, Chief. This place is giving *The Secret Garden* vibes." She admired it before unbuckling her seat belt, opening the passenger door, and stepping out.

Goddamn it, if she called me Chief one more time …

The magic words went straight to my groin the moment they left her full, pouty lips. She might as well be talking into it like a microphone.

"Yeah, I, uh … I grew up here," I stuttered as I stepped out of the vehicle.

The loud slam of my car door closing concealed my nervous swallow. *Thank God.* I met her where she stood and prayed my dick behaved long enough to get me into the house before she noticed my testosterone-packed teenage-boy behavior.

Get it together. Fast, I thought.

"No kidding? Lucky getting stationed so close, huh?" Elle looked my way before glancing back at the house.

The way she made small talk to show her appreciation was adorable. She didn't have to thank me. I should be thanking her.

"Very lucky." I closed the car door behind her.

Together, we climbed the three small steps and approached the front door I'd walked through countless times before. My large frame towered over hers. Our size difference was on full display, forcing me to imagine how easily I could cocoon her body in my arms. How safe I could make her feel if she ever asked me to.

How vulnerable she made me.

"Welcome to Hotel Carterson. I hope you'll excuse the mess. The housekeeper called in sick today," I announced.

Fuck, that was lame.

I shook my head, silently cursing myself, and unlocked the door before entering first to ensure she didn't feel trapped between my body and her exit. Making sure she felt safe was my top priority. Keeping the blood as far away from my cock as possible was a close second though because seeing her walk into my house nearly killed me.

Like a superhero and his semi-depressed sidekick, we walked deeper into my foyer. She closed the door behind her, sighing.

My house was tidy—I'd made sure of it. No speck of dirt remained on the wood floors. No shelf was left undusted. A spoon and coffee mug were the only things left in the sink by design, so my preparations weren't too obvious.

I couldn't have predicted if Elle would see my place in her time here, but you bet your ass I had been prepared in case she did. Her perfectly sculpted eyebrows formed a veil of suspicion over her face.

Was she onto me?

My heart thumped against my rib cage.

"I'm searching for the mess you excused, but I can't find it. This place is immaculate," Elle said. The tension in her face released, relaxing her forehead as she inspected her new accommodation.

"Almost ten years in the military will do that to a man. Wait until you see how crisp and tightly tucked the sheets are in the guest room. You'd think I'd written a textbook on bedmaking in my last life."

"Wait, are you serious? I'm a total sucker for good linens. Towels, fresh sheets—they're kind of my thing ..." she said.

A knot formed in my throat. I visualized Elle wrapped up in nothing but a towel after a hot shower. What would it be like to see her almost naked, only comforted by the softness kissing her skin while the exposed parts of her body dripped wet?

I'd die to find out.

"You've come to the right place then. The guest room is just down this hallway to the right." I gestured past the kitchen and pivoted, hanging my cover and peacoat on the hooks lining my entryway. My scalp thanked me for allowing it to breathe.

Elle stepped deeper into my house, leaving a stream of brisk air that still flowed out from under the door behind us.

The forecast called for a major cold front in the coming days, that infamous Windy City chill making itself known. Was my Florida girl ready for it?

Her jacket must be back at the hotel, along with the rest of her luggage. I made a mental note to remedy that as soon as possible.

She followed me down the hallway and stopped when I did without hesitation. I nodded, assuring her it was the correct door.

"I'm not sure why you're being so kind to me. But I can't tell you how much I appreciate everything you did for me today," she voiced. I froze, a pang of guilt finding me before she continued, "If it's all right with you, I might hibernate and catch you in the morning when I'm more rested." A fatigued exhale followed.

She'd had enough for one day. Her smeared lipstick, darkened under-eye hollows, and the stray hairs that remained stuck out of place from the others on her head further supported my theory.

If things were different, I'd take a warm shower with her. I'd dry every drop of water off her skin, wash and blow-dry her hair, cook her dinner, and then put on her favorite movie. But those things weren't an option yet. Would they ever be? For the time being, my only job was to help her comfort herself. To be there for her *only* if she needed me.

The ultimate test of my restraint.

"Everyone deserves respect. That's why I'm being so nice to you," I offered. "I'll be across the hall if you need me, but I won't come in unless you ask. The space is yours, along with the private bathroom attached."

Her fingertips gently grazed my forearm in appreciation while her tired smile penetrated its target—my soul. I wasn't prepared. Our contact was quick, ending before it ever really began, but every touch from her meant something to me.

This one meant she felt safe in my presence.

Austin: 1, Jesse: 0.

I pulled the door closed behind her after she vanished into the room that hadn't seen a guest since I'd moved back into the house. She didn't need to know that though. You'd think I managed a high-end resort with how much preparation had gone into ensuring the room and bathroom were perfect in case she found her way into them.

To my amazement, she had.

Somehow, my dream girl had fallen out of my dreams and landed in my life for the second time.

Maybe one day, I could start calling her my angel instead.

NINETEEN

Elle

HOW IN THE WORLD DID *the most significant emotional blow of my life land me in another man's house?*

The inside of the bedroom door listened intently to my inner thoughts while I stood frozen, staring at it.

When we had arrived at Austin's house, I'd expected a messy bachelor pad, riddled with piles of dirty laundry, dishes overflowing from the sink, and an unrecognizable smell—much like Jesse's apartment. Instead, I'd stepped into a retreat. A storybook setting, of sorts. Not a hint of bachelor life in sight.

Bachelor was likely an understatement, considering how Chief Carterson's impressive height and eyes alone could execute whoever they landed on. Throw in the uniform, and he could have been married yesterday.

If he were flying solo, it was by choice.

Austin's invitation for me to stay at his place had told me he lived alone. That didn't stop me from double-checking the back seat of his Jeep for a car seat or left hand for a ring. The last thing I needed to do was accidentally disrespect a wife or girlfriend. The unfortunate scenario had *just* happened to me. I'd *never* throw that indescribably shitty feeling at another woman.

At anyone, for that matter.

When my host for the night had removed his uniform cap upon our arrival, his rich brown hair had been set free. Funny, his hairstyle was the opposite of Jesse's—shaved tight to his scalp on the sides while remaining just long enough on the top to hold a few waves.

A sneaking suspicion told me the rest of Chief Carterson was far less manicured.

Hard to pinpoint exactly why, but he seemed less particular about himself than Jesse ever was. More rugged. *Natural.* He didn't have time to stare into the mirror every time he passed one because he was busy with other things.

Like helping me.

I'd been so excited to see Jesse in Chief Carterson's getup, with a classic military fade and the swagger that came along with it. However, picturing *him* in the uniform instead of Austin now made me want to throw up. He didn't deserve my nausea.

He absolutely wouldn't play a part in any more of my fantasies.

After a slight delay, Austin's retreating footsteps disappeared down the hallway, alerting me that I was alone—free to explore my new surroundings. I unpeeled my purse's strap from my chest and placed it on the edge of the bed. The thickest, smoothest, whitest duvet cover and matching pillows I'd ever seen topped the full-sized mattress.

My idea of heaven.

Dominated by a wrought-iron bed frame and a tall gold-rimmed mirror hanging across from it, the space's modest size and the long wooden beams jutting across the ceiling only accentuated its charm. Lace curtains covered the window, overlooking a wooden shed and an overgrown hydrangea plant. Its periwinkle blooms, which reminded me of cotton candy, were easily seen from across the room.

Their allure drew me in.

Cotton candy reminds me of the fair; fairs make me happy; Jesse used to make me happy ... I thought.

Ruthie would not approve of my inner monologue. My head shook back and forth because neither did I.

Time and rest were the only antidotes that had a fighting chance of curbing my addiction to Jesse and the future I'd thought we had. Fortunately, time and rest were my only resources for the evening because the rest of my life was back at the hotel. No pajamas, no toiletries, and no Jesse. Just me, my bleeding heart, and a protective sort of stranger down the hall.

My ass sank onto the bed, and my nose burrowed into my palms. The sobs I'd fought hard to contain were released. Not only had Jesse left me, but he'd left me so stranded that another man had to swoop in and clean up his mess. A tight wad of condolences for my wasted energy and dedication over the last few months gathered in my throat.

Where did we go wrong?

I let the tears flow until none remained.

Ten minutes later, I slowly rose from the ashes of my sorrow, reached around to the back of my sweater, and unclasped my bra through the material. The tension that released from my ribs and chest felt like freedom.

Freedom to breathe.

A narrow door by the window led me into a bathroom with a shower and the porcelain claw-foot bathtub of my dreams. It sure beat the mold-kissed bathroom tiles back at the hotel.

Hell of an improvement ...

Triggered by my walking over the threshold, a row of auto-sensing lights illuminated the base of the basin. Invitingly, the amber glow welcomed me deeper into the moody scene like a hug with open arms.

I stripped down to nothing while contemplating bathing in the tub like a queen whose kingdom had just fallen. What I needed though was to wash my future with Jesse down the drain and hop into the bed calling my name so the day would finally fucking end. The shower would have to do. I ran the water for a moment to let it warm and stepped inside.

Steaming water splashed my skin while I stared, puzzled, at the eucalyptus hanging from the showerhead. The scent, overflowing from the rising steam cloud, enveloped me. It was calming and earthy, and I vowed to replicate it back home because it felt like a damn spa treatment. Stubborn tension oozed from my shoulders and neck, vanishing instantly. *My God*, it was therapeutic.

High-end shampoo, conditioner, and a brand-new razor stared at me from the shower sill as I scrubbed my skin. Lather from the apple-scented soap bar I'd found dripped down my body and mixed with my curiosities before racing toward the drain.

Was Austin used to women staying the night? Why else would these curated comforts be here?

Screw it.

I was only here for one night. No stray thought could stop me from smelling like an organic Granny Smith and herbs from the farmers market.

After an unreasonable amount of time exploring Austin's shower, I sat and curled into a folded ball, feeling defeated and confused as the water drenched my face, chest, and legs. At least I was clean.

I tried to cry—again—but no tears remained. If I had to guess, they were too busy rebuilding my self-esteem to show.

Regardless of Jesse's justification when I talked to him, not an ounce of his reasoning would mean that something was wrong with me or the way I loved him. I had to hammer that into my conscience with everything I had left. If I didn't, it would break me.

Despite my doubts before he left, I'd given him my all and stayed committed because I knew he was human and that humans weren't perfect. That was what made them unique. *Beautiful* even.

Jesse was no longer the beautifully imperfect human I had known. He was something far worse.

He was a liar.

And a coward who couldn't even own up to it.

When the hot water expired, I found a towel folded neatly on a stool nearby and wrapped myself in the only thing that would hold my body for the night. The thought was unequivocally depressing.

Mostly dry, I walked back into the bedroom and over to the closet, leaving a path of moist footprints behind. I wasn't one to snoop, but borrowing whatever clean clothes might be available to wear to bed instead of putting my dirty outfit back on sounded acceptable. Austin wouldn't mind, I assumed.

A row of perfectly pressed T-shirts and a collection of uniforms faced me when I slid open the closet door. Boots, dress shoes, and a few pairs of sneakers lined the bottom of the space while several stacks of folded boxer shorts and other accessories sat high on the top shelf.

Am I at the dry cleaners?

Austin knew how to do laundry as if it were his job, obviously.

Either that or he had a full-time housekeeper, and she really had taken the day off ...

I peeled an extra-large white T-shirt from the farthest hanger, slid it over my head, and inhaled as it rolled down my back and chest. A scent so fresh, so fucking manly, smacked me in the nose. The triple threat of spearmint, sage, and sandalwood almost brought me to my knees. Whatever detergent Austin washed his clothes with was mature. *Sophisticated*, unlike the headache-promising body spray Jesse wore.

My heels left the floor while I balanced on my tiptoes, grabbing for a pair of boxers on a shelf just out of my reach. They were way too big. However, being naked from the waist down in someone else's house didn't sit right with me.

Ruthie would call me a pussy for that.

Embracing my morals, I pulled the shorts up my legs and knotted them on one side, securing the waistband around my hips. When I turned, my reflection in the mirror across the room showed me a version of myself that resembled a kid playing dress-up—a far stretch from the lingerie and orgasms I expected to be knee deep in by now.

Unexpectedly, a dizzy spell shifted my focus. *Ouch.* I gripped the edge of the closet door to steady myself. Tension headaches weren't new to me, so I knew it would only intensify if I didn't eat or drink something soon.

Should I sneak into the kitchen and at least grab some water or attempt to find something sweet to keep it in check?

Austin was probably showering or relaxing in his room.

My gurgling stomach told me it was a risk worth taking.

Optimistic, I went to the door, jiggled the handle, and pushed it open. There was a porcelain *clunk*, and something solid on the ground prevented it from fully opening. Peering around the door, my eyes landed on two glasses and a large plate on the ground. An appreciative grin painted my face.

A dish with a chicken salad sandwich, sliced pineapple, and two glasses tempted me. I snatched them like a raccoon ravaging a dumpster and retreated to the bed to devour every bite. The sandwich was delicious, but not as delicious as the nutty amber liquid that followed my first bite. Tequila was my liquor of choice, but the whiskey went down just as smoothly. The ice water in the second glass was a welcome counterpart. My skull thanked it for dialing back the throbbing pain pummeling my forehead.

After finishing my feast, I gathered my mess and headed for the kitchen, unable to decorate such a pretty bedroom with dirty dishes for the night. No, I wasn't in the mood to chitchat, per se, but my mother had taught me to always be a good houseguest, which meant cleaning up after myself.

What made a terrible houseguest though was sneaking into someone else's kitchen while wearing their stolen—or should I say, borrowed—clothes. At least that's what she'd tell me.

"Shit!" I shrieked.

Everything in my hands dropped to the floor, shattering Austin's concentration. No, I wasn't surprised to see him in his own house. What shocked my nervous system was his massive, shirtless silhouette, accentuated by the endless nautical tattoos that climbed up his arm, wrapping around his shoulder blade. He turned toward me. His uniform had covered most of his body earlier.

Nothing from the waist up was concealed anymore.

Appearing swollen, his bicep and trap muscles bulged—muscles apparently made of steel because supporting arms and a back of that capacity was a full-time job, plus overtime. His body wasn't the kind sported by heartthrobs in the '90s. It was the kind that chopped wood in the wintertime and threw around bales of hay like they were made of papier-mâché.

Holy shit pulsed through my veins.

What the hell had crawled up my spine? It felt like a mix of chills and something else I couldn't put my finger on. Whatever the zing was monkeyed around to my front and perked up my nipples, leaving them on full display through the shirt that struggled to contain them.

"*Fuck*. I'm sorry I ... I thought you'd be asleep by now," Austin explained, placing the bottle of whatever he had been pouring onto the counter.

His deep voice reached into my stomach. Austin's body further rotated to face mine. His expression stayed neutral. His flushed cheeks when he noticed my impromptu pajamas gave away his amusement.

"I'm happy you found some clothes. Help yourself to anything in the house to get you through until we can grab your stuff tomorrow." He smiled, though something prohibited it from reaching its full capacity.

"Yeah, I, uh ... I didn't think you'd mind," I uttered, crossing my arms against my chest in a poor attempt to hide my erect tits.

"Trust me, I don't mind. They look better on you anyway."

A long-winded swallow strangled my response. He was just being a good host.

That was all.

"Let me clean up my mess before one of us steps on a piece of glass," I offered, sinking to the floor and rounding up the broken ceramic shards that stung my fingertips with each gentle pass.

"Absolutely not," he said. Austin shuffled toward me. "If it's okay with you, I'd like you to get some rest and let me pick up the pieces tonight. You've been through enough today."

His words were not a suggestion. They were a command, camouflaged in kindness. I could see it in the veins climbing his neck, pulsing with every second longer my pause stretched.

"Are you sure? You shouldn't have to do that. I mean, you already made me dinner. I don't mind …"

Could his eyes talk? Because I swore those sage fields spoke to me.

"You're right. I shouldn't have to, but that doesn't mean I don't want to." His confession was practically verbal therapy, stealing my ability to look away. "Go get some sleep. We'll make a plan in the morning to get your things."

I nodded, quickly agreeing to honor his wishes before turning away.

"Thank you again for everything. I hope you have a good night," I added over my shoulder. "Pretend like I'm not even here. I'll try not to make any more messes for you to clean up …" I released a chuckle.

The silence that followed did something to me.

Had he taken my words at face value? Or was he overthinking them? Accepting his lack of response as my signal, I retreated to bed and left him alone.

I was used to cleaning up Jesse's messes, not the other way around.

Boy, did it feel nice to have someone clean up mine for once.

Twenty

Austin

Elle was in *my* house, wearing *my* clothes and drinking *my* goddamn whiskey. I lay stunned, frozen in the realization that she was so close to me—just down the hallway. My gaze remained plastered to the ceiling. The clock on my nightstand approached two a.m., reminding me that only a few hours separated me from seeing her again. No amount of exhaustion, physical or mental, could put me to sleep.

Thick adrenaline coursed through my body.

I was a calm, collected man. Usually so poised that I prided myself on it. Losing control was not a functioning part of my wheelhouse.

But Elle was a different breed. She did things to me I would never understand. Everything about her sucked my usual tranquility back into the endless undertow.

My shirt, my boxers, *nothing else*. The oversize clothes she had borrowed from my wardrobe could never hide her perfect body from me. I tried my damnedest not to stare, but the outfit's simplicity only added to her overflowing innocence, taunting me from across the kitchen. Barefaced and braless, she strolled in like she belonged there.

For a moment, a trail of broken glass was the only thing that separated us.

Thank *fuck* for that glass because a visible, sharp line was precisely the reminder I needed to take things slowly. *Cautiously.*

For so long, I'd hungered for the sight of her standing before me, like a shark starved of blood. The moment it had arrived, it'd shredded me into nothing but a broken bucket of chum.

How did we get here? A mix of gratitude and hesitation drenched my thoughts.

Half of our story was written by the coincidence that had brought Jesse into my division when he reported for boot camp. His bad decisions and my memory of her forged the other half.

I'd found their letters when I cleaned out Jesse's bunk after catching him sneaking around with—no, *fucking*—Rita Camellino, a female recruit from another division. Elle's name and address were waiting for me on the top left of each envelope. The key to her I'd been searching for.

My curiosity convinced me to read them to see how she was doing.

Instead of alerting her about Jesse's delay, fate bribed me to write back to her in his name. Although it hadn't taken much convincing.

I knew she would find out about her ex-boyfriend's indiscretions, regardless of when or how. But reading her letters, witnessing her desperation for reassurance, and seeing her gorgeous face in the pictures she had sent told me not to let her slip through my fingers again.

For two years, her face had taunted me. I no longer had to sit back and let it. I was a reasonable man, but sometimes, reasons weren't meant to be understood. There was a reason I never forgot her face.

What better reason could there be than us?

Her future mattered to me as much as my own; her happiness mattered to me more than my own. Helping her get over Jesse, whether we had a second chance or not, was the least I could do.

Jesse's words had been riddled with lies, false hope, and bullshit. But once they had started coming from me, they were nothing but truths.

My truths were meant to provide her comfort and support until I could tell her face-to-face.

My truths were the ones that could end up pulling her deeper into the darkness if I wasn't careful.

My truths were the ones I vowed to ensure she understood before she went home.

Twenty-One

Elle

Morning rays of sunlight penetrated the drapes, their bright flicker robbing me of my drowsy peace. I stretched into the mattress, my spine carving into the memory foam. My thoughts resurrected with every heavy blink that woke me. Yes, the day was new, but Jesse was still a liar. The realization hurt a little less on the comfortable guest bed, which supported my body better than he ever had. Still, waking up without Jesse by my side reminded me I'd be alone for the foreseeable future.

Something I hadn't faced in over two years.

The only thing stronger than losing the future I'd thought I knew was knowing I could create a new one. If I were honest with myself, I'd admit I had seen it coming. None of that mattered anymore. It was the first day of my new life.

Waking up on Haroldeen Lane was not a bad start.

The blinking battery icon illuminating my phone screen evidenced my lengthy text exchange with Ruthie the night before. Our conversation had lasted well into the early morning hours. Her texts were my lifeline—another reason I needed to grab my charger back at the hotel.

Buffering my worries with positive self-talk was how I chose to start my day—something I often advised others to do in their therapy sessions.

Your healing starts today, Elle. You've worked too hard to let a boy give you crippling anxiety, intrusive thoughts, and fractured confidence. When the right man comes along, you'll know. And you knew it wasn't Jesse "Jizz-Faced" Jenkins.

Cool air kissed my skin when I adjusted the comforter and freed my legs, planting my feet on the floor like an unsteady baby bird. The wood chilled my toes as I tiptoed across it.

Too bad I don't have any slippers. Or clean socks. Or a change of clothes, I thought before noticing a note on the dresser by the door.

Didn't want to come in while you were asleep.

I ran out last night to grab something for you to wear today.

I couldn't have you going out in my clothes, not that they didn't look like they had been made for you.

Come to the kitchen if you're hungry.

—A

Austin's sweetness dissipated the Jesse fog that continued to follow me. Grinning, I opened the bedroom door and found an overflowing plastic bag hanging from the handle.

A pair of black flannel leggings, an olive-green sweater, knee-high socks, no-show thong underwear, and a puffer jacket fell onto the bed as I emptied the bag's contents. The items were things I would pick for myself. Things that complemented each other.

How is he so good at this?

Austin was polite, but not shy about it.

A refreshing combination.

After carefully ripping the tags from my new clothes, I dressed and ran my fingers through the ends of my hair, wondering if the style I'd worked so hard to perfect the day before had stuck around. For some reason, I didn't feel the need to hide my true self in front of Austin. He'd already seen me at my lowest.

Chief Carterson's kitchen was as endearing as the rest of his house; its charm welcomed me as I approached it. Cabinets and shelving made of oak lined the modest room, utilizing the space in a way that I imagined a good interior designer would. The dark river-rock backsplash rested vertically, meeting glossy, well-polished countertops. Their shine showcased Austin's effort to preserve the space's natural beauty.

It was the kind of kitchen that begged you to cook in it.

Austin had a shirt on, but his stance was no less intriguing than the last time I had seen him. He faced the stove while his right hand gripped a frying pan's handle. He flipped two sizzling eggs without a spatula.

Impressive.

His free hand reached for a plate, lined with bacon and toast, on the counter beside him, shaking it gently to make room for the eggs. When I looked at Austin, the effort he was putting forth, my anger toward Jesse tripled.

How could someone I barely knew care for me in a way that my boyfriend of two years never had?

"Smells amazing. Should I call you Chef or Chief this morning?" I greeted Austin, doing my best not to startle him.

"My one and only houseguest can call me whatever she'd like." He turned, exposing bedroom eyes and the darkened bags supporting them.

He'd had a late night. Guilt stung my gut when I remembered he had run out to get me clothes.

He continued, "You think the smell is good? Just wait until you taste it."

"I can only imagine it'll be as impressive as that one-handed egg flip," I complimented, appreciating his icebreaker.

He was good at warming otherwise cold situations, like the first show of flame at a bonfire.

"You sleep well?" He walked toward the table and set an overflowing plate down next to a glass of golden juice before returning to the stove.

"I did. And thank you so much for the clothes; I couldn't have picked better myself. You didn't have to. But I can't lie; I'm grateful that you did." I pulled and released the shoulder of my new sweater.

"I see we have similar tastes. Hopefully, that also applies to breakfast because this is the Hotel Carterson special." He beamed.

Austin returned to the table and placed two sets of silverware and a matching dish across from mine. A carafe of coffee and two mugs filled the rest of the surface between us. We sat at the same time, joining each other.

"You do this for all the girls you bring home?" I asked, looking down at my plate instead of up at him.

I had been ballsy enough to ask the question, but not to look him in the eye while he answered. He didn't owe me an answer anyway.

"Huh? No. Are you kidding? I haven't cooked breakfast for a girl in years, but I do love your faith in me."

He bulldozed my doubts while planting new ones in their place. How was that possible? There wasn't a single thing about Austin I didn't like so far, making it hard to comprehend how someone like him wasn't in a relationship. Maybe he just wasn't the marrying type? Was he divorced? He was certainly more established than I was, suggesting he was somewhere in his thirties.

The scent of freshly griddled protein landed in my nostrils, reminding me that none of it was my business. Besides, I was starving, and the cooking-magazine-esque meal tempting me needed my attention.

"I'm not kidding." I finally looked up at him, unable to resist a bite of bacon before finishing my thought. "You just seem like a good guy with a lot to offer. I get the impression that your solitude here is intentional." I swallowed, triggering a change of expression across his face.

A shadow fell over his eyes just before a top row of perfectly imperfect teeth distracted me through his slightly fallen bottom lip. Instead of looking fake and veneered, his teeth had a slight crook and a natural brightness that reminded me of the smile made famous by Tom Hardy.

Rugged and meant to be his.

His prolonged pause told me his mouth had more to tell.

"You're right about that. I like my solitude." He sipped his juice, nodding. "I appreciate peace and order because my childhood didn't always provide it. That's why I chose the military." Austin's tone amplified his confidence. His pride in knowing how far he'd come.

My heart turned to jelly.

"Sorry, that was a little personal of me to ask," I admitted.

"Are you more akin to chaos and disorder, Ms. Madelyn?" he asked quickly.

Dryness coated my windpipe. The question struck me from left field.

"No, not at all. Although chaos and disorder seem to have found me lately …" I poured steaming coffee into his mug and then mine, avoiding looking at his face while my blush simmered.

"I've learned that the best way to find what's meant for you is to leave the things disrupting your life in the past and stay open to new things that might help re-center you." Austin clearly spoke from experience.

"You make it sound so simple."

"It takes time. But time is something that you can't get back. So, I try not to waste mine on the wrong people."

Austin's mossy eyes chilled me when they met mine. He sipped his black coffee, transforming my hopefulness into something far less cheery.

How much time did I waste on Jesse? I thought.

Far too much.

I nodded, even though the statement stung.

Austin continued, "I know that sounds harsh. I just … I believe in you. You're going to get through this time in your life and look back at it when you realize it led you to where you were meant to be."

A lone tear struck my right cheek. I stuffed a forkful of eggs into my mouth to avoid responding to his powerful words. He noticed and offered me a sympathetic nod.

"Anyway, I thought you'd like a ride back to your hotel. You're welcome to stay with me again tonight, and I hope that you do, but I thought you'd like to collect your things at least," he said.

Austin's invitation to stay another night wasn't off the table. Besides, staying in the Jesse and Elle love shack didn't excite me any more than it had the day before.

I had time to think it over.

"I'd love to get my stuff. I do have another question though," I added.

Based on our interactions, I knew Austin wouldn't like what came next.

I asked him anyway.

"Can you tell me where Jesse is?"

Twenty-Two

Austin

"Can you tell me where Jesse is?" Elle didn't look up at me. Instead, she hid behind another bite of the soul food I'd poured my heart into.

I had known the words were coming. Even so, my stomach stiffened when they hit my ears. I could tell she didn't want to wonder, but she had wondered enough to want to know.

Nausea punched my gut.

"Jesse's in holding. There's a separate division for recruits who have been rolled back due to injury or trouble. He'll stay there until his Captain's Mast, where he'll learn the consequences of his actions," I answered honestly. Maybe it would be enough for her to know where he was.

"What do they do while they're waiting?" Elle asked. She leaned forward, giving me her full attention.

She cared more about his situation than I preferred, but I couldn't blame her. Her feelings were genuine, unlike his.

She noticed my annoyance before adding, "I don't want you to think I necessarily care to see him. I just … I'm curious about where he is now."

"Honestly, it depends on why a recruit was rolled back. Usually, they help maintain the base, clean the facilities, do landscaping, stuff like that. Pretty much whatever is needed until their next stop is decided. For Jesse, that will likely be a discharge from the Navy. The timeline is indefinite."

Elle's brows kissed the middle of her forehead at the word *indefinite*.

"Is the girl from the video in holding too?"

The taste of bile crawled up the back of my throat like a demon from the depths. I watched her put her fork down and realize there was a chance they were still seeing each other, still communicating, and still having sex. Worry bleached the color from her complexion. Unsure how to respond, I decided honesty was the best I could do.

I already had too large of a lie waiting for fire to load more into the barrel.

"She is. There are separate barracks for males and females. You see how hard that is to enforce with one hundred percent accuracy though."

Could my sarcasm lessen the reality of the situation?

Her eye roll told me it couldn't.

"It's very unlikely that Jesse is still in frequent contact with Ms. Camellino. Surveillance is doubled in the holding divisions for many reasons."

I watched the wheels turn in Elle's head like our minds were connected. Defeat was evident in her exhale, but her resilience found a way out through the angry flare of her nostrils.

"I want nothing more than to start moving forward, Austin. I'm just afraid I won't be able to do that without talking to him and getting more closure. Do you know when I might be able to do that? Respectfully, you're the only one who can answer that question, so I would greatly appreciate it if you could provide me with all the information you can. I won't tell anyone. I promise."

God, she could melt me.

Not only did she deserve to start moving forward, but she also knew how to reason with me *respectfully*. Although entirely inappropriate, I imagined her in my bed—*respectfully*. Naked—*respectfully*. Backing up the creamiest, most mouthwatering ass I'd ever seen against me—*respectfully*.

My thoughts were so out of line that they even surprised me. I couldn't remember the last time I'd craved something so desperately that it felt like I would die if I didn't devour it. It was clear that I would do anything she asked, whether I wanted to or not. All she had to do was say my name or the word *respectfully* at the end of a sentence, and I was a dead man.

Like *dead*, dead.

I adjusted my spine toward the top of my chair, attempting to convey the strength and honesty I knew Elle needed. The last thing I needed though was Jesse clouding her head and interfering with the possibility that she and I could become something more.

Preventing them from ever speaking again was impossible. Jesse would gain access to a phone sometime soon, and Elle would be the first person he called. As much as I didn't want it to happen, I knew it needed to.

It would be better if I attended their inevitable reunion.

"I'm sure this is incredibly frustrating, and I understand that you need more closure. I really do. It's not my place to stand between you and Jesse, but there's only so much flexibility that my position allows before I put my career at risk. Showing you the security footage was a major gamble," I reminded her.

I wanted to give her everything in my power. But my power could only stretch so far.

"I know. And I appreciate everything you've done for me. Truly. You've gone above and beyond. I understand you're in a difficult position." Her posture softened, like she'd just fought a battle and lost.

Stop fucking this up, I warned myself.

"Can we make a deal?" I offered.

Her eyes lit up at my change of pace.

"I'm not due back on base until Monday at the earliest, Tuesday if I take the extra day off they allow after a graduation weekend. Showing up before then would look suspicious. If you have time before your flight, I'll take you to talk to Jesse before you leave." I hesitated.

Their meeting had to happen for both of our sakes.

She was right.

"Really?!" she exclaimed, swiftly scooting her chair away from the table.

"If it will help you, I'll do my best to make that happen. I want you to have what you need to move forward."

Her slow-growing smile was a mix of appreciation, realization, and terror. She knew it meant facing Jesse head-on.

And I knew it could mean confronting my truth.

She placed her hands on her thighs and steadied herself before her eyes found mine. Was that what she would look like, sitting before me, if she felt about me the way I felt about her?

She really was breathtaking.

"Thank you, Austin. Seriously. I ... I don't know how I could ever repay you for everything you've done to help me."

"You don't have to repay me. All I ask is that you finish your breakfast before we go back to your hotel. The noises coming from your stomach are distracting me," I insisted playfully.

She needed nourishment. Unfortunately, food was my only way of getting that into her for the time being. Maybe when she grew to trust me more—when she knew the truth—I could nourish her in other ways.

God, I wanted to give her everything she needed.

Everything she deserved.

After breakfast, I followed Elle out the front door and opened my driver's door for her. The dropping temperatures kept her arms secured around her chest.

"You want to drive? Let The Ol' Green Goddess take your mind off things for a while," I asked. "Usually works well for me."

As if I needed something else to love about her, without hesitation, she agreed and hopped into the driver's seat. She drove us back to her hotel in my baby, like it had been made for her, while I gave directions and fought every urge to spill my truth.

I was the one writing back to you, I begged my mouth not to say, admiring the freedom lacing her smile.

Someone had waited their entire life for the unspoken connection we shared.

And it wasn't Jesse Jenkins.

It was me.

Twenty-Three

Elle

Elle: I just got back to the hotel. Grabbing my stuff. I'll let you know if I end up staying here tonight. I reeeally don't want to, but I don't want to overstay my welcome with Mr. Navy Man either …

Ruthie: Have you seen the news, girl? It's everywhere. Even made the 5:00 here in P-cola.

Elle: Do I even want to know what you're talking about?

Ruthie: Midwestern states are expecting a cold front with record snowfall for this time of year. You should DEFINITELY shack up with Mr. Navy Man again tonight. He'll keep you warm …

Elle: You're full of shit. Also, it's been one day since Jesse. I'm not letting Mr. Navy Man keep me warm. Do you know me at all?

Ruthie: I'm telling you ... put the news on. I'll bet you fifty bucks your flight tomorrow gets canceled, sis. Also, I'm a big believer in the power of a good rebound, so don't close that clam up just yet. There may just be a pearl inside, waiting to be discovered by a worthy sailor ...

Elle: LOL. You're sick ...

Ruthie: Can I at least see a picture of new and improved Mr. Navy Man? Does he have social media?

Elle: No, and I don't know. I've been too busy picking up the pieces of my broken heart to ask.

Ruthie: If I ever see Jesse again, his balls will be topping our Christmas tree.

Elle: Like, so sick ... you need a doctor.

Ruthie: Does Mr. Navy Man have a name?

Ruthie: I need to see a picture of him!

Ruthie: You said he seemed older, but, like, HOW much older are we talking? Older guys are soooo hot. It's giving DADDY, if you know what I mean.

My phone chimed on after I slipped it back into my purse. Ruthie could only be serious in her support for one day at most. Apparently, that day had been yesterday because her new approach overflowed with sexual references, rebound suggestions, and questions I expected only from her. She had a point though.
How old was Chief Carterson?
Austin and I approached my hotel room, stopping at the door. My nervous system electrocuted itself. The only thing more

embarrassing than dismantling this room would be doing it with someone like him standing next to me.

"Do you want to wait for me in the lobby? Great coffee bar down there," I lied.

Embarrassment wasn't a strong enough word for what I was about to experience. *Death by pathetic sex dungeon* was more like it.

"No," he said, straight-faced. "If you let me help you, we can get it done faster."

It made sense, but not enough to convince me.

"Mmkay," I mumbled sarcastically, my effort missing the mark by a mile.

Austin could do a lot of things well. Taking a hint wasn't one of them.

"Does this mean you're staying at my place again tonight?" His tone told me he'd prefer it that way.

"I haven't decided yet. I figured I'd see how this went and go from there. Is that all right?"

"Of course. I just want you to know that you don't have to stay in this room if you don't want to or if it's too much. You're welcome at my place for as long as you need."

Austin leaned against the wall, his posture relaxed while he patiently waited for me to open the damn door. It was the first position he'd assumed that resembled that of an average man instead of a naval chief.

With no way around it, I nodded, took a deep breath, and retrieved the room key from my bag. The door to room 102 opened with a subtle *click*, giving Austin a direct view into my hopeless devotion. The stunned look on his stupidly handsome face when we entered suggested he regretted joining me. It was too late to extinguish that fire.

I let the shame burn me instead.

"You know what? This was a bad idea." I halted and turned to shove him back out the door.

Despite my best efforts, he remained still, even as I pressed all my force into his chest. He was a brick wall. My petite frame stood no chance against his trunk of a body.

"Where should we start?" he asked.

He was here to help. No matter how uncomfortable the sight made him, it was apparent he wasn't leaving.

"I don't know. I ..." My gaze ping-ponged, and I noticed all the things I hoped he didn't.

What task could I possibly give him that wouldn't continue to embarrass me?

"Ruthie mentioned some bad weather coming in. How about you turn the news on while I gather my things so I can decide where I'm staying tonight? It would help if you didn't watch me right now," I confessed.

He stared down at me without blinking, killing my embarrassment and replacing it with something much more profound.

Understanding.

"I can do that. I think you've already made that decision though. And I agree with it."

Austin could command a room without even trying. A man of few powerful words.

Damn.

They froze me.

Ruthie was right, and so was he. There was no reason to stay alone at the hotel tonight when I could stay in a comfortable bed while Austin cooked for me, took me to see Jesse, and drove me back to the airport. No taxis, no staring at what could have been, no shitty continental breakfast or stale coffee, no unnecessary hotel charges, just peace.

And safety until my flight home.

"I don't have to help you if you don't want me to. But I'm here if you need me. I'll check the weather on my phone while you decide. Either way, it's no problem."

His right arm rose from his side, and he gently cupped my shoulder. I stared at our connection.

The quick movement left me feeling like a scolded little girl. But the unexpected jolt it evoked from my chest was a sensation understood only by a woman.

"Okay ..." I barely whispered.

Where is my breath?

Austin took it with him when he turned and sat on the floral-fabric chair in the corner of the room and got busy with his phone. I turned, hiding *whatever the hell* was blossoming over my cheeks.

Quickly, I gathered the lingerie, massage oil, and vibrator—the most embarrassing items within Austin's radius. He didn't appear to be watching me; his line of sight remained pinned on his phone. However, he did a terrible job of hiding the smile that could have only come from realizing what I was doing. I'd grab the rose petals later, but at least the big-ticket items were out of view.

Fifteen minutes later, I emerged from the bathroom with a fully stocked toiletry bag. Austin no longer held his phone. Instead, he sat back in the chair, his legs spread as wide as his rugged pants would allow.

His whole body greeted me.

"Feeling less embarrassed now that the bandage is off?" He smirked. His arms remained glued to the armrests, like a king on his throne.

Statuesque was his stance. Thumping was my fucking chest.

"Yes. But I didn't really have a choice, now did I?" I challenged.

"No choice but to get it over with and move forward, right? One step closer to the future you deserve."

I nodded at his statement. Without a doubt, he was making one.

"Can I confess something?" he added.

"Sure."

"This is so fucked." His confession barely found me before he erupted into equal parts berating and humorous laughter. It didn't feel like Austin was judging me though. Instead, he laughed with me in realization.

Relief riddled my exhale.

"Tell me about it." I rolled my eyes. They went right back to staring at him. He was the only one in the world who knew *all* the details of what I was dealing with. The only one who had seen the video, the deceit.

The only one who could laugh with me when all I wanted to do was lose it ...

"Could he be any less of a man?"

What is his point in putting Jesse down?

Did he think it would lift me up? Because his repeated attacks only made me feel worse. Like I was some idiot for trusting Jesse in the first place.

"Look around you, Elle. You stayed dedicated to him for months while keeping up with your own life, came all this way, and were even thoughtful enough to bring rose petals and other ... *things.*"

I laughed as he avoided naming the other unmentionable things he'd spotted around the room.

"It rattles me to my core that someone like Jesse would do this to someone like you."

"What do you mean, someone like me?" I asked, inching toward him.

Did he think I was better than Jesse or the other way around?

"You're a beautiful person—obviously on the outside, but clearly on the inside too. It bothers me so immensely that I can only laugh at his stupidity. He'll get what he deserves. And if I have anything to do with it, so will you."

His statement left me flushed, flattered, and stunned, among other things.

My body sank onto the corner of the bed before my face dropped, my gaze aligning with the patterned carpet beneath me. What was he alluding to? Potent and reassuring words from someone of his esteem carried weight, leaving whatever was between us heavy. So heavy that I felt the air evacuating my lungs as his statement crushed them.

Austin spoke about me the way I imagined a husband would brag about his wife when she wasn't in the room—effortlessly and with force behind every syllable. On occasion, I'd felt I deserved better than Jesse, but, damn, Austin made me want to believe it.

"Look at me," he commanded.

I lifted my chin and obeyed long enough to watch another man rise and take Jesse's spot next to me on the edge of the bed.

"It's his loss, and you'd better believe that."

This man was used to commanding a room. *Yes, sir*, were the only words I wanted to say. But nothing came out.

"Do you believe it? That you deserve more?" His words were surprisingly soft. His attention rose.

"Not yet," I replied honestly.

How could a man I hardly knew take my breath away so easily? The answer contained reasons I couldn't pinpoint.

"Mark my words," Austin promised. When he stared into me, his sage fields returned, letting my warm, sunny irises water them. "You will."

Twenty-Four

Austin

I APPEARED CALM AND STILL, much like the static coastline we passed on the drive back to Haroldeen Lane. Still, the desires burning within me could set saturated fields ablaze. My desire to care for Elle collided with my desire to rid her mind of Jesse, leaving me lost in our unknown future.

I so badly wanted to tell Elle everything I knew to be true—that I would do anything to make her mine, that she deserved better, and that I was the one who'd written her the letters. The girl who lived in my dreams had no idea she'd kept me afloat like a buoy for so long.

Would she ever be ready to know?

Would I ever be ready to tell her?

Sneaking a peek at her in my passenger seat, I bit down on my tongue to keep it quiet. It was abundantly clear in the immense effort it took that my truths were desperately searching for their way to shore; they were searching for their lighthouse. *She* was my lighthouse.

My truths belonged to her.

I imagined us sharing a home someday, perhaps the one we were sharing now, and how hugely her simple existence within it would impact my life. Could I even fathom what it would be like to wake up next to Elle Madelyn, possibly naked and in love with me? Legendary was what it would be. To endlessly fuck away our weekends, wishing our weekdays away like ice cream in the summer sun, just to do it all over again. To cook breakfast in our kitchen, much like I had done this morning, except I could serve her a side of honesty with her eggs instead of a lie.

My hips sank further into the heated driver's seat, warming my already sweltering thighs. It all sounded phenomenal, but the question remained: could she love someone like me after discovering the truth?

The salty old chief who'd kept to himself for a decade and waited so long for her that he forced fate to side with him.

I'd still be tied to the Navy for at least another year. Deciding to reenlist or not wasn't a choice I'd yet made. Having someone waiting for me on the other side of the decision would make it easier. Age was another factor to consider. She had to be in her mid-twenties if she was well into a graduate program. My age—thirty-three—still felt young to me. Would it be too impactful of an age gap for her?

If she wanted to travel the world, live in a mansion made of envy, and lead a life of delirium, I couldn't provide that. I wasn't the type of guy who could keep up with the Joneses, nor did I want to be. However, I was overqualified for the job if she wanted to live a life of loyalty and infatuation, where she'd be cared for in ways so pure and unspoken that they'd feel tantric. To me, a well-lived life had little to do with money, although I had enough of that to give her the things that mattered too.

I wanted to give her everything I had.

Elle's exhales clouded the passenger window she rested her head against. The soft sound of her breath stole my attention as I grounded my thoughts and surveyed the Jeep. By design, "Crash into Me" by Dave Matthews Band pulsed through the audio system. Noticeably quiet after leaving the hotel, Elle remained lost in her thoughts. She'd had high hopes for that room; I couldn't blame her.

Were they as high as the hopes I had for us?

Doubtful.

Mine were sky-fucking-high.

"I forgot to ask; how did the weather look when you checked?" She straightened, finally turning her attention my way.

The forecast wasn't unusual for April. We usually got a few good snows before the real spring weather officially kicked in. The news had indicated colder temps and heavy snowfall throughout the night though, which would likely ground flights for at least a day or two.

I hadn't mentioned it earlier because it excited me endlessly.

Being snowed in with Elle sounded like a fantasy; being unable to act on it was my worst nightmare. Elle could stay with me as long as Mother Nature wanted her to, as long as Mother Nature agreed to help me keep my testosterone in check.

Acting normal around her was getting harder.

"If I'm being transparent, it looks like we may get some heavy snow tonight. I didn't want to worry you. If your flight gets canceled tomorrow, it's not a problem. You can stay as long as you need," I reassured her.

"Great ..."

Her apparent sarcasm stung me. She'd rather leave tomorrow. I could feel it.

"I know that's probably not what you wanted to hear, but there are worse places to be stuck, right?" I nudged her arm.

"I didn't mean it like that." Her fingers brushed my forearm before landing on my hand. I froze. "I'm just ready to be back in my own space to cope with everything. I need to take my mind off things, and being here keeps me close to the day I want nothing more than to forget." The fingers on her left hand retreated from mine and intertwined with her right ones, like she was keeping something safe between her palms.

It felt ... different, having her ride shotgun next to me. It was peaceful, like the calm before our inevitable storm. Deep down, I knew there was a real possibility it could be one of our last rides together. I needed our night to count. She had nowhere to be, and I had nowhere better to be than beside her. Plus, the weather wasn't due in until late into the night. We still had hours to take advantage of.

"I have an idea," I announced, admiring the disheveled hair she'd layered into a messy bun atop her head. The style screamed off-duty model.

She could be a three-eyed alien, and I'd still find her insanely attractive. It wasn't only her outer beauty that choked me. It was the whole damn package.

"Let's hear it," she said, unamused.

"I wish circumstances were different, but I have to say, this is the most enjoyment I've gotten from another person in a long time."

I heard the distinct sound of the *gulp* she attempted to bury in her throat as the words left my lips. Redness kissed her knuckles as they tightened. Were my words making her nervous?

"It's your first time here; I'm a native, so it only makes sense for me to show you around, right?"

"That does make sense, yes. Only I look like shit, and I'm not sure I'm up for being your little tourist right now," she admitted.

I can show you places you've never seen, little tourist.

"Sorry. That was rude of me." She laughed after a pause. The sound exposed how well she knew her feelings and how little she knew mine.

It was sexy.

"No, it wasn't rude; it was honest." Unlike Jesse, I wanted her to express her feelings freely. It meant she felt comfortable enough around me to tell me how she really felt. "Life has been cruel to you lately—I get that. But …" I paused, hoping to entice her curiosity.

"But … what?" She took the bait.

"But I know a place that might make you smile through that cruelty. A place where you can't help but feel good."

"And where exactly is that?" The muted glow in her eyes sparked brighter than I'd seen all day. It was brief, but apparent to someone who paid attention. Operation Cheer Up Buttercup was underway.

"It's a surprise," I revealed too quickly.

I desperately wanted to share my optimism with her. If she let me, I'd show her an unforgettable night.

"I'm not sure I'm up for any more surprises this weekend, but I'll give it a try," she said.

Once again, she stared out of the passenger window. Fatigue pulled her shoulders down. Her expression followed the setting sun.

"Oh, I think you'll be up for this one."

Twenty-Five

Elle

A KALEIDOSCOPE OF COLORS, PULSATING music, and excitement lit up Navy Pier and Austin's sculpted face. Featured in one of my favorite movies, *Ferris Bueller's Day Off*, the attraction was famous in Chicago and in my search history. The popular tourist destination had piqued my interest when I researched the trip, my heart badgering me to add it to the list of things I wanted to experience with Jesse. Looking back, I realized he should have been planning those things for me, not the other way around.

Another reminder that forever had never been in our cards.

The balls of my feet took a beating while I bobbed on them to see my surroundings better. Austin and I paced closer to the action, the vibrations around me meeting the swirls of anticipation swimming around my stomach. If I let unease win, I'd never be comfortable again, so I allowed the dancing lights and intensifying energy to draw me in.

It was time to get comfortable with being a little uncomfortable.

Besides, the only way to get to a different room was by walking through a different door, *right?* Standing next to Austin at a place I'd thought I'd experience with Jesse was a *very* different door.

Yet one I was surprisingly interested in entering.

Guilt could have turned me around before we approached the entrance of the pier, but Jesse hadn't cared that Rita Camellino wasn't me when he fucked the decency out of her. Why should I? I muted my guilt and admired Austin's effort. He'd chosen this place as the backdrop to my lousy weekend. It was thoughtful of him.

I was grateful for the distraction. And for the heavy pep in his step.

In the distance, a giant illuminated Ferris wheel invited us to the farthest end of the pier, steady in its enormous, sweeping motion. Several other amusement rides swirled around it, creating an enticing arrangement of motion and sound. The place mimicked a county fair, mixed with a lakeside boardwalk, on steroids.

Live jazz music pumped from a stage positioned off to the side of our path. A woman, wearing colorful hippie-style clothing and charm-embellished dreadlocks, swayed around two sitting musicians, allowing the breeze to take hold of her body and sultry vocal cords. She sang and moved with confidence and admirable freedom. I smiled at her enviously. For a moment, I was hypnotized, marking the first moment I'd allowed myself to fully think of something other than Jesse.

Austin knew what he was doing, bringing me here.

"Well, this is incredible," I said, turning to catch a glimpse of Austin through my crystalized breath. It froze in midair, something I wasn't used to. The goose bumps sprinkling my skin told me the temperature had dropped significantly.

"I knew you'd love it." He smiled, almost tripping me with his charm.

It didn't matter that hundreds of people were among us. The way he communicated with his entire body made it feel like it was just the two of us. His mouth, chest, and frostbitten words said so much.

"How could you know that?" I asked.

Like he was in a designer cologne commercial, Austin buried his left hand into his front jeans pocket and rose briefly on his toes. "It's vibrant and cheerful, full of life. Like you."

"That's sweet, aside from the fact that I've *literally* been the opposite recently …" I added.

Did he receive my subtle admission? Perhaps I shouldn't have felt bad about the mood that had engulfed my normally warm, appreciative demeanor all day. But I did. None of my situation was Austin's fault.

Jesse was the only target for my sharpened comments and daggered annoyances.

"Can you try something for me?" The statement read more like an order than a suggestion. Austin adjusted his stance, zipping his jacket before stepping closer toward me.

"Like?" I asked.

On his approach, Austin's sweeping upper body crowded my view. I craned my neck back, peering up at him to take in his entirety.

"Look, I know we don't know each other very well, but can I show you what kind of night this was supposed to be for you? You're so in your head, and it's fine. *But* ..."

"But ... what?" I asked curiously.

His pause stoked my interest before he finally continued. A wide breath expanded his chest.

"Maybe you can step out of that head for a few hours tonight and step toward me. You deserve to have fun and enjoy yourself. Let me help get you there."

His words were immaculate, almost rehearsed. Mostly though, they were convincing because how the hell could I say no to a request like that?

A handsome-ass, respectable-ass, tall-ass, muscular-ass, military-ass, established-ass *man* wanted to show me what I deserved. Even if just for a night, he wished to pull me into a world where I could let a man lead instead of feeling like I was leading one.

Not one single reason to say no came to me. Besides, it was a learning opportunity.

An opportunity to learn what it could feel like to experience Elle without Jesse for the first time in years.

A blurted response leaped from my lips without caution. "You know what, Chief Carterson? I'm in. Besides, your chivalry is unmatched so far, and if I'm honest, I think you can show me a better time tonight than Jesse ever would have ..." It was unlike me, releasing a line like that so shamelessly. If Ruthie were with me, she would be smacking my ass at the confidence I often had a hard time projecting.

It felt amazing.

The grin that erupted across Austin's face revealed the teeth that had taunted me earlier at breakfast. His right thumb met the corner of his parted smile before he gracefully swiped it across his bottom lip. Nature had undoubtedly designed his phenomenal smile and full lips.

A mouth that was hard to say no to.

"I must say, I agree. *Heavily.*" He laughed too loudly, rocking back on his heels.

A rare moment of awkwardness found us. He was so smooth, but his Adam's apple fell as he swallowed whatever else he wanted to say. Making him nervous made me nervous.

It was exhilarating.

"You probably didn't imagine my first move of the night to be leaving you alone, but can you wait here for a few minutes? Give me ten, and I'll be back." The wink he shot me as he turned and walked away told me that whatever he was up to would be worth the wait.

I sat on a nearby wooden bench, bouncing my legs to the beat of the music. An older couple passing by released warm laughter into the air. Their hands remained as intertwined as their memories likely were—a glimmer of hope that enviable, sustainable relationships still existed in the world. My chest ignited. It was my turn to enjoy what the night had to offer.

If I let it.

Several minutes later, as promised, Austin approached me with overflowing armfuls of every carnie-style treat I could imagine. In the crooks of his elbows sat two tubular light-up glasses, each filled to the brim with blue slush.

For the love of God, please tell me those contain alcohol, I thought.

Cushioned between his thick biceps and forearms, a funnel cake, pink cotton candy, and two steaming hot dogs balanced strategically. I smiled, my expression greeting him and the mountain of delicious junk food he presented.

How the hell did one person carry that much? I didn't care.

My stomach sparked with as much enthusiasm as my eyes did.

"I knew you'd be hungry, so I had to cover all the bases. I got something sweet, something salty, something fried, and something alcoholic. Take your pick, *doll.*" He accentuated the word *doll* with an old-school, bad-boy accent, straight out of the movie *Grease.*

My all-time favorite movie.

"As tough as that decision should be, it's easy. I'll take one of each." I stood and retrieved a frozen cocktail from his arms before sitting back down and bringing it to my lips, allowing my tongue to guide the multicolored swirly straw into my mouth. Blue raspberry flavoring overwhelmed my taste buds with each long sip.

"Shit, that's good," I released between slurps. Eager to reap the benefits of the liquid courage hiding inside, I sucked the straw harder.

A few drops of sugary saliva overflowed from the corner of my mouth.

Austin's hawk-like stare while he watched my tongue find every fallen drop told me he was pleased with himself. He appeared to enjoy watching me enjoy things. He placed the rest of our treats down next to me.

"Napkin?" he asked, bringing a clean square from his back pocket to my chin.

I nodded.

Cleaning up my messes yet again …

Someone like him could probably drown a woman in her own cum. I could tell he was a natural pleaser. A pleasure protector, if you would.

The heat of the forbidden thought found my thighs, as unexpected as the thought itself.

Am I a bad person for having dirty thoughts about Chief Carterson?

Or was I simply observing the opposite sex for the first time in a long time?

Besides, anyone with a beating heart could recognize his potential to rock someone's world in bed. He could fling a woman around any way he pleased.

Was that why he'd just called me *doll?*

I bit down on my tongue, hoping the sharp pain would capture my inappropriate thoughts.

He sat beside me. The bench shook below us as it worked overtime to support his stout body and my hungry one. I claimed the cotton candy as my own while he started his feast with the funnel cake. We ate together—silently. I'd never eaten a hot dog so fast in my life, allowing the sugar, alcohol, and calories to layer in my stomach like sand art. Austin ate every last crumb of his delicacies and then finished whatever I couldn't of mine.

The man could eat.

"What now?" I broke the silence as our indulgences came to an end.

Austin collected the trash from our feast and threw the wrappers into a nearby garbage can. "Come with me." He offered me his hand

and a softened expression, anticipating my unsteadiness before I stood.

I rose, leaving my inhibitions at the bottom of my empty cocktail glass.

My fingers relaxed into his when I took his hand. Even when I was fully upright, he didn't let go.

"Let's decide what's next together. I've been taking trips here since I was a kid, but this is all new to you. I want to know what's drawing you in."

Rich gold, spirited oranges, and lively shades of raspberry illuminated the sky behind the giant Ferris wheel at the pier's edge. Heights hadn't been kind to me—mild turbulence had made me vomit as a child—but I'd always wanted to ride on one. To let it take me higher.

To a place where I'd have no choice but to get comfortable with my fear.

"Okay, Mr. Smooth. See that Ferris wheel?" I tilted my head in its direction.

His ears perked up, and he nodded curiously.

"I don't care what we do first. I just want to end up there." I pointed to the highest point at the top of the wheel. "I've always been too scared to ride one, but I kind of want to make it my bitch …"

His laugh was the sweetest sound. Deep enough to remain manly but raw enough to sound genuine.

It was the kind of laugh you never forgot.

"You got it. Sounds like a good opportunity to go after something you've always wanted," he said. I agreed. "Let's wander, maybe get a bit lost, and then we'll go show that thing who's boss."

I could tell he enjoyed my admission of being a Ferris wheel virgin.

His stride moved at half capacity, mimicking my smaller paces.

His hand never left mine.

Twenty-Six

Austin

WITH EVERY SECOND THAT TICKED on, reality surprised me with how vulnerable Elle's presence made me feel. My new favorite hobby was watching her peruse souvenir shops and select thoughtful touristy trinkets for her parents and Ruthie. I bought her a Navy Pier sweatshirt—hopefully the first of many things.

The kindness I'd noticed in her letters was evident in how the heartbroken girl still tried to bring some happiness home to others. My girl was the sweetest, always giving to those around her.

She'd make the best lover, I thought as she asked if thermals were warmer than fleeces.

Had she been just as giving to Jesse?

The thought chilled my bones more than the cold sweeping the boardwalk. The Windy City was living up to its reputation, showcasing the characteristic wind chill, made famous by how hard it pierced unassuming skin. I'd gotten used to it after a lifetime of enduring it.

Elle, however, was a Florida girl. Her hand trembled in mine, her mouth chattering in the unforgiving breeze.

I refused to let go of her hand unless she needed to use it. Our finger-laced embrace lasted far beyond its expected expiration. There was no way I wasn't soaking up every second of feeling her hand in mine—something I'd fantasized about for way too long.

Challenging the chill by lighting the fireplace when we got home sounded nice, except it wouldn't be because taking her in front of raging coral flames on my living room floor was another fantasy I'd been carrying for weeks.

Years, truthfully.

Hell, just holding her hand had more than overwhelmed me for the last hour and a half. I couldn't imagine what touching her body in other places would do to me. Her straddling me with the ass that I couldn't help but notice would probably kill me on impact.

At least then I could die a very happy man.

I so badly wanted tonight to be just for her, to relieve the emotions she'd experienced the last few days and see her have some fun. But who was I kidding? Our little arrangement for the evening was equally as favorable to me as it was to her. I got to fill her hand with mine, fill her stomach with deliciousness, and fill her heart with temporary peace, all while staring at her.

Admiring her in person instead of on paper.

I showed her off to everyone who walked by. Seeing other men and women stare at Elle as we passed them reinforced that we weren't a real couple. *Yet.* Other people could stare at her, *want her*, and eventually ... she could want one of them back. I couldn't let that happen though.

Nothing would stop me from making her mine.

After a trek down the boardwalk, we approached the Ferris wheel and the newly darkened sky. Her fingers had slicked with sweat, slipping from mine in anticipation. I was just glad to be beside her as she faced her fear. She didn't need to feel intimidated next to me *or* by the amusement ride. If she let me, I would always catch her if she fell.

"Next in line," a young gentleman bellowed, indicating it was our turn to enter the next available seat car on the paused wheel. He was busy with line duty while a second guy manned the controls from a booth a few feet away.

The famous structure had been updated over the years, but the glass-enclosed seat cars still exposed riders to a three-hundred-sixty-degree view. Suddenly, Elle sank to the pavement to tie her shoe. Funny, because her boots had no laces. She needed a minute. So did I.

To memorize her.

Her plump, pouty mouth bit down on itself while she glanced around her feet for laces that didn't exist. The voluptuous ass I fought hard not to stare at as she bent over captivated me.

I couldn't help myself.

Golden eyes that could pierce the blackest night looked up at me in hopes that I hadn't noticed, widening with the playful *oops* expression lighting up the rest of her face.

Does she realize how mind-blowing she is?

I cleared my throat, desperate for distraction. "You ready? We've got people behind us." I outstretched my hand, ready to steady her lower back and propel her forward as she stood.

She didn't need me to though.

My girl walked through her trepidation and approached the halted car, scooting into it with force. Her sluggish steps told me she'd moved before she was ready. Impressively, she did it anyway. I added *watching Elle conquer her fears* to the growing list of things I loved about her and joined her in the swaying enclosure.

My weight vibrated the glass and metal, no matter how still I remained. Grabbing her hand wasn't an option because she'd already formed a double-handed death grip on her seat. She stared at the floor, quiet. With her need for support clear, I gripped her kneecap. One hundred and ninety-six feet in the sky was high.

Would the grasp of the beast be enough to calm my beauty?

"You sure you want to do this?" I asked.

Her chest rose and fell like a tired trampoline.

"Just shut up and ask me again when we reach the top," Elle whispered, breathless.

She closed her eyes and inhaled deeply, her knuckles paling from gripping the bench so tightly. I wanted to wrap my arm around her and kiss her. Take away her fear and replace it with something else that could fuel her adrenaline.

Without notice, the door closed, and a sharp crank propelled us forward, leaving no room for her to change her mind as we jolted into motion. Our path was set to the top of the wheel, where Elle could face her fear.

And I could face my desire.

Twenty-Seven

Elle

FUCK, FUCK, FUCK, FAAAACK. I was doing it.

Austin was taking my Ferris wheel virginity. The massive wheel lifted us into the sky while he continued gripping my knee like it was his. The alcoholic slushy from earlier must have relaxed me because I finally admitted to myself that I liked it. I felt less guilty and more at ease when I noticed Austin staring at me from just outside of my view. It was easier to focus on him than down at the disappearing pavement.

Experiencing the moment with Austin felt right. Loosening my attachment to Jesse was also starting to feel better. Sure, the whiplash of emotions I'd experienced over the past two days was intense. But my self-respect was stronger.

Austin's heavy hand shifted slightly higher up my leg, his palm landing on the middle of my thigh. The action was smooth, unlike my breathing when I realized how close we'd become. The sheer size difference in our thighs stared up at me.

It was astonishing.

The ground below us evaporated as the people on the pier shrank with each movement forward and upward. Instantly, the busy boardwalk below transformed into a silent film. Fifty feet off the ground and growing, the widening view of the Chicago skyline and Lake Michigan dissipated my nerves more than expected.

I shivered. Were my body's unstoppable vibrations caused by the city lights, the atmosphere growing colder with every foot we rose, or Austin? He noticed my weak tremors, transferring his warm touch from my thigh to my shoulder.

"Thank you," I whispered, touching his knee in answer. "This is really something …"

"I should be thanking you. I haven't been on this thing in ages. I love the rush." He looked past me. His gaze left the glass box that lifted us to another world, where sunsets were traded for the stars freckling our horizon.

Silver moonlight backlit his piercing emerald eyes. The ones that captured me, even when they focused elsewhere. For a moment, he looked broken.

Is he holding back?

Desperate for his expression to find me again, I faced him. Looking away felt impossible. Perhaps the evergreen vastness in his eyes—the endless possibilities hidden behind them—kept me entranced.

Maybe Jesse's screwup had been my path to a man who could make me feel things other than doubt. A man like Austin. I'd have to let him in if I ever wanted to find out.

I shrugged my shoulder free from Austin's grip, making the man next to me shrivel.

His chin lowered, his immaculate profile angling toward the floor while his hands searched aimlessly for a new resting place. Austin's jaw pulsed, and his arms stiffened before he froze. A look of concern darkened his demeanor. His body language told me he was desperate for the reason I'd pulled away.

We were out of time, out of space.

About to step out of line.

None of that mattered. My vision tunneled, homing in on the only mouth I could picture tasting. His lips had already taught me so much.

"Do it, bitch," imaginary Ruthie whispered into my ear.

The heart that kept me alive plunged. I tilted my head and leaned forward, crashing my mouth into his without a second thought. The motion was spring-loaded with softness and desire. Eager yet tender. Austin's hands quickly magnetized to my cheeks, proving he hungered for more than just a peck.

How could a kiss be so perfect without rehearsal?

There was nothing artificial about the way his tongue purposefully swam around my mouth, like each slow pass sweetened the taste of our connection.

Our taste.

"Fuck," Austin released into my mouth.

I welcomed it, parting my lips slightly wider. His throaty groan entered my bloodstream, confirming my suspicions. He wanted me.

And clearly, I wanted him too. At least for tonight.

His right hand left my cheek and proceeded to wrap the base of my skull before his fingers slithered upward through my hair. They tightened, securing his grip. Shudders dripped down my spine like molten lust as we tasted each other deeper. I'd never *ever* been kissed like this. So passionately.

So perfectly.

He tasted so fucking good, his saliva laced with spearmint and a sweet drizzle of alcohol.

Tingles pinballed around my stomach. Austin gently bit down on one side of my bottom lip, moving across it with several small nibbles. Jesus Christ, it felt phenomenal.

I panted into his mouth. Intensity, heat, and a plethora of other foreign feelings collided between my thighs. For once, I let the sensation melt me.

Please don't end, I begged silently, fiercely kissing him back so he knew exactly what I needed.

Him.

His chest widened, pressing against mine with every powerful inhale he could find between tongue tricks. No way would I be the one to end our connection. It felt too damn good.

He broke it first.

In unison, our lungs gasped for the air we'd stolen from each other.

"Are you sure about this?" he panted. Panic paused on his hungry expression. His jaw hung slightly open while something that looked like terror filled his face.

"Would you think less of me if I asked you not to stop until we reached the bottom?" I admitted.

If kissing Austin was what it felt like to fly, I prayed my feet never touched the ground again. Screw being afraid of heights; leaving the moment behind scared me more.

Austin grinned suggestively, instantly releasing my remaining hesitation into the endless darkness surrounding us. He leaned forward, this time toward the exposed skin under my chin. It didn't matter that the sweater and jacket he'd bought me covered some of my neck; his fingers moved the fabric obstacles out of the way to make room for his hunger.

His longing.

The cool air, mixed with his heated tongue, was heavenly. He lifted my chin to accommodate the greed controlling his movements. And mine. Sensations sparked through my entire body in a way I'd never experienced, pushing me past the guilt I no longer felt for a man who had never made me feel the way he did.

"Do you know how long I've waited for this?" He spoke into my neck.

My head spun, my body quivered, my breath quickened. I wasn't dizzy though.

I was free.

I wrapped both arms around his neck, and my fingers explored the tousled waves cresting across his head. I made sure to apply enough pressure to his scalp to ensure my intentions were clear.

Selfishly, the little explorers attached to my palms found their way to his thighs, colliding with the muscular quads I had known would be waiting there. Hard as goddamn stone.

He softly grazed the sensitive stretch of nerves along my lower back, leaving a slew of goose bumps and my nipples on edge as his touch trailed my skin. Every movement was intentional.

Do his job duties in the Navy include soaking panties?

They were known for conquering the seas after all.

Kissing his way from my neck back up to my lips, he hovered over them and stared into my eyes like they were a book he couldn't stop reading. I'd be his personal fucking library if it meant he kept going.

"I have to stop. I'm … I'm sorry … you're too damn much for me," he let out, not so nonchalantly moving a hand to cover his prominent erection.

The bulge growing in his jeans was the only thing thicker than the sexual tension between us. I hadn't thought much about his cock until that moment, but it was safe to assume it was impressive.

Okay, maybe I had thought about it.

Okay, I'd definitely thought about it.

"If it makes you feel any better, you're too damn much for me too. That was …"

"Legendary," he answered for me, raising his fingers to his mouth to capture one last feel of my lips on his.

I swallowed what was left of him on my tongue.

"Legendary."

Twenty-Eight

Austin

The ride back to my house was heaven and hell, tangled together in a beautiful mess. The heaven of tasting Elle for the first time was a moment I'd dreamed of for far too long—her thick, sweet lips; the softness of her skin; the flavor of her. I would never forget it for as long as I lived. I needed more, but couldn't stop thinking about how far I should let things go before telling her my truth.

That was my hell.

"As the cold weather event of the season sets its sights on northern Chicago and the surrounding areas, local airports brace for extensive delays. Expect temperatures to plunge overnight and into tomorrow morning," a woman's voice spouted from my TV above the fireplace, formally delivering the news I couldn't wait to hear.

Not only did it mean I'd have more time with Elle, but it also meant her reunion with Jesse would be delayed.

Both scenarios delighted me more than they should have.

"I hope Hotel Carterson has a vacancy for a few more days because this isn't looking good," Elle hinted.

She sat on the couch beside me, twirling a stray thread still attached to her pants. Her reclined position told me she was cozy in the sweatshirt I'd bought for her. She knew she was welcome to stay as long as needed. Her continued playfulness after our kiss let me know she was as comfortable with the situation as I was.

"I'll have to ask the manager, but I'm sure he won't mind having a pretty blonde hanging around a few more days ..." I teased. *Was that lame?*

She smiled. God, did she smile. I could think of a million other words to use instead of *pretty*, but she truly was the prettiest woman I'd ever seen. Her shoulders and cold-kissed cheekbones rose in tandem.

When did I start noticing weird things like that on women?

Oh yeah, two years ago, when she had walked into my office and fucking rocked my world in an instant.

"This is the coldest weather I've ever experienced, and it hasn't even started yet. Should I be worried?"

Her plaid blanket vibrated, her thin Florida skin unable to warm her fully. The heat was on now, which I rarely used because who didn't prefer a fireplace? I wasn't lighting it unless she specifically asked me to though because it would start an impossible-to-extinguish frenzy deep in my groin.

We sat on the same corduroy couch in my living room that my body had relaxed on thousands of times before. Only this time, Elle sat close enough for me to touch. To practically taste.

To worship, if she'd let me.

I shifted, covering my umpteenth cock bulge of the day with a second throw blanket. Resisting her was becoming increasingly more difficult, especially after I'd learned she enjoyed our kiss as much as I did. Her excitement fueled my unrelenting desire.

My grandmother had taught me that life was about timing, like how lobster bisque tasted better after you spent a long day out on the water. And as much as I wanted it to be the right time for us to take another step, I feared it was too soon for Elle. Patience was the name of our game.

I needed more practice playing it so I didn't mess things up.

"So, Chicago boy, what do you usually do when you get snowed in here?"

She lightly sipped the hot chocolate I'd made for her when we got home, leaving a creamy sheen on her top lip. My secret was topping it with cereal marshmallows instead of regular ones—a game changer. Her secret was keeping her eyes glued to mine while she repeatedly sipped as if she were sucking my ...

How could I get through the night without touching her again?

I couldn't.

"You wouldn't know this because you're a Florida girl, but as long as there's firewood to keep warm, that's all you really need," I answered.

"What about food? Water? Entertainment?" Concern circled her brows as they crowded the middle of her forehead. She gripped the top of her blanket and pulled it, along with her knees, closer to her, like she was listening to a scary story at a sleepover party.

If she thought I wasn't prepared to keep her safe in the event we got snowed in, she was mistaken. I could keep her safe forever.

"If you have wood to keep a fire going, you can hunt and gather, cook food, boil water—not to mention the fun of chopping it. It keeps you plenty busy. You don't need electricity or internet. If you have heat, you have life." I beamed.

Survival scenarios made me feel closer to my grandfather, who'd prepared me for almost anything.

Aside from my self-inflicted, Elle-centered predicament, of course.

"You look like you chop wood, but I didn't realize you *actually* chopped wood. That's cute," she chirped, grinning through another sip of chocolate comfort.

"Cute?"

My dream girl did not just call wood splitting cute.

"I meant ... manly," she corrected, likely in response to my foul expression. "It's a super manly activity. I just ... I sort of tried to imagine Jesse chopping wood, and it's quite comical to picture. More on the cute side." She paused before adding, "He was never really the outdoorsy, chop-his-own-firewood type."

Relief overtook the cuteness she had referred to because I agreed. Jesse chopping wood would be pretty cute.

The opposite of what I looked like while doing it.

"Maybe when we run out of my stash there"—I pointed at the stacked stockpile crowding the corner of the room—"I can show you my woodshed and how me splitting wood is anything but cute." I bit down on my tongue to physically stop it from detailing what I wanted to do to her in there.

Every step deeper Elle took into my world made things feel more intimate. I could no longer picture my life returning to the way it was without her.

"Wait, you have a real woodshed? That's amazing. I'd love to see it!" She looked toward the ash-ridden fireplace and then back at me. Her face grew puzzled.

Don't ask me to light it, don't ask me to light it ... I thought.

"I might be a Florida girl, but to burn through logs, don't you have to light them first?"

Damn it.

"Yes, that is how it works. I thought we'd hold off until tomorrow. You know, to celebrate you being stuck here and all." Another lie.

"Smart. Better save our resources, huh?" She nodded.

I loved how she followed my lead.

She trusted me.

"Exactly what I was thinking," I said. However, it *wasn't* exactly what I had been thinking because what I was thinking involved lighting the stupid fireplace immediately, staring at every inch of her naked body, and studying the light that danced across each curve. My tongue was dying to do the same thing.

Elle broke my trance when she yawned, stood, and emerged from the blanket she'd cocooned herself in. She placed her empty mug on the coffee table. Chocolate hid in the corner of her mouth.

Yeah, you know where I'm going with that ...

"Would you mind if I took a bath and changed into something more comfortable? Now that I have my suitcase and pajamas, that fancy tub in the bathroom is calling my name. I need to touch base with Ruthie anyway. She was supposed to pick me up from the airport tomorrow."

"Of course. Take your time." I cleared my throat. Hearing the word *bath* come out of Elle's mouth made me picture her in it. Sprawled out and covered in suds. I ground my molars together, hoping she wouldn't notice how aggressively my nostrils flared. "Should I wait up, or should we call it a night?" I asked. My voice echoed, my remaining composure fighting for its life as she walked away.

The way she looked back toward me could have killed me, almost like she didn't want to leave me behind.

"I won't keep you up, but I'll come and say good night."

Her words were free of the caution I'd expected. Instead, a silent promise ran through them. A promise that our night wasn't over quite yet.

Sleep Sweet

I exhaled. "I'll be here."
I'll be here all right.
Thinking about her.

Twenty-Nine

Elle

"Are you freaking kidding me?!" Ruthie's voice crackled through the waterlogged speaker of my phone.

Its descent into the bathwater after Ruthie's loud, "*Ahhh*," into my eardrum when I told her about the kiss hadn't helped the already-cracked screen or busted front speaker. As usual, she was more excited about updates on my love life than I was. And, boy, did I have updates.

"No, I'm not kidding. It was … I can't even describe it. It was perfect. And I initiated it! I mean, who am I right now?" I bragged, scrunching my nose in celebration and sinking deeper into the heaven that was Austin's guest room tub.

Bubbles and heat surrounded me while my best friend kept me company.

It was the exact therapy the doctor had ordered.

"I don't know, but I'm sad I'm not around to witness it in person. I hear so much growth in your voice. I'm just happy you're not still crying over that douchebag. I know y'all were together for a long time, but that big of a fuckup gets you off the hook for feeling guilty about anything you choose to do to deal with it."

Ruthie had always believed in rebounds and moving on quickly and mercilessly from men who had done her wrong. I, however, was known for taking things slow and letting empathy guide me through relationship troubles. Was that my downfall or hers?

"I feel like I didn't choose this though. It's like it found me. Like *he* found me. I mean, what are the odds that I end up kissing Austin at the exact time and place I'm supposed to be kissing Jesse? It seems fast, way too fast, but it feels right. I can't explain it …" Vulnerability wrapped my admission.

I resubmerged my washcloth and situated it flat on my chest, allowing the warm water to reheat my core.

"All I'm saying is that you can't puss out now. I know you, and you're probably all up in your pretty blonde head, thinking of every reason not to explore things with the big, mysterious sailor man. Am I right?" She paused.

She was absolutely right. My lack of response answered her question.

"But let me ask you something. Did Jesse think about you before he stuck his stupid cock in someone else? *No*. So, why the hell should you? Let him sit wherever he's sitting, and we can only hope he caught something itchy and scratchy as a parting gift," she said, her voice echoing through the bathroom.

"First of all, ouch and eww." I chuckled.

Her delivery made it hurt less than it should have.

"Sorry," she added quickly, taking responsibility for the harshness shadowing her unrivaled words of wisdom.

"Secondly," I continued, "I hear you, but I've never slept with anyone besides Jesse, and I'm freaking out. I've only ever *complained* about my sex life in the past—the lack of intensity and realness—but Austin is … intimidating and passionate and also incredibly manly. Not to mention, he's massive; he could probably break me in half with one single thrust. The kiss almost killed me—let me tell you," I divulged.

Zaps shot through my limbs at the plethora of naughty images bombarding my brain.

Austin shirtless.

Austin shirtless, chopping wood.

Austin with his dick out.

Austin on top of me with his dick out.

"Goddamn it, do you hear yourself? That sounds amazing!" she squealed, coughing on whatever beverage she was sipping on back home.

"I miss you, Ruths. I feel so weird. Like I just entered a completely new world. I need my sexpert to talk me through this!"

Pulling the phone from my ear, I pressed the speakerphone button, set the busted screen face down on a nearby wooden stool, and gripped the tub's sides with both hands.

Was I lost? Or was I stopping myself from fully exploring my new surroundings? The surroundings I wouldn't be in if it wasn't for Jesse.

Or Austin, for that matter.

"Promise me something, Ells ..." Ruthie quieted.

Was she about to be serious? Doubtful.

"You know I don't promise anything without knowing what I'm agreeing to first. That's Elle 101. You know me better than that."

"That right there—that's your problem." She sucked her teeth. "Too much thinking, not enough doing. Going in for the kiss was a start. I'm proud of you for that. And letting him make the next move is okay too. But, Christ, Elle, the man sounds like an orgasm in a uniform. He's been caring for you, cooking for you, kissing you like there's no tomorrow. If the opportunity arises, I hope you enjoy yourself and seize the chance. You deserve all the good things, but you gotta take off the pussy shield and let those things in." Her hilariously unimpressive speech was anything *but* the moment the words *pussy shield* came out of her mouth.

She had a gift though. Because no matter how unserious the off-duty teacher sounded, she was right. It was time to open myself up to new things and people because navigating my life without Jesse would take practice. And I couldn't think of someone more perfect to practice exploring than Chief Austin Carterson.

"I'll think about it," I blurted.

Was there a real chance that the girl who had come here for Jesse could share her heart with someone else so soon? It sounded like the opposite of everything I stood for.

So, why did the idea tempt me so much?

I stared across the bathroom, collecting my thoughts, before a wooden figurine I hadn't noticed caught my attention. Above the doorway hung a palm-sized anchor. It looked hand-carved. Anchors always reminded me of home. Was it a sign? That I belonged in the tub, the house, and the moment?

"So, what's the final word on your flight for tomorrow?" Ruthie asked, steering our conversation in another direction.

"It's officially canceled. The airline told me they were hopeful it would only be delayed a day or two, but who knows?"

"Snowed in with a sexy sailor. Now that sounds like a bestseller!" she gushed.

"Knock it off!"

Our laughter echoed through the small, humid space. For a moment, she was splashing around in the tub with me.

"As much as I miss you, I don't want to keep you. I do expect a *full* update tomorrow. Keep me posted on your new flight so I can arrange to pick you up. Oh, and stay warm!" Ruthie hung up before I could protest.

She was my brand of crazy—the type of crazy that was convincing enough to make me take notice of Austin and what I felt around him.

Excited.

Nervous.

Attracted.

Panicked.

But mostly, I felt like someone with a whole new future ahead of me.

Was there a chance that Austin could be a part of it? The man's endless actions proved he respected me. I had to accept that he made me feel good. His touch and heavy hand steadying my thigh earlier had felt good. His mouth on mine had felt more than good. Being around him just felt plain ... good.

Perhaps it was about time I let myself feel good again too.

Thirty

Austin

ELLE NEVER SAID GOOD NIGHT. Routine woke me up early to a cold couch and an empty living room, void of the warmth she radiated. The frosted windowpane told me the weather had declined overnight, as promised.

Was yesterday too much for her? I thought. *Did I scare her?*

I outstretched my arms and sat up from the couch, recalling how I'd overheard Elle laughing on the phone with Ruthie last night through the walls. I did everything in my power not to listen. Sadly, my restraint failed.

Respecting her privacy was one thing, but my girl wasn't exceptionally quiet during her phone call. She likely had never stayed in a house without hurricane-proofed walls to buffer her late-night conversations.

Her innocent unawareness and Ruthie's lack of volume control had gifted me an incredibly important piece of information—Elle had never slept with anyone besides Jesse.

I didn't know whether to thank my lucky stars or feel sorry for her that her primary source of pleasure was most definitely herself. To my displeasure, I'd watched Jesse have sex with Rita Camellino. It had been clear that his needs took precedence over his partner's.

Elle deserved a man who found more pleasure in giving than taking.

If I could give her a glimpse into a future with me, she'd see that Jesse and I couldn't be more different in that way. In many ways. A draw from his tarot deck would reveal The Fool while mine would show her what it felt like to pull The Lover card for once.

I rose, foggy sunlight from the window illuminating my path into the kitchen. I stepped softly to avoid waking Elle. God, how I dreamed that my arms were tangled around her while she woke, sleepy-headed and clinging to my body for warmth.

The universe didn't allow me to cook breakfast for her again because, to my pleasant surprise, Elle was already seated at the table in my kitchen when I entered. She waited for me with a pot of coffee, two omelets, and steaming nut-covered bread. The smell was heavenly, but the sight of Elle twirling her hair with one elbow leaning on the edge of the oak tabletop was what drew me in.

She noticed me, stood, and walked my way, stealing the breath I should have been taking from her. She'd added light makeup to her already-flawless face, enhancing the feminine features that organically hypnotized me. Something was different about her; she looked refreshed. *Radiant*. One thing remained the same: she still blew me the fuck away.

"Good morning, Chief," she chirped, pulling out the chair across from hers before sitting again.

I loved it when she called me that.

"Thought I'd snoop through your pantry and throw together breakfast to make up for not coming to say good night yesterday. I hope you eat omelets and banana walnut bread."

"If you made it for me, I'm eating it," I vowed.

Her smile grew at my response, which had one job—to hide my growing urge to shatter every plate before me and eat her for breakfast instead.

"By that, I mean, it looks and smells delicious, and I know it will be if it's made by you. Is it weird that I can't picture you being bad at anything?"

Her chest fell to its usual resting place while mine expanded to accommodate my excitement.

An entire day of being snowed in with Elle, possibly longer.

It was all I'd wished for since the day we'd met.

"I can think of a few things ..." She smirked and forced a bite of omelet into her mouth. A string of melted cheese stretched like a tight rope from her glossed lips.

My pants tightened.

"Like?" I asked.

"Like saying good night, apparently."

Her nose scrunched. I found it adorable. Was she admitting to her crime in the cutest way possible? Yes, she was.

"Okay, you might be kind of bad at that." I cushioned her admission with a matter-of-fact brow raise. "Don't worry; all is forgiven. I was tired too. Long day—I get it."

One bite of steaming banana bread was all it took to confirm her cooking skills. "Have you considered a culinary career? Because this is next level." A low, "Mmm," left my chest as I swallowed.

"Yesterday was … incredible," she released. Her smile told me the change of subject was deliberate.

I agreed, *obviously*. Our date was incredible. But our kiss? It was mind-blowing. A kind of perfection I'd never known.

"Today can be incredible too," I chirped. "I know we're stuck here and all, but …"

"Can I be honest?" She placed her fork down on the napkin next to her plate before continuing. She meant business.

I nodded, craving her honesty just as badly as I craved every other part of her.

"I can't think of anyone else I'd rather be snowed in with. I just want you to know that," she revealed before exhaling a heavy breath. "Feels a little weird to say, but it's the truth."

She chased it with a sip of her coffee; I noticed she took it with light cream, so I could re-create it for her the next day. No way was she doing this again; that was my job.

"I first came to Haroldeen Lane with you because my unfortunate circumstances had brought me here and I felt like I had nowhere else to go. But now …" A giggle left her lips while her golden gaze held mine. "I *want* to be here, and I'm glad I'm here with you."

Her hand flipped onto its back on the table, willing me to grab it. I obeyed. My palm kissed hers, triggering my heart rate to crescendo. Our hands looked good together, our fingers laced. It was a simple gesture. One I could tell she enjoyed when she gently dragged her thumb across my skin.

"Well, if *I'm* being honest, I like to think there's a reason we ended up here." I cleared my throat, feeling like my grandfather, spitting wisdom. "Maybe being snowed in together can help us figure that out."

I'd never been with a woman I was afraid to lose. It didn't matter how we had come to be. All that mattered was that, somehow, we were together. No more wishing. No more drifting aimlessly through my life, further from the shoreline.

It was time to make Elle mine.

And prove to her that I was worthy of being hers.

Before she found out the truth.

Thirty-One

Elle

MY FIRST SNOW DAY, AND I'd hardly noticed the damn snow. Sure, it was delightfully pillowed around Austin's house, staring me down through every window. Like wool, it blanketed his yard, driveway, and every plant in view. But not even eyes virgin to the frosted landscape could pull my attention from Austin Carterson.

The way he moved, moved me.

Our day was filled with close encounters as we shared his space. Our tangled fingers and short-lived shoulder brushes left me wanting more. He sat beside me and gripped my leg while we watched too many reruns of *The Nanny* to count, his callous hands scratching against the fabric of my leggings. We didn't kiss again, but our hours together were anything but wasted. We swapped stories about our childhoods and hopes for the futures we envisioned. Getting to know him felt intimate, almost more intimate than the two years' worth of my time wasted on Jesse.

I would never have thought Austin had had it tough as a child. In his words, his grandparents' unconditional love had shifted his trajectory. The way he spoke about them melted me. They sounded incredible. Genuine and selfless. I also finally found the balls to ask how old he was.

"Thirty-three years young," he admitted.

I'd expected it. Perhaps his six years on Jesse were why he was galaxies more mature. Eight years of life separated my and Austin's timelines, not nearly enough to deter me.

Hours flew by, yet my mind remained fixated on the man standing next to me at the sink.

Iridescent reflections of silver found us through the kitchen window as the moon replaced the sun, adding depth to Austin's immaculate profile. His angular jaw, Grecian nose, and thick lips, surrounded by just the right amount of weekend stubble, needed no help. The light set his rugged features ablaze.

Is Austin the most attractive man I've ever seen? I thought, unable to recall when exactly my pull to him knotted this tightly.

I couldn't avoid kissing him again much longer.

Conditions outside were worsening, but I didn't care. I craved whatever our night would bring. And here it was, greeting us as we stood in his kitchen with stomachs full of lasagna and a sense of connection I never expected.

His grandmother's recipe, which Austin had so graciously shared with me while we prepared dinner together, was one worth taking note of. The right level of al dente mixed with the ideal amount of ricotta—a mountain's worth.

"Snow days are more exciting than I thought," I admitted, placing our clean forks back into the silverware drawer. "There's something very serene about them."

I suspected any day spent with him would be enjoyable though.

"It's the snow *nights* that really zap the life out of you. Cabin fever is real when you're alone. Thankfully, I have you to keep me company," he bantered, smiling while drying the last dish. After placing it on the drying rack, he set his dish towel down.

"Can't be worse than the hurricane blues."

Hurricanes were one of the only things I hated about Florida. Evacuations, wind damage, flooding—it all sucked. Being snowed in with him sucked far less.

Austin's hips moved within inches of mine as he turned to face me. I placed a hand on his chest, shifting my weight from one foot to the other while holding on to the countertop behind me for balance.

Touching him made my knees act stupid.

"Can I make a request?"

"Let's hear it," he invited.

"Can we finally light the fireplace? It sounds … nice. I've never even been in a house that has one. I need the full experience!"

Fireplaces weren't a thing in Florida.

Plus, it sounded hot. And not just because of the heat of the flames.

Austin's body hardened, except for his eyes. They darkened faster than a fresh bruise. I could tell the fireplace made him uncomfortable, although I wasn't sure why because it didn't make sense with his love of wood splitting. Like a serpent, his tongue slid across his top teeth.

"Yeah, all right." Something somber tugged at the corners of his mouth.

"Is there something wrong with the fireplace? We don't have to. I just … I don't normally get the chance to …"

Austin's response cut me off. "It's fine. I love lighting it," he sighed, clearly not loving it.

His right hand smoothed over the bedhead he'd sported all day, and his nostrils flared with unknown intention. I'd never fought so hard not to look at someone. Something I couldn't pinpoint worried him.

"Is it cool if I shower first?" he continued. "I'll be quick."

It was his house, his fireplace, his life. He could do whatever he wanted without asking me. But how gentlemanly that he had.

He cared. He wanted me to know he'd be back.

"Yeah, of course it is. I'll do the same. I promise to come back this time." My joke gathered no response, and I quickly turned to avoid whatever wall Austin's hesitation was building between us. I needed more of him before the snow on Haroldeen Lane thawed and reality found us again. "Thirty minutes, same time, same place?" I looked back reassuringly. Heat flooded my cheeks as images of what our night might hold flashed before me.

"I'll be ready for you." His sharp inhale surprised me. "I mean, *it'll* be ready for you. The fireplace. *Fuck* … sorry." He scrambled, tripping over the words I'd lick from his mouth if he let me.

I loved his slipup and the confidence boost it provided.

"Don't be sorry. I'll be ready for you too." I chuckled, smirking softly at his verbal foreplay.

I might have hidden from us the night before, but I was done hiding.

I was done running from things that made me feel alive.

Thirty-Two

Austin

My scarred knee bounced with spastic anticipation. A chainsaw accident when I had been seventeen left it marred with visible scar tissue. Would Elle discover those personal, hidden parts of me tonight? I needed to know before I drove myself insane. The only thing I knew for sure was what I needed—and it was her.

As much as I'd avoided it, I lit the damn fireplace. The flames before me raged as thick as the blood pooling in my dick while I waited for my girl to return. The time had arrived for me to pull out all the stops for her, just in case.

In several of her letters, Elle had mentioned her favorite singer, Jewel. I'd snagged her record from a vinyl shop in downtown Chicago weeks ago. "Who Will Save Your Soul" crackled from the record player nestled in the corner of my living room. The buttery-smooth voice had made me feel closer to Elle when I wrote back. Like I knew something about her that only her closest confidants did.

I shook my head, thankful that I no longer needed to do weird shit to feel closer to her because she was here, in my damn house, getting ready for me.

Placing another log in the fire, I overthought every detail of our kiss, our current situation, the truth I hid, and how in the world I would stop myself from diving into her when she came back into the room. My resolve thinned by the second, challenging the mental strength I'd worked hard to build.

Not even a dusting of that resolve remained when Elle emerged from the hallway half an hour later in pajamas purchased from the Devil himself.

No fancy lingerie shop could design something so intriguing, as if there were secrets sewn into the material. Elle held the secrets to my goddamn soul.

The fabric wrapping Elle's body was the opposite of what I'd consider winter wear. Instead, the silky sleep shorts and matching spaghetti-strap top, lined with lace and sex appeal, didn't stand a chance at warming even the sun.

She rounded the couch, stepping closer to the warmth.

"Sorry I took so long. I hope I didn't keep you waiting …" She froze before the fire. "Wait … is that Jewel I hear?"

Excitement lit up her face more than the nearby flames. Too bad I couldn't focus long enough to form an answer. Unassuming shades of cream and baby pink complemented her skin and the absurdity that was her body.

Holy hell …

I wrapped my hand around the base of my neck, absorbing the intensity of the utter perfection overpowering my pulse.

There was no bra underneath the top that rose and fell with every breath she took. The outline of her small nipples penetrated the thinly stretched fabric. Dizziness delayed my response.

"Austin?"

"Yeah, I, um … I love Jewel. She's my girl," I lied without thinking.

The soul singer wasn't my girl; Elle was. But looking at her while saying, "She's my girl," felt so damn good.

"I can't believe this. I freaking love her! 'Intuition' single-handedly got me through my teeny-bopper phase. She sounds especially smooth, coming from a record player. I've never heard her voice that way. Nice touch, Chief Carterson." Her enthusiasm assured me she wasn't fighting the moment. She was enjoying it. Dare I say, enjoying *me*?

"I bet she's your type. If I were into girls, she'd *totally* be mine. She's musically gifted and a badass philanthropist, all in one gorgeous package. Must be nice to have it all …" The sparkle in her eyes told me she idolized the artist who had seemingly gotten her through many a middle-school heartbreak.

"She's great, but, no, she's not my type. She certainly doesn't have it all," I articulated confidently, aiming to dull the envy in her words. No way was I letting her think any other woman in the world had shit on her.

"Do you have a type?" she asked quizzically.

Is she testing the waters?

"Not exactly. I rely more on someone's energy. Their vibes."

"Well, what is your vibe then?" She stepped closer.

Electricity struck my stomach.

"You," I whispered. "You're my vibe, Elle."

Thirty-Three

Elle

Bingo. I had him. His vibe was Elle Madelyn, and I was starting to realize mine was …

Austin. *Fucking.* Carterson.

Residual heat from the burning wood and my growing desire permeated the tension around us. Pensacola sometimes got chilly, but it was never fireplace-worthy or blanketed with snow. I couldn't tell what was warming me most though. Was it my internal desires or the fever that Austin infected me with?

His hair, still damp from the shower, glistened in the ambient orange glow. It begged me to tangle my fingers through it, to lace my arms around his neck and straddle his wide waist while he was wearing only pajama pants.

To give in.

"Did you know I've never seen snow? Like ever?" I admitted, breaking free from the compulsive thoughts restraining me. "Never played in it, never even felt a snowflake touch my skin."

"What?! How is that possible?" Austin straightened, looking away for the first time since I'd stepped into his view.

"I don't know. I guess my family opted for tropical beach vacations and cruises instead of mountain views and ski resorts when I was a kid."

"Unacceptable. We're remedying that right now. How did you resist going outside all day today? I never would have kept you inside if I knew that."

He stood, forbidding me the chance to refuse his order. His stance thickened the air between us. Was that why it was so hard to catch my breath?

"Let's turn this into more than just the trip where you had your heart broken, shall we?" His eyebrow rose, meeting the occasion.

"We shall." I nodded excitedly.

"Grab my peacoat and some shoes. They're in the entryway by the front door. You'll need them." The words oozed demand.

Why did authority turn me on so much? Was it the type-A rule follower in me, begging for a break? Or was it the fact that Jesse was the complete opposite?

Letting someone else be in control for once felt incredibly liberating.

Austin led me into the entryway. I threw the arms of his coat around my body, slipped on his boots—which, as promised, waited next to the door—and followed him onto the dimly lit porch. Blistering wind blasted me in the face as we left the familiarity of his house.

Surprisingly, following him into the darkness brought me a sense of safety. Austin didn't flinch at the wintry rush flooding the porch. He slowed before we reached the top step, waiting for me to stand beside him instead of behind.

Of course he did.

Of course he'd brought me outside to experience my first snow. It didn't matter that he'd seen it a thousand times before.

"It's like a wonderland out here. It's gorgeous," I chattered through stunned windpipes, processing frost-thickened oxygen for the first time in my life. "I'm happy I get to experience it with you."

"How lucky am I to have the honor of showing it to you?" He grabbed my hand and tugged me closer until I was positioned in front of him with my back against his chest. Two heavy arms draped over my shoulders, drawing me in deeper.

"The woman who has never seen snow and the man who lives in one of the snowiest places in the country. An unlikely duo, huh?" I rattled aimlessly.

His stance behind me was intimate by design. Formulated to get my blood pumping. He was close enough for me to feel his words, his breath, on the exposed stretch of skin behind my ear. My fingers curled in on themselves, fiddling with some of my building stimulation. I fought to remain upright. Slowly, I drifted my head closer to my left shoulder, hoping to kill any remaining space between us.

Stone-carved hands ran up the arms of the coat that concealed my goose bumps. No part of him made direct contact with my skin, yet his presence behind me gave off such potent alpha energy that it was enough to send traces of arousal through my veins.

Austin had let me initiate our kiss on the Ferris wheel, but I'd suspected it was solely to ensure I was emotionally ready for it. Would he let me initiate anything first ever again?

I hoped not.

"I'd like to grab some more firewood from the shed. You want to come with?" he asked. "It's just over there." His index finger directed my attention to the structure he'd mentioned yesterday. It was the one I could see from my bedroom window. "I promise you'll be warm soon enough."

He stepped out from behind me and recaptured my hand, not taking no for an answer. I nodded. It was cold, but not cold enough to stop me from exploring whatever he wanted to show me. A man of his stature didn't need help carrying logs inside. There was an impressive pile next to the mantel anyway. Perhaps he wanted to show me a side of him I hadn't yet seen.

His hand stayed in mine as we walked through inches of snow to get to the side of his house, where the free-standing structure stood.

When we entered, I noticed neatly stacked firewood lined the inside of the shed's perimeter, piling halfway up the walls like nature's wallpaper. A chunky stump—the width of a large recliner—sat, sliced and rooted through the ground, in the center of the shed. A well-loved axe, positioned upright, was stabbed vertically into the ground next to the pedestal. Did Austin use the old half trunk as a splitting slab?

He'd created a working surface from an old tree and used it to butcher new trees, surrounded by a shed built by his efforts. Was there anything more primal than that? He didn't just *look* like he split firewood, but he *actually* split fucking firewood.

No wonder he wanted to show me his workshop.

My thirst grew as I saw what he could do with his hands, as if I hadn't already been impressed by everything else about him.

"I know; it's … a lot," he sighed, looking around at his borderline obsession encircling us. "But splitting wood is a great workout and helps me clear my head when I'm stressed. I like being self-sufficient and having the things I need here at home."

"Is that why I'm here?" I shattered, speaking without thinking. My heart rate skyrocketed. Anticipation knotted in my core.

His mouth fell open, lengthening the sharp jaw that could cut my life short.

"Never thought of it like that, but yes. Maybe that is why you're here, Elle. Maybe that's how you ended up here." He stepped toward me, closing the gap between our bodies before continuing, "On *my* base, at *my* house, and now in my woodshed, wearing my coat. Is there somewhere else you'd rather be?" Darkened emeralds scanned me up and down like they were trying not to eat me.

Had the big bad wolf walked me right into his territory?

"No, there's nowhere else I'd rather be than here with you …" I swallowed, nearly gagging on my throat's dryness.

His stance invited me to fall apart, surrounded by his strength.

"Can I show you that there's nowhere else I'd rather be than right here with you too?" He wiped a stiff strand of hair from my face.

"Show me." My lustful nod let Austin know just how deeply his statement penetrated me. A cloud of frozen breath left my mouth.

His job and rank demonstrated that he was accustomed to being in control. His sudden stampede toward the shed door proved it. Austin threw it shut and latched the handle, startling me. Hands of steel barreled back toward me. They stole his coat from my body and threw it onto the hay-topped floor. I shivered when a fresh wave of below-freezing temps infiltrated every newly exposed pore.

My nipples tightened, and a warm rush of heat replaced the emptiness between my thighs. Still sporting Austin's boots, my feet remained cemented in place and time, leaving only my impulses to forecast his next move—an unanticipated one that swept me off my feet. He scooped me out of his boots and into his solid arms. One swift motion was all it took.

He had a plan.

Even if I didn't know exactly what it was, the disheveled groan that left his throat as he effortlessly balanced my body weight on his forearms told me it was improper, indecent, and insatiable.

All the things I craved finally stared back at me.

Thirty-Four

Austin

BEFORE SETTING ELLE DOWN ONTO my splitting slab, I peeled my coat away from her body with the animalistic force I could no longer contain. Self-control wasn't at the forefront of my mind anymore.

Ravishing her was.

Waiting any longer to see her fully exposed wasn't an option. I'd waited long enough, held back long enough, and dreamed of her long enough. It was time to show her how a real man showed up for his woman.

I wanted to keep her in the woodshed just long enough to show her how arousing the frostbitten air could feel when mixed with the heat of the moment, how the only warmth she'd ever need again could forever come from me. Usually, the logs I collected and stashed were placed on the smooth surface in the center of the shed before I split them open, using pure, unfiltered strength.

I was ready to do the same to her.

Elle's full teardrop breasts escaped from the bottom of her top when I tugged it over her head, which was more than enough to get my blood pumping. The hot liquid pooled in my boxers with arousal so intense that it felt like the first time, but better. Seeing her topless, resting back on bent elbows, staring up at me on the flat surface, clouded my vision.

Jesus Christ ...

Perky nipples, possessed by the frigid draft creeping in under the door, gave her tits a look I could only describe as fucking luxurious. If she ever graced a topless beach with her presence, no doubt she would become the cover model for the travel brochure. Men would do terrible things to witness a chest like hers.

Me included.

"I'm f-f-freezing," she chattered, with a look that told me she wasn't used to the feeling but didn't hate it.

I nodded, acknowledging it before my knees buckled. I sank to the ground before her, leveling my face with her slightly spread thighs. My hands—no longer controlled by reason—gripped opposing sides of her silky shorts. Pulling forcefully, I shredded them from her hips before removing my shirt to show off my tattoos and the veins filled with longing that pulsed just for her.

Maybe she didn't expect it from the honorable Chief Carterson, but the sneaky smile creeping across her face showed me she liked how feral she made me. How easily her presence possessed me.

Like blowing out a candle, I pursed my lips and let out a long-winded breath the moment I realized the panties I'd expected to find were never there. Their absence left her shaven pussy vulnerable—her purest form fully exposed to me.

I'd never seen a more mouthwatering sight.

Adrenaline-packed saliva slicked my tongue, fighting to stay inside my mouth. I swallowed. As hard as my dick begged me not to peel my eyes away from the most intimate part of Elle's body, I couldn't overlook her sultriness, her longing, silently begging for me.

She'd flashed me with her gorgeous teeth moments before. The stare she'd paired them with was anything but innocent. Her expression was desperate and bold, letting me know she needed me just as badly as I needed her. It was a realization that left me utterly untamed.

Broken by her.

Am I dreaming?

It was hard to tell when I straightened and leaned forward before my tongue crashed into hers. It wanted to dive deep into her soft pink lips, but my brain advised them to kiss her on the mouth first, like the gentleman I could never be in her presence again.

Her heated breaths entered my mouth. Every sweet puff cemented my addiction to her. I got lost in her taste, unable to stop unleashing greedy nips on her tongue before they evolved into hungry bites, their placement dropping from her tongue to her bottom lip. Eventually, they fell from her chin to her neck in the primal passion that overtook me like a whitecapped wave.

Nip.
Lick.
Suck.

The pattern continued.

"Oh my God," she hummed, throwing her head back.

The low, addictive sound barely registered over the anticipation coiling through me.

I stood and inched forward, assuming a dominant stance above her. She remained on her back, waiting for me to pounce. The view from above amplified our vast size difference. I loved that I could devour her in one bite if I pleased.

Her lengthy gasp let me know she loved it too.

Nothing but pajama pants hung from the deep V of my hips. Elle was every bit the proper little princess, searching every bulging muscle of my body for rescue.

But I wasn't the prince, swooping in to save her. *No.*

I was the dragon, coming to unleash fire on everything that had come before me—to destroy Jesse's memory in her mind and replace it with one worthy of taking up space in her beautiful head.

Elle no longer wore her silken pajamas, yet a similar texture remained between her legs. The smoothness of her skin tempted my insatiable fingers, among other things, begging for a touch as they roamed her thighs and hips.

A sneaking suspicion told me my girl liked to be handled.

"Austin … I'm cold. I need your body to warm me back up … come closer." Elle shivered, every inch of her vibrating.

Her request magnetized my mouth to the heart-shaped freckle just under her collarbone. An intimate detail about her that instantly hardened my already-stiff cock.

The sound of my name leaving her suck-swollen lips while I explored her body let me know my actions were right in line with her desires.

What we'd both been longing for.

"Did you know the human tongue holds strong around ninety-nine degrees?" I asked. Briefly, confusion crossed her face. "I bet it would feel amazing against your chest—don't you think?" I added, grinning suggestively down at her. Her eyes met mine.

Our staring contest never broke, even while I allowed my starved tongue to taste her chest and make its way down her stomach. My saliva painted a slick line on her body in its wake.

Her rib cage bobbed with broken exhales, forcing me to stiffen my tongue on its downward path of destruction. That was, until it reached its final destination between the thighs she'd spread just for me—fully exposing her irresistible, glazed cunt.

"Christ, Elle ..." I growled, undeserving of such utter perfection.

I paused just long enough to take a meditative inhale of her sweet scent, savoring the moment. Between my girl's slick inner thighs, I found the connection, the nourishment, I'd forever longed for, like nectar to a hummingbird. Sweat, excitement, frostbite—I didn't give a shit what had made her glisten; my tongue craved a taste. It craved a whole damn meal made of her.

And it was dinnertime.

"I like to cool my meals off before devouring them," I rumbled, surprising her with my sudden, upright movement.

"Wait. Don't go!" She panicked, angled up, and pulled her knees inward—the opposite direction I preferred.

She didn't understand why I'd stood. But she soon would.

That's right, my little snow angel, I thought. *Beg for me.*

"I'll be right back," I assured her, placing my hand against her chest and inviting her to relax back on her bent elbows again. She did, accepting my invitation. Inching toward the door, I looked over my shoulder at her once more and admired her like the goddamn masterpiece she was. "Two seconds. Don't you fucking move," I warned.

An unnervingly cold breeze electrocuted my boner when I stepped out of the woodshed and frantically grabbed a handful of snow. It wasn't much, but the growing collection of flurries that had accumulated atop the nearby hydrangea blooms provided enough to serve their purpose. Quickly, I returned to the shed, closing and latching the door behind me.

Before the icy handful could melt, I resumed my position, knelt before her, and leveled my eyes between Elle's legs, setting my palmful of snow onto her now-swollen, pulsing clit. The heat enveloping her pussy quickly liquefied the flakes and stole my movement. I watched them melt and glide down her hungry, throbbing slit.

"Fuuuck," I groaned gutturally. Firmly.

I'm done fucking around laced my profanity, and the blowing sensation was just bothersome enough to leave her panting for relief when it reached her velvety skin.

Her stomach quivered.

My shoulders flexed. I knew the sight before me would leave me hungover for months to come. I sweltered in the heat of the moment, but evidence that the temperature was affecting Elle was all over her body. She was naked after all. And it was below freezing. Her body shook uncontrollably, chills stretching from her head to her pedicured toes. Time to heat her back up.

"Austin, please …"

Two words.

Two words—my new aphrodisiacs—were all it took to melt my tongue into her clit and give her the hot relief she was desperate for. I drenched the pillowy pink skin between my girl's legs, using every ounce of raw energy I had to unleash my fantasies into her. The tip of my tongue became a wild flame, flicking her from side to side.

I devoured every drop she gave me.

The taste was otherworldly, an intoxicating mix of femininity and freshness that would forever live in my mind as a delicacy.

Like the first bite into a summer-ripe peach, her flavor was as refreshing as it was alluring. I dived deeper into her for a better taste. Sucking sounds filled the shed as I made out with the captivating pussy that spoke to me more than a mouth ever could. I swallowed every pulse, savoring it as it coated my throat.

Every flex.

Every drop of her.

"Holy f-fuck. Yes …" she moaned, breathless in her conviction.

"You taste so damn good." I slurped. "I could eat … you … forever." Each individual word of my confession came in waves between the soft, slow, drooly kisses I placed onto her center.

Tasting her made my rock-solid boner as hard as a diamond. I felt pre-cum collect at the tip of my dick. Stroking it wasn't necessary though because her scent alone kept me lost in a fog I never wanted to escape.

Her scent and taste stroked it for me.

Instead of touching myself, I slid one finger inside of her, gently circling in my pursuit of experiencing an even deeper part of Elle.

Immediately unable to resist, I stole my finger back and sucked it before adding a second into her tight cunt. Her walls were tender and scorching as I dipped in and out of her.

After a minute, my jealous tongue returned to replace them.

The endless sensations unleashed something wild in Elle. At least, it seemed that way when her left hand grabbed the handle of the tall axe stuck into the ground beside her. Like a handlebar, one hand gripped it for dear life to get through my feast while the other slithered through my hair, teasing my scalp. The pressure from her fingertips adjusted to match the tongue-lashing she was taking. I could eat her all night and never tire of her. On the other hand, I needed to suck her cum into my mouth like I needed air to breathe.

It was time to hear what Elle Madelyn sounded like when she lost total control.

Breaking the in-and-out pattern that crumbled her walls, I softened my tongue, flattening it over her clit as I nursed it back to health.

No, I wasn't a doctor.

But I knew how to get the job done.

"Come for me. I need more of you," I demanded, the growl in my voice leaving no room for rebuttal.

"I'm close, Chief ..." Her grip tightened on my hair.

The admission hardened me so much that it was beginning to hurt. *Throb.* With my saliva, I created swirls of chaos. I spit and licked up my mess, repeatedly lapping up every last drop of desire I'd released onto and into her slick skin.

It was delicious.

"Yes ... *ahhh.*" Her hips bucked uncontrollably when she cried out.

She fell to pieces on my lips, and I died inside, only being brought back to life by the creamy glaze filling my throat. Delighted, I swallowed, ensuring not a single drop escaped.

Our desperate cries echoed together through the shed.

Seconds later, I scooped her naked body into my arms, inhaling her residual moans into my lungs before kicking the woodshed door open in one sharp, lock-shattering motion.

It was finally time to carry Elle into my living room, lay her in front of the fireplace, and—if she wanted me to—take what I hoped would always be mine.

"We're just getting started," I whispered into her ear, presenting her through my front door like the queen she was.

The most unforgettable smile emerged through her postorgasmic bliss.

Thirty-Five

Elle

Hot relief flushed my body in shades of pink as Austin carried me into his living room. The heavy breaths I blew onto his chest were no longer frostbitten; exhales drenched in heat took their place. I'd never felt stronger, *more powerful*, or safer than in his arms. What Austin had shown me was something completely new. To be wanted so fiercely, so intensely, that my body screamed for more.

It didn't matter that the man made of stone had just milked every ounce of my orgasm into his mouth; the hunger circling his pupils and the intensity overtaking his expression told me we were about to enter uncharted territory.

Austin's thick arms unraveled, resting my body onto a plush throw blanket on the floor in front of the fire. The motion wasn't soft, but his smile still was. He held nothing back. I sure as hell didn't want him to start. A man at war with his desires but still gentle enough to show a woman he cared was a major turn-on.

The Adonis standing over me stepped back, admiring his prize while he shimmied off his pants, revealing briefs stretched so tight that they looked uncomfortable. Still swollen from his down-below magic show, his mouth bit down on itself. Carnal lust laced his half-lidded gaze.

"You're perfect—do you know that?"

The sweet words would have brought tears to my eyes if they weren't hyper-focused on my first clue that Austin had a huge cock—the sheer size of the bulge staring back at me. My second clue was the impressive pool of liquid arousal seeping through the tight gray fabric, trying hard not to evaporate from the heat of his muscular thighs.

I had no words to describe his body because none would have done it justice.

The moment the briefs disappeared down his quads garnered a moment of silence for my poor, poor pussy.

Have I only been fucked by a boy?

What I saw was something reserved by God for only the worthiest of women.

Finally freed, the thickest, most incredible dick I'd ever seen—including in porn—bobbed toward me. Every step Austin took forward brought me closer to my downfall. Heavy, swollen balls complemented their master and screamed for me to cup them.

To *kiss* them.

To *suck* them.

What would it feel like to feel their forceful slaps slam into me from behind?

I licked my lips.

My heart rate crescendoed to an unhealthy beat, shocks of electricity reeling through my stomach and chest. Between his immense thighs and the size of everything else crowding the space below his waist, I'd nearly have to do a split to accommodate him between my legs. We were about to have the best, most mismatched game of Twister in existence.

Could I volunteer to be the sore loser?

Austin's sexy-as-sin, vein-riddled hands stroked the masterpiece I was glued to.

"Wow …" I whispered, hypnotized.

Hands were one of the first things I noticed about a man, and although I didn't want to admit it, I'd had an initial inkling that his long, thick fingers were attached to hands full of magic. You could tell a lot about a man's dick through his hands.

His had told me everything I needed to know.

Lowering, Austin spoke into my mouth. "If I'm dreaming, don't wake me up." His tongue slithered between my lips and slowly dragged from left to right. "I can't decide which lips I like better. They both taste like fucking heaven."

With that, my heart rate had to be critical.

"Austin, please …" My stomach dropped as I cursed—or shall I say, blessed—his name, my tongue vibrating along with the rest of my body.

"Are you ready for me to show you what you deserve?" he asked into my neck before licking the length of my collarbone.

My spine arched, tingling at the sensation his saliva left behind.

"And what exactly is that?" I returned his call, hungry for the answer to his praise-filled question.

I always knew I had a praise kink, but Austin brought that fantasy to life in ways I never could have imagined.

Ways I'd only wished for.

"To be fucked like the angel that you are." He gently sucked a nipple into his hot mouth while his hands roamed my stomach and hips. He was learning me. "To be cherished for every inch of perfection that is your body and to ruin me so I can never look at another woman again because I've had you." His expression was carnal, and his tongue was sharp, only softened by the compliments showering my soul.

"How can I know if I'm ready? I've never had that …" I revealed, clinging to every word.

Austin set both forearms on the blanket, one on either side of my head. They caged me in a dungeon of muscles, nautical ink, and erotic fire. I tasted both of us when he kissed me, a delicious combination of soft and strong.

Austin and Elle.

Unexpectedly, arms—bred from years of strength training and dedication—flipped me onto my stomach, leaving my jaw on the floor and my body aching for what came next. More seconds passing without him inside of me was no longer acceptable.

"I need you. Like I've never needed anything else before in my entire life," I said into the blanket. "I didn't know I could need someone like this …" Blindly, my fingertips swept back, up, and over my collarbone and found the muscular dip between his shoulder and the side of his neck. I needed to touch him.

"Almost like you'd do absolutely anything to have me, right?" I couldn't see his face, but I knew he was grinning because I felt his lips harden behind my ear as he unleashed the intoxicating sentence.

"Anything," I answered.

I smiled because a more accurate question had never been asked.

Fire and my insatiable longing transported me to another world where only he and I existed. I felt his breath gather in the middle of my shoulders and cascade down my back as he made his way south. He peppered kisses and tiny licks down my spine like I was melting and he might never have the chance to taste me again.

He didn't just lick.

He *savored* my skin.

Inhaled my scent.

Memorized me to recall later.

He had me right where he wanted me—under the weight of his power. Our trust allowed me to relax in a place I'd never been comfortable in.

A place where someone else was in control.

Sensually, his hand moved around the side of my face, his fingers stopping on my lips as he worked to spread them apart. I opened my mouth, and Austin slid two inside, stealing the wetness from my tongue while I sucked them in answer.

In one swift motion, his fingers slipped out of my mouth and crawled into me from behind. They filled me with friction as they made their way around my pussy like they'd been inside dozens of times before. His contrasting strokes left me shaky, pushing me closer to my second orgasm of the hour. He hadn't even stuck his cock in yet, and it was already the best night of my life.

"Yessss," I moaned, humbled by his skill.

"That feels good, doesn't it? I'll give you anything you ask for. *Anything*, Elle." Gliding over me, into me, through me, he and his movements were as effortless as his words.

Flutters electrocuted my heart.

"Oh my God, please don't stop. *Ahhh.*" I panicked, knowing I would die if he changed his pacing or pressure.

Moments later, I shattered around him, my clit as swollen and satisfied as the rest of me.

My legs trembled as ions soared through my nerves and slayed any remaining ounces of lingering anxiety from the last few days. Satisfaction won.

But the race wasn't over yet.

Ever so slowly, Austin flipped me onto my back again and stroked the back of his hand against my cheek. The reality of his totality—his overwhelmingly captivating body and the surprising amount of tenderness and care that came with it—came into full view.

"Has anyone ever made you come three times in one night? I'm already addicted to it."

I had a feeling he already knew the answer. I tried to respond, but couldn't, way too lost in whatever universe Austin and I existed in.

He spread my legs apart with his and inched forward, the tip of his dick praying to my clit.

"Are you on birth control?" he asked.

A light layer of sweat coated his face. Every inch of him glistened.

"Yes. I have an IUD," I whispered.

"And you're sure you want this?" He paused. "This is your decision, and I'll honor your choice. You've been through a lot, and I ... I don't ..."

"I need this," I released truthfully.

There was nothing I wanted more than to feel him inside of me. To accept my fate because fate was the only thing that could have brought us together in such a monumental way.

Austin nodded, kissed my forehead, and then shifted his hips back. He took his time slowly filling me.

I opened for him with every inch he crept forward, feeling nothing but tightness. He worked into me with equal parts restraint and care. I spread my legs wider, giving him the permission his desperate, clenched jaw told me he needed.

Permission to ravage me.

Austin's thrusts grew deeper—faster, hungrier, and all-consuming for both of us.

There was no way I could take all of him at once without practice. Several inches still overflowed from me.

A bead of sweat slid down his forehead, free-falling before landing on my cheek. He attempted to wipe it away, but I shook my head. I wanted all of him—every last drop.

The glaze blurring Austin's eyes overtook me, stealing my breath and leaving my mouth dry as flames from the fireplace beside us, reflected on his sculpted chest. I tried to smile at him, but my mouth could only moan, inhale, or suck.

He mesmerized me.

Austin snaked his arm around my body in answer, supporting my hips as we rocked, and he dived deeper. His free hand roamed, desperately lost between my breasts, shoulders, and seconds later, my hair. Using his mouth as my lifeline, I inhaled greedy kisses from his mouth. The only place he allowed me to take a breath from was him.

I gasped for more.

"I'm full of you." I beamed. "Your cock, your air …"

"That's right. Let me consume you," he instructed, rocking his hips forward and back.

His lips forbade me to look away.

His touch told me I'd never be able to again.

I reached for his face, and his pumps intensified. He planted his forehead against mine.

"This is the best night of my life," he said, reinforcing every word with a deep, filling thrust. His chest heaved.

"I'll never forget tonight, and I'll never forget you," I echoed, filling the space between us with truth serum.

Forget Chief Austin Carterson?

We were far beyond forgetting each other.

The room around us disappeared, and all I saw and felt was him. His dick pulsed, releasing heat into my core and the last sensation I needed to lose myself once again.

We came together in an immeasurable moment that could never be defined by something as finite as time. For an unknown number of minutes, we stared at each other. Silent and in awe.

Even after we disconnected, I knew our night would leave us forever entwined.

When the fog cleared, Austin scooped me up from the blanket and carried us both into what I assumed was his bedroom. I leaned my head against his chest, his heartbeat still running wild as my ear found it. The level of exhaustion I'd reached was completely new. The kind that only came from a triple orgasm with a powerful, generous man—something foreign to me.

We settled into his bed, complete with crisp white sheets. His scent bombarded me when he rolled a fluffy down comforter over my body.

Nothing had been more perfect than our night.

Nothing looked more hopeful than the emergence of my new life, one rid of past crutches.

Sleep Sweet

Throwing an arm around my chest and a leg over my thigh, Austin rolled into me and whispered into my ear, "Sleep sweet, Elle."

Thirty-Six

Austin

MY BED WAS A CONFESSIONAL, the ceiling my priest, as I lay frozen, silently confessing my sins.

God, if you're there, please let my slip of the tongue get past her ... I thought.

I wanted nothing more than for Elle to remember our night for the perfection it was. We'd spent the last few hours in heaven, but my panic quickly descended me into hell as I thought about the lie that had brought us together. The one that could easily tear our night—and us—apart.

"What did you just say?" she asked. A ribbon of concern wrapped the question.

She didn't shift from my embrace. Instead, she burrowed her nose further into my pounding chest, as if she didn't want to hear my answer. What was I supposed to say to Elle that wouldn't hurt her? This wasn't the right time, but would it ever be?

There would never be a good time to face the possibility of losing her.

"I said, sleep well ... in these sheets," I lied. *Another lie.* Panic engulfed my euphoria.

"Oh ... okay." She further stilled, to the point that her breathing was no longer detectable, stuck in something I prayed wasn't realization. "I'm sorry. I must've misheard you. It sounded like something else." She swallowed. "Something a friend used to say to me a lot ..."

Her loose hair cascaded down her back—a view I'd envisioned for months.

One I wasn't fucking worthy of.

The liar, the lesser of the two of us. How could I keep the truth hidden inside while she bled all her remaining trust into me?

Would she ever trust me again once she knew?

"Tomorrow is a new day," I whispered, kissing her cheek. "Get some rest. Your body will thank you."

A moment of silence passed.

"Thank you for the best night I've ever had."

Fuck me.

Was she crying? Her body trembled weakly.

"Don't thank me." I squeezed her tighter against me, where she belonged. "Just tell me you'll do your best to keep your heart open for me," I added.

She shifted before her grip tightened around my waist. As if I were modeling clay, her hands had the power to mold me into whatever she needed.

We lay, facing each other, our limbs tangled and hearts thumping in unison. Our position was the most intimate of the night.

"What do you mean by that?" she asked.

I was tense, knowing that every second that passed brought our time together closer to its inevitable end. How could I ever prepare for that?

"You've been through a lot, and I know it's too soon for you to think about a future with someone else."

She winced at the honesty that salted my words.

"But you're an incredible woman, and I hope that when you're ready, you'll give me a chance to be more than a distraction. I'm not the type of guy who wants to pressure you. But I can't pretend it wouldn't hurt me if you forgot about us when the weekend faded and you found yourself back in Pensacola." I sighed. "This isn't the weekend I'm sure you were expecting and …"

She smiled, cutting me off with that gorgeous, sparkling beam that could lead a midnight crusade.

"The only things you've distracted me from are my stagnant taste in men and the relationship I thought was keeping me afloat, Austin." She shook her head. "You're right though. This weekend wasn't what I'd expected …" Her shoulders softened.

I held my breath, hoping to cushion the blow of what came next. I wanted her truth, but just as mine could hurt her, hers could hurt me.

"It was better." She kissed my chest. Her fingers traced my tattoos, tickling the ink with mutual understanding.

"Way better," I whispered.

The moment obliterated every preconceived notion I'd had about how the weekend would go. She'd surpassed every hope I'd had for our short few days together.

My chest reinflated. I could breathe, knowing I'd made the right choice in writing back to her and showing her the video of Jesse and Rita. How could we be anything but made for each other?

"You think we'll be able to get out a bit tomorrow?"

No. No, no, no. Don't ask to see him. Tell me I've given you all the clarity you need and that you never have to speak to his pathetic ass again …

"The plows usually come throughout the day after a big snowfall. We might be able to, but no promises."

"I'm sure they prioritize the base though, *right*? Can't imagine they wouldn't start there," she guessed.

Her guess was correct.

"Right." Disappointment clung to my face like a mask.

"Will you have to work tomorrow? It's a weekday."

"Instructors get a few days off after their division graduates. I can take the overtime, but I wasn't planning on it since you're here."

"Would it be a good time to talk to Jesse?" She stared past me and out my window. "I feel like I finally have the information I need to face him and close that chapter of my life for good."

"Yeah. That might work," I said flatly, pretending her words hadn't almost just killed me.

I had to get him out of her head somehow, even if it meant taking her to confront him myself.

She noticed.

"I want to leave him here. It has nothing to do with you, okay?"

I hadn't had a lick of reassurance on anything in my life since my grandparents had passed.

It felt good.

"I understand." I didn't. "If we can get there tomorrow, I'll take you to him. But you have to promise me something."

I quieted and ran the backs of my fingers down her spine. My hands refused to be empty of her.

"Anything."

Her confident response to my blind request told me she felt safe with me.

"You can't let him hurt you again." I shook my head, replaying her pain from memory as if it were my own. It felt like it was.

"I won't … I didn't let him hurt me the first time though. I hope you realize that."

She was right.

Fuck, why did I say it as if it were her fault?

"I know it wasn't. It *absolutely* wasn't. The first time is never a choice, but it could be if you let him in again."

"I'm done with liars, Austin. I want nothing more than to help myself heal and move on to bigger and better things. Things meant for me. Things that come into my life for a reason, not a selfish season."

Oh, I was screwed. I smoothed the hair resting on her temple and inhaled her scent, the apple aroma immediately calming my pulse.

If she was done with liars, what would she do when she found out she was sleeping with one?

"What's meant for us will always find us. My grandfather taught me that. The tides always bring you back to shore if you let them."

"Well, I believe him," she said matter-of-factly. "And I believe you were the exact person who was supposed to relay that to me this weekend." She yawned.

I kissed her lips, quietly giving her the permission she sought to fall asleep and hopefully dream of me. Minutes later, she lay still in my bed.

In my *arms*.

In my *life*.

In my *heart*.

In my *head*.

It had only taken two years of waiting for her, less than two months of writing to her, and two days of experiencing her to know I was in love with her.

"I love you, Elle," I whispered. "I hope you can forgive me someday."

Sweet sleep had pulled her too deep into her dreams for her to hear me.

Thirty-Seven

Elle

I WOKE UP ON TUESDAY, alone in Austin's bed, to a text alert that my flight had been rescheduled for the next morning. Only one more day in Illinois, which meant only one more day with Austin.

One more day to confront Jesse and move on with my new life.

Sure, things were moving quickly, but what was the alternative? Overthinking everything and letting things linger? Ruthie would be proud.

A note dropped gracefully onto the floor when I rose from his bed, greeting me like an old friend.

I went to see if the roads to the base were clear.

Ran you a bath. Enjoy it.

There's a cup of coffee in the bathroom for you. Light cream, just how you like.

Get dressed when you're ready. I'll be back to pick you up in an hour.

Last night was incredible.

You're incredible.

The man had a way with words, but the three I'd heard last night still haunted me. I could have sworn he'd said, "Sleep sweet, Elle."

But how could he have known those words? The ones Jesse used to sign his letters with.

The ones only we'd shared.

Was I hearing things that Jesse used to say because the time to confront him was approaching?

Maybe I'd close my argument with those exact words, using his against him. *Sleep sweet, Jesse. You're a fucking prick. Buh-bye!*

I laughed and clutched Austin's note to my chest before bringing it into the bathroom. There was no way his verbal sugar syrup was not coming home with me to replace Jesse's letters. Those things were going straight into the burn pile for Ruthie and me to enjoy s'mores over when I got home. I'd never felt more ready to move forward. Out with the old, in with the big, handsome, thoughtful, deserving new.

As promised, Austin pulled into his driveway an hour later and greeted me while I waited on his porch. His tan work uniform, peeking out from under an unzipped parka, was one I hadn't seen him in before, one the thirsty girls back home referred to as the "peanut butters." Which made total sense since my eyes were stuck to it like glue. I salivated when he stepped out from behind the Jeep and into view.

"Good morning, Chief Carterson. You look incredibly hot," I chirped from the top porch step, swinging back on my heels.

He approached and brought his lips to mine. They lined up perfectly while he remained on the lowest step. His gloves brushed my arms, stopping just before they reached my hands.

He gently gripped my wrists when he said, "And you look incredibly refreshed."

"You might have had a little something to do with that." I winked.

He'd had everything to do with it.

"Roads are clear to the base. It's a nice drive. My Florida girl is going to enjoy the view."

"I agree. It's *quite* the view." I scanned the *view* before me again, committing it to memory for later use. The snow lining his driveway and topping the hydrangea shrubs was nice too.

Austin loosened his grip, grinned, and locked his front door before we loaded into his Jeep. He didn't offer to let me drive this time. Something heavy kept him quieter than usual. No music played to keep the mood light; the low hum of the heater was the only sound surrounding us. He never reached for my hand as we drove.

"Is everything all right?" I asked. My chipper mood was melting like the salted ice on the highway.

"Yes, everything's fine." His short response didn't feel directed at me, but I had a hard time believing it.

He didn't look my way when he said it. Instead, his statement reflected the gravity of the situation we were driving into. Surprisingly, I wasn't overly nervous about unleashing my rage on Jesse. He deserved what was coming to him. The absence of Austin's usual softness worried me more.

"I'm sure you're feeling uncomfortable about this whole thing. I doubt you're excited about me seeing Jesse again, and I get that. I'm not overly thrilled either. But I want you to know how much it means that you're helping me get what I need to move forward." My confession loosened his shoulders and the death grip he had on the steering wheel. "With you," I added.

Austin slammed on his brakes a yard premature of the incoming red light, jolting us forward.

"What do you mean by that?" he asked.

"What I mean is that I know we live states apart, and things are moving fast, and that brake slam isn't the only thing giving me whiplash …" I reached for my neck, ensuring it was still attached. "But I've never felt the way I feel with you. I want to try, but I need to erase Jesse from my head and let him know that his actions carry consequences. Losing me is the first one."

"Don't fuck with me." Austin sucked his teeth. He pulled off the road and put the car in park, giving me his undivided attention.

"Why would I be fucking with you? You've turned what would have been the worst weekend of my life into the best I've ever had. You've taught me that life keeps moving. I won't let Jesse sink me. Today, I take back my power. You're helping me do that."

Seriousness stiffened his jaw, an unreadable expression meeting his widening eyes.

Without notice, his hands grabbed the sides of my face. He leaned over the center console and brought his mouth within inches of mine. Warm breath heated my lips as he stared wordlessly at me and digested my truth.

"Things never felt right with him. They feel nothing but right with you," I admitted. "I don't want to rush things. I just—"

He kissed my statement short.

"We don't have to rush." He spoke into my mouth. "I can't lose you though. When you go back to Pensacola, we can't be over. We're just getting started."

I hugged him like a friend but inhaled him like a lover. He helped me feel again.

"Look at me," he commanded with a softness as caring as it was fearless.

I obeyed.

"No matter what happens today, I'm here for you. I'll be here for you as long as you let me."

I nodded, believing him fully. "Let's get this over with, okay? My flight leaves tomorrow morning. Besides, there's only one more night left for you to teach me how to use that axe in the woodshed."

"*Yeaaaah*, I don't think so. Leave the splitting to me." He laughed, emotionally collected enough to shift into drive and merge back onto the road.

Minutes later, Chief Carterson flashed his military ID card, along with my driver's license, at one of the uniformed men arming the gate. The young man scanned them both and nodded before returning them to Austin. It wasn't the main gate my shuttle had entered through on graduation day though. This one brought us around the back of the base, presumably for service members only.

Massive trees lined the concrete roadway, guiding us through shadows and a mix of steel and brick buildings that all shared the same exterior features and a covering of snow. A few minutes later, I recognized one with a row of large overhead doors where Jesse's graduation and Austin's office were housed.

Austin parked in the same parking lot we'd left from last time and stopped in front of a metal sign that read *Instructor Parking Only*.

He tapped the hood of his car as he walked around it to open my door.

"Instructors don't typically bring civilians into these buildings," he warned. "We'll go right to my office. We can't kiss or hold hands. No PDA. I'm sorry, but we'll need to act like this is official business."

"Yes, Chief Carterson. My God, we've only just met," I chirped sarcastically. I brought my hand to my chest in a fake show of appall before adding, "That means no looking at my ass on the way in."

"We can't touch. Doesn't mean I won't be staring at you the entire time." Austin gave my butt one swift smack before straightening his collar, putting on his knit beanie, and shutting my door. "Follow me, ma'am," he added sternly, pairing it with an authoritative glare.

Without realizing exactly what I was following him into, I looked at the gray-clouded sky and whispered my mantra for reasons entirely different than before, altering one word for the occasion. "Keep me calm, keep *him* calm, keep us together."

Thirty-Eight

Austin

Elle was a vision in winter wear. Before me—in jeans, the sweater I'd bought her, and a fleece coat—she sauntered down the hallway, each step bringing us closer to the unknown.

It was a sight I'd pay to forget.

One that scared me because it could be the last time I ever saw it. I needed Jesse and Elle's reunion to be over before it even began. My heart thumped erratically, acknowledging my struggle.

"My office is the next door on the left," I announced as coolly as my unease allowed.

"I know. I've been there before. The Heartbreak Room," she sassed, topping her sarcasm with an eye roll.

My breath hitched when Elle stopped in front of the door and looked back at me.

We'd arrived.

Our conversation on the way over had eased my worries, but only enough to get me through the drive to base. I feared our end could be closer than she realized and, silently, begged whoever had brought us together to keep us intact. Maybe it was God, or perhaps my grandparents had had a hand in it. My sole hope was that it hadn't been the Devil, lurking in my life, like he had when I was young, waiting for an opportunity to tear me away from the woman I loved.

The answer would come soon enough.

"You'll have to wait in here while I grab Jesse from the holding division. If anyone knocks, don't answer." I looked left and right to ensure we were alone, unlocked my office door, and let Elle enter first.

"That won't be a problem." Elle nodded as she entered the aptly named Heartbreak Room, the tenderness of her voice mimicking the calm she'd brought into my life.

I shrugged off my parka and beanie and hung them behind my door. She followed suit, handing me her coat for safekeeping.

"Remember, this is against policy, so everything that happens today must stay confidential," I reiterated.

I'd do anything for her, but compromising my security clearance was a big risk. I never did shit like this.

I'd never felt the way she made me feel though.

"You can trust me. You know that, right?" She plopped into my desk chair and spun in a circle. It was carefree. *Innocent and pure.*

Guilt wrapped its broken wings around me.

I knew she was trustworthy. So, *how* could I have let my lie go so far? I was the one whose trust she should be questioning, not the other way around.

I cleared my throat. "I'll be back in a bit. I've got to come up with a good excuse to pull Jesse from the rest of the group and bring him back here with me." My hand found her shoulder. "Try to relax."

Before kissing her, I jiggled the handle to my office door, ensuring it was sealed shut, encapsulating our last moment before I left to get Jesse.

"It's funny; I thought I'd be freaking out before seeing him." Elle turned and ran her palm across the framed award sitting next to my computer monitor, the title *Most Influential Instructor of 2011* engraved across the glass protecting the manila parchment.

"Are you not?" I asked.

Her bobbing knees hinted otherwise.

"No … surprisingly. I'm just ready to hear his why."

She looked past me momentarily, tremors of the memories she and Jesse had created likely reemerging in her mind. They needed to fuck off and regenerate themselves with the new ones we'd made the last two days.

"Fair warning: standing by and remaining professional while you two talk is going to be extremely hard for me. I can't promise not to interject …"

"You won't have to say a thing," she assured me. "So far, you've only seen me weak. I think you'll be impressed when you finally see me stand strong." Her gaze cemented our fate.

Would she stand strong against me, too, when the time came? I swallowed, the thought threading around the knot already making a home in my throat.

Our night together replayed in my mind, the only scene that gave me enough confidence to leave her alone in my office. Regardless of what happened as our day unfolded, we would never be done.

There was so much more to learn about each other. To build together.

It was time to go and get the last thing standing between me and my girl. The same thing that had brought us together.

Jesse Jenkins.

"Where are you taking me, bro?" The crackle in Jesse's voice showcased what a little bitch he was as we navigated the hallways leading back to our futures.

Addressing his ex-instructor as bro was about as disrespectful as a recruit could get. We weren't brothers, not even friends. We were enemies as far as I was concerned.

An enemy was something I wasn't used to having.

I didn't respond, allowing his anxiety to build naturally. If I could avoid it, I'd give him no time to prepare to see Elle face-to-face.

Surprise, asshole!

"I'm aware you've never liked me, but I deserve to know where I'm being taken. You don't oversee holding, and I'm pretty sure this is against procedure," Jesse fired.

"You aren't aware of the procedures of my job, *shipmate*. Addressing me correctly isn't even something you're capable of. So, if I were you, I'd keep my mouth shut and keep walking. You'll know where we're going when we get there." Annoyance overtook me.

Just the sight of him was enough to curdle my usually hardened stomach.

It was hard to comprehend that Jesse had ever had the honor of owning Elle's attention. For two years, he'd touched her like I had, probably tasted her like I had. But had he ever made her feel safe enough to come three times in one night like I had?

Common sense told me he didn't have it in him.

Rage told me he'd better fucking not have.

"Can you at least tell me when I can contact my family? My girlfriend? Anybody? Were they even notified about my delayed graduation date?" He shook his head back and forth. "I figured they would realize something was wrong when they stopped receiving my letters. For God's sake, they probably have no idea what happened to me or if I'm okay. It doesn't matter what I've done. I deserve basic freedoms until my formal review. Prisoners get more liberties than I do!" Jesse's tone rose like the hives racing up his neck.

By my design, the unknown—which was clearly suffocating him—was part of his punishment. I'd notified his parents of his delayed graduation and safety. Sadly—but luckily for me—they hadn't seemed to care.

Still, my panic sprouted like seeds from the clearance aisle of the local garden center—never blooming, just rotting away in my mind. If Jesse's mouth was good for anything besides tongue-fucking Rita Camellino's cunt, it was giving Elle way more information than she needed.

"You know what? When we get where we're going, you'll be able to explain yourself, I promise," I hissed.

"What the hell is that supposed to mean?" he barked.

"It means ..." I paused. Was it the right time to reveal what he was about to walk into? Moments later, as we approached my office door, I realized it was as good of a time as ever. "It means that Elle Madelyn is sitting in my office, waiting for an explanation from you as to why you had sex with someone who wasn't her."

The accusation drained the blood from Jesse's face faster than a leech ever could. His sunken eyes found the floor. His jaw followed.

Yeah, pal, that's right. You're fucked.

I gave him only seconds to accept his self-inflicted fate before opening the door. Elle sat perfectly still where I'd left her, her ankles crossed. It took incredible self-control not to grab her hand or walk over and kiss her. To comfort her.

But she needed to do this alone.

A sturdy nod was the best I could offer to keep our relationship out of Jesse's sight. The less he knew, the better.

"Oh my God, Elle!" Jesse lunged forward, entering my office more enthusiastically than the occasion required.

I entered second and shut the door behind us.

Watching him drop to his knees and wrap his arms around my girl's legs was a cruel and unusual punishment. My teeth gnawed at the inside of my cheek before a metallic taste spread across my tongue, annoying my taste buds.

"That will be the last time you touch me for the rest of my life," she revealed calmly.

Elle let him conclude his selfish embrace before unleashing her first wave of fire.

Jesse pulled away and straightened his white T-shirt. Quickly, he stood. A far less hopeful look masked his face than the one he'd walked in with, as if he were two different people in the span of a minute.

Dr. Jenkins and Mr. Hide.

I leaned back against the inside of my closed door, blocking his only way out of the mess he'd created.

Elle stood, facing her opponent.

"I'm going to let you pretend like you have valid reasons for screwing the girl who you must've mistaken for me. And then you can explain to me why you chose her and answer the questions that have filled my mind for the last few days." Elle cleared her throat, seemingly making room for the strength her words conveyed.

"How did you even find out?" Jesse asked frigidly.

How pathetic.

"Seriously? That's your first concern?" A scoff left my girl's lips. The ones Jesse would never taste again. "Your main concern is how I found out about your little affair, if you can even call it that, instead of how badly it hurt me or how quickly it destroyed us?" She stepped forward, scanning Jesse's downturned face for the fucks he didn't seem to give.

"Let me make this crystal clear for you. You will *never* see or hear from me again after you give me the closure I'm asking for. I'll wish you well, pray you'll find the decency you lost, and let your parents know you're safe. I'll remember our good times for the temporary fill that they were, but those will be the last things to tether me to the Jenkins family, Jesse." Again, she stepped closer, her face inches away from Jesse's before delivering the final blow. "We're fucking done."

A single tear fell from Elle's left eye. She swatted it immediately. *Angrily*. But she wasn't sad.

She was pissed and in full-on Mafia-wife mode.

"I ... I really ... I can't justify my actions," Jesse rambled, gearing up for some bullshit justification. He continued without catching his breath, "I've thought about this moment a thousand times, and I haven't come up with a single logical reason why. No reason is good enough." Tears welled in Jesse's eyes before falling and dampening his cheeks. "Maybe I did it to cope with being away from you. I don't know."

"Wow, strong coping skills!" Elle smiled and nodded relentlessly. "You'd think dating a psych major for two years would have taught you a thing or two about how to deal with emotions in a healthy way. But, hey, at least you're right about one thing: no reason will ever be good enough because I deserve so much better. I know that now. Clear as day."

Elle glanced at me in a brief but powerful moment of connection forever engraved in my soul.

"You didn't do anything to deserve what I did. I know that." Jesse lifted his head and faced his fate eye to eye for the first time since we'd entered my office. "But this mistake will stick with me for the rest of my life, trust me."

"Trust you? Yeah, right. I can't trust a word that comes out of your damn mouth, Jesse. I can't believe I ever did. I was willing to uproot my life for you after graduation. You know everything about me, my family, my life, but I don't know who you are anymore. Did I *ever* know the real you?" she asked.

"I don't know who I am anymore either ..." He trailed off. "And I'm not afraid to admit that I'm scared ..." Jesse's voice shook. His hands came together as he brought them to his face and covered his nose and mouth like a surgical mask.

"Scared? Of what?" Elle asked unsympathetically.

You should be scared, asshole, I thought. *Scared of being without Elle for the rest of your life, scared of getting kicked out of the Navy, scared of ...*

"Rita's pregnant."

My girl's mouth fell open faster than mine at the information that was brand-new to both of us.

Information that changed the way I felt about the broken young man before us.

Information that made Jesse look a lot like I imagined my own piece-of-shit father looking when he'd found out my mother was pregnant with me.

Thirty-Nine

Elle

OH MY GOD. MY TEMPLES pulsed with anger as all my newfound confidence drained from my body.

Not even Austin's strength supporting me from across the room could lessen the blow of the news.

"You have got to be kidding," Austin interjected.

I had no words left to give.

"I wish I were." Jesse reached for my hand.

I stepped back, away from his tidal wave of chaos that tried to pull me back under.

"When did you find out, and why wasn't I notified?" Austin barked.

He seemed just as shocked by the news as I was. Although I also noticed a hint of something else behind his forest eyes. Something almost ... *empathetic*?

"How would I know why you weren't notified? You're supposed to be the one in charge, *Chief*. It's easy to lose track of time here ..." Jesse scoffed at Austin. Their uneven power dynamic was alarming. "I found out a few weeks ago maybe. Long enough to sit with it and let the thought scare the hell out of me. I don't even know when I'm getting out of here. How am I supposed to support Rita or be a dad?"

My guts dropped onto the speckled linoleum floor at the admission. Jesse's life was more different now than I'd ever seen coming.

More different than I ever could have imagined.

"How could you keep writing back to me and never mention this?" I asked, begging for clarity. "You wrote to me like everything was fine. You let me work extra shifts to ensure I had enough money saved to get here, and not once did you mention a delay, that you were struggling, nothing. Am I not worth that decency?"

The skin between his eyebrows pinched. Jesse's expression morphed from hurt to confused before he looked at Austin. The three of us exchanged a triangular moment of silence. Austin inhaled loudly, and I glanced at him. His jaw hardened in a way I hadn't seen while both of his palms clenched to the point of white knuckles.

"I had no way to communicate after the incident, Elle. I honestly can't believe you still came after not hearing from me for so long. Since they caught me with Rita, I haven't been able to contact anyone—no letters or calls. I haven't written to you or received mail in over a month ..."

Jesse's words penetrated my heart like a dagger, jaggedly slicing the organ like it was made of thin, wet paper. He scratched his neck and ran a hand through his disheveled hair. In answer, I rocked, unsteady, on my legs.

He'd written to me the entire time he was here, aside from the pause of a few weeks when no one in his division was permitted to send mail.

I wrote back.

Those things I knew to be true. We'd talked about personal things, things only we would know. I'd sent intimate photos. We'd made plans.

What the fuck is going on?

"But ... but you said you earned computer privileges. You said you could write me more letters, not less. We talked about how the distance made us stronger and how things would be better when we graduated because you had a new appreciation for our time together. For us. I'm confused ..."

Suddenly, a jolt of realization filled me.

Followed by sheer, unfiltered panic. The kind of panic that scarred.

I looked at Austin—my lighthouse, my tide through the chaos of the weekend—puzzled. Desperation ate away at his face, one I'd fallen hard and fast for—the one I'd trusted so easily.

"What's going on here?" My line of sight ping-ponged between Austin and Jesse.

Silence.

More silence.

"Somebody say something!" I screamed. My face found stability between my hands that flung up, landing on either side of my temples. "Why wasn't I notified that Jesse's graduation was delayed, and how did I get letters when he wasn't allowed to send them? Who the fuck have I been talking to if it wasn't you, Jesse?" The dryness peppering my throat choked me. Nausea crawled through my intestines like a fish with no fins.

When did I become a pawn instead of the queen?

"What the hell did you do, asshole?" Jesse finally spoke.

The stare he bored into Austin could have turned him to stone. Instead, it cemented my confusion.

"I protected the woman's heart that you had no problem destroying. That's what I did."

The second the words left Austin's lips, I wanted to disappear.

"What ... what do you mean?" I gripped the desk behind me to keep myself upright.

"Yeah, Chief, we'd love to know what you mean by that," Jesse spat sharply.

Austin's Adam's apple rose and sank like a boat lost at sea.

"Jesse, it's time for you to go back to holding. I don't need to explain shit to you." Austin swung open his office door. "I'll be right back, Elle. I can explain everything. It will all make sense, okay? Please, you've got to believe me ..."

Hopelessness blanketed his face. He didn't touch me, but I knew he wanted to. His saddened stare pummeled me before I looked away.

"I'm not sure I can believe anything from either of your mouths ..."

Austin grabbed Jesse's arm and tugged him through the doorway before he could say anything else.

He peered around the door. "I promise you, it will all make sense. Please, I'm begging you, don't leave this room," Austin added frantically.

I didn't respond. I couldn't.

The door slammed behind him, trapping me in the office I hoped held the answers neither Austin nor Jesse had fully revealed.

How many minutes did I have to find them before he came back?

It was time to break apart the Heartbreak Room.

Forty

Austin

Thankfully, no one was within earshot. Any words exchanged between Jesse and me needed to die quickly. If they accidentally escaped the space between us, we were both screwed.

"What the fuck did you do, asshole?" Jesse grumbled as we walked through countless hallways on our way back to his temporary hell.

"Don't worry about it," I snapped, clenching my teeth.

We moved quickly. Testosterone overflowed from the silent daggers we repeatedly exchanged.

"It would be in your best interest to keep my name and anything said in that office out of your mouth because if you don't, the consequences and your future will be far more depressing than they're already looking …" I paced, stopping just short of the holding division and into a semi-private area where we could finish our conversation.

Getting back to my girl was my priority.

"So, let me get this straight. First, you caught me with Rita, and instead of letting it slide, you ruined my entire career. And now you've done God knows what to Elle." Jesse smiled deviously. "What, were you intercepting my letters and getting off to the pictures of *my* girlfriend in your little office? Is that it? You act like I'm the monster. Why don't you look at yourself before pointing the finger, you fu—"

"Watch your mouth! None of this would have happened if you hadn't been stupid enough to sneak off with Camellino after I told the entire division on day one all about the surveillance cameras planted around this place. What were you thinking?!" I growled.

"I don't have an excuse, okay? The only thing I have now is a fractured future, no clue when I'm getting out of here, and a little white stick that stole the freedom I never had." Jesse's *poor me* mentality was draining. "I don't even know when I can see the mother of my child, who I would imagine needs some support too."

As much as I disliked him at a cellular level, Jesse's new circumstance multiplied my compassion toward his case.

He really was screwed.

How was I not informed that Rita was pregnant?

It made sense though. I had no overreach into the female divisions, so why would my colleagues have provided me with confidential medical information on one of their recruits?

"Your Captain's Mast is coming up in the next few weeks. If you can keep your mouth shut until then, maybe I'll consider that you're going to be a dad soon when I give my disciplinary recommendations to the captain. Trust me, I want you gone as much as you want out."

"Oh, how kind of you … not like I have much of a choice now, do I?" Jesse mocked, topping it with a scowl and an eye roll. The muscles in his face tensed as he fought against his unmistakable urge to say more.

A nod was all the kid deserved—the only thing I could offer him. I extended my right arm forward and motioned, urging him to join the rest of his bunkmates behind the double doors leading to his division. His hand paused flat against the door.

Hurry the fuck up, I thought, desperate to get back to Elle so I could explain myself.

Jesse needed to go away.

"What is it, Jenkins?" I inquired, giving him one last chance to get whatever he had to say off his chest.

"Just remember, Chief." He looked over his shoulder at me glaringly before continuing, "She was mine first."

Jesse flashed his middle finger before entering.

What a prick.

"Just remember, Jenkins, she'll never be yours again," I fired.

Sleep Sweet

Would she ever be *mine* again either?
I sprinted back to my office to find out.

Forty-One

Elle

Like an addict scrambling for their next fix, I spent my time alone in Austin's office looking for anything that could numb my unknowing until he returned. I couldn't access his password-protected computer or get into his locked filing cabinets, which defeated me.

"I can explain everything. It will all make sense." Austin's empty words replayed in my brain, taunting me.

I needed clarity like I needed air. Only *he* was the air that had kept me alive since Jesse.

Had I foolishly allowed him to steal my breath and revive me at the same time?

My hands quivered while I inventoried the small room for anything useful. A metallic flash near the ceiling caught my attention, drawing me toward the tall mahogany bookshelf against the wall next to Austin's desktop. Five bracketed shelves—overflowing with accolades, historical books, and figurines—faced me.

The first four shelves were filled with Blue Angel mini models, a globe crafted from opalescent pearl and jade, and handwritten letters addressed to Chief Petty Officer Carterson, thanking him for his contributions to the naval boot-camp program.

The top shelf housed a lone, framed photo of a couple, who I recognized from some of the pictures that hung at his house on Haroldeen Lane. His grandparents.

The one in his office was different though.

Framed in pewter, the dapper couple, captured in black-and-white, embraced on their wedding day. Their love radiated from the glass-preserved memory, tapping into my unease. Austin's grandparents had saved his life. I wanted to believe *he* was as good as they had been made out to be—that he sought a love like the one they shared. Too often though, photos of strangers concealed things the naked eye could never see.

I assumed the one staring back at me was no different.

I pulled the photo off the shelf to get a closer look, revealing a deep tin, the size of a shoebox, situated behind it. After grabbing it and flinching at its impressive weight, I placed it on Austin's desk before settling into his chair. Before removing the lid, I closed my eyes and found a deep breath.

No matter what, you'll be okay ... I thought.

The contents of the box said the opposite. The stack of letters I'd written to Jesse sat neatly piled inside.

Every *letter*.

Every *photo*.

Every *detail* of my life over the past two months had been stolen and stuffed into the box my adrenaline-weakened hands could barely grasp, a metallic prison holding the most intimate parts of me.

"No," I released. "This doesn't make sense ..."

Since I'd arrived, my heart had endured so much pain, my spirit drained. I'd be damned if I didn't take back what was rightfully mine, this time without the help of a man.

Austin wasn't my knight in shining armor after all. He couldn't be the villain—Jesse had already filled that role. The role of jester was up for grabs though, and if Austin wanted to play games, the queen of hearts was ready to meet him at the front gates with ropes made of velvet to strangle him with.

I vowed never to allow someone to trick, deceive, or turn me into a love-blind fool ever again.

I collected the letters and photos of myself and stuffed half into my purse and the other half into the pockets of my coat, replacing the tin box and wedding photo on the shelf where I'd found them. My discovery didn't explain everything, but it explained enough.

Enough pouring my all into people who couldn't be trusted.

Enough questioning my future.

Enough allowing others to dictate how I felt.

Enough.

Sleep Sweet

I'm not calm, no one is safe, we're better alone than together. My mantra might have changed, but one thing remained the same: I needed a way to cope.

I chose the strategy I should have explored when I realized Jesse wasn't at his graduation.

I left.

Forty-Two

Austin

"Elle? Elle, please ... OH MY God. No!"

Desperately, I flung the paperwork covering my desk across the room as if my girl were hiding under it. Stray paper clips bounced onto the floor, magnifying the emptiness that remained in her absence.

Again.

I nearly tripped over myself before peering down the hallway. Left, right, the ceiling, the floor. My neck winced. More emptiness. The narrow corridor to hell couldn't show me what I wanted to see, what I needed to see.

Her.

Slamming my office door, I immediately searched for the box behind my grandparents' wedding photo, the vault where my secret lived. Where I'd fallen for her. It was there.

But it was empty.

"Fuck!" I shouted.

Was I being punished?

I pounded both fists on my desk, rattling the surface so intensely that a thin crack emerged in my wake. Adrenaline and anger pounded against my forehead, concocting a rage I'd never experienced. Tears stung my eyes as they found the air.

I wasn't a crier. I never cried.

But Elle slipping through my fingers for a second time was something I couldn't handle. Something I hadn't been trained or prepared for. The rib cage holding my heart in place burned, its grooves infected with red tide as the toxins of Elle's absence stung my chest.

"I can't do it. I can't lose her again," I whispered, pressing my fingertips to my temples in hopes it would blur my vision enough to skew my reality. It didn't do a damn thing.

I sank to the floor.

My *heart* followed.

Then my *stomach*.

And finally the picture of my grandparents as I threw it. Shards of splintered glass shattered across the floor.

"Fuck the tides. The tides don't pull people together. They rip people apart!" I cried out, helpless, hoping it was loud enough that Grandpa Joel could hear me wherever the hell he was.

"Trust the tides. The tides will take you where you need to go," he used to tell me.

Bullshit.

Maybe that fantasy had worked for him, but there was no boat in my case. No anchor, no tides. There sure as shit was no sweet tea or lobster bisque waiting for me at the dock. I was alone, a message disintegrating without a bottle.

Void of her and the lies I'd told to ensure our paths crossed again.

Jagged metal corners lightly pierced my palms, the sharp pain not registering when I brought the box that had once contained the messy road map to Elle to my chest. Emptiness replaced its contents. The same emptiness that filled me.

Five silent minutes later, a quiet resilience cloaked my shoulders while I stared numbly into the nothingness. It was a heavy feeling, reminding me of the very thing I'd told myself the day I found Elle's letters under Jesse's bunk.

That giving up on my girl was not an option.

"You're a crazy bastard—you know that?" I cursed myself.

When would I learn to let Elle Madelyn go?

The toes of my thickly treaded boots thudded together repeatedly, their solid *thumps* calming my nervous system before a sour reality punctured my denial.

It could take days, months, or even years to experience Elle again. If I chose to wait, what kind of wait was I in for? Could there be an *us* ever again? Would the years turn into decades? Would she even be open to talking to me in the future, let alone forgiving me? Wanting to be with me?

A lifetime without her meant an eternity in purgatory.

I would never lie to Elle again or push her past the boundaries she'd set. She deserved more respect than that.

I was a better man than that.

A liar was not the Austin she needed, nor the Austin I wanted to be. The Austin I wanted to be was one who honored Elle's wishes and gave her what she asked for, even if what she asked for was a life without me. I swallowed my instincts, my next thought sinking my hopes like a poisoned anchor.

"If she's ever ready, you'll know." I adjusted my collar before dousing myself in necessary restraint. "For now, you give her what she wants and leave her alone."

Forty-Three

Elle

Eight Months Later

"Keep it up, ladies! You're doing great! Next, we'll move into boat pose. It works several large muscle groups, so be sure to take a good, long stretch before moving into it." Brielle, Coastal Pensacola College's resident yoga instructor, beamed.

The distinct scent of foam mats, sweat, essential oils, and determination permeated the on-campus yoga studio. I inhaled deeply, intentionally, before transitioning into my resting position of choice—child's pose. When I lengthened my spine, tension oozed out of every vertebra.

"Oof," I groaned.

"Will she ever quit torturing us? Or do you think she gets off on watching us suffer?" A chaotic top knot and floral headband secured my best friend's wild, curly hair. Entirely ass-up in a downward-facing dog, Ruthie still found a way to protest. Perhaps it was an eye roll or a huff and puff; regardless, my best friend never ceased to make her least favorite positions known. Ruthie complained often, yet she hadn't missed a class since we'd started practicing together eight months ago.

Deep down, I knew she loved coming as much as I did.

The boat, reserved for the end of each class, was a pose that required insane strength, balance, and coordination. Luckily, since returning to Pensacola, I'd dedicated much of my free time to improving those three things. I couldn't blame Ruthie for dreading it; the boat was among the most challenging poses for new yogis.

For that reason alone, it was my personal favorite.

"Now, after fully settling into your position, I want you to meditate for a couple of minutes. Close your eyes and visualize something in your life that makes you feel safe. It can be a place—somewhere you've been before or maybe somewhere you hope to go one day ..." Brielle sat in the front of the heated studio and gracefully extended her legs, as if it required no effort, wowing me with her incredible body. Her arms followed suit.

Her golden, glistening quads and hamstrings stiffened in unison, competing with the tight abs visible through her second-skin tank top. She was stunning, in her early forties, strong, and naturally gorgeous. I envied her and her full head of virgin red locks.

"Or it can be a person," she continued. "Sometimes, it's not the location that matters; a person's presence alone can often provide you the safety you seek ..."

A bead of sweat swam down my forehead, leaving a salty taste on my lips before falling into my cleavage. I imagined our instructor's sweat probably tasted more like gummy bears and glitter.

Mimicking Brielle, I used every ounce of my inner strength to sit upright on my butt and find and hold my boat. My lower abdomen pulsed after only a few seconds, humbling me.

Yoga, for me, was about leaving my ego at the door, accepting myself in the form I showed up in, and honoring my practice, no matter what it looked like.

Today, I feared it looked like *him*.

"Squeeze, everyone. *Squeeeeze*. If you think you're about to lose your form, squeeze harder," Brielle echoed.

I stiffened on command, challenging myself as the burn burrowed deeper into my core.

"She's lost her damn marbles." Ruthie's boat rocked on her teal mat to the right of mine, vibrating the floor with her efforts.

I giggled at her imbalance before visualizing my safe place. Mild pain gripped my body while each tendon and muscle supporting me tugged deeper. The moment I closed my eyes, the warm aches grew cold.

They eased.

It didn't matter how hard I'd worked to cleanse my mind of the memories or how much of myself I'd thrown into coursework, my future, or new hobbies.

I always saw him when I closed my eyes.

Strong arms and a shoulder kissed with ink.

Ivy-green stares that tangled around my mind, no matter how many times I uprooted them.

The uniform.

The pier.

The fire in his house and his soul.

The woodshed.

The snow.

The letters.

He reached out and touched me, grazing my neck and hair. He kissed my stomach, smiling up at me from my bare waist. His teeth nibbled the skin protecting my hip bone before he licked a path down to the middle of my spread thighs. I was hot and desperate for him …

"Austin," I whispered, clenching my eyelids as hard as possible to keep them from overflowing.

I bit down on my tongue, silencing the moan searching for its way out.

"Elle." A voice called my name.

Lost in my safe place, I ignored it.

Why did you do it, Chief? We were perfect for each other. Show me how you never meant to hurt me. I need you. I've needed you since the moment I left you …

"Sheesh, Elle. Snap out of it!"

A hand grazed my arm, far daintier than I recalled his being. I wasn't ready for the fantasy to end, but it was ready to end me.

Austin shook every inch of my body. I let his memory infect me like venom, slowly and designed to destroy. My limbs quivered, reminding me of the last night we'd spent together at the house on Haroldeen Lane. The pose I still held made me tremble the way only he could while the memory of him that I clung to made me feel things that only he could make me feel.

"Elle, seriously, are you okay?"

Failing me, my body collapsed. I flattened onto my back like a plank. Hot flames rode the nerves up my neck after the back of my head tapped on the foam mat beneath me, protecting my skull from the hardwood floor. Emotion poured from my tear glands. Like a heavy storm cloud, they could hold no more.

I winced, not because of the pain. But because when I finally opened my eyes, the only person left in the room with me was Ruthie. One of her arms supported my back; the other brought the straw of my glass water bottle to my lips. A discerning look replaced her typically playful one.

"When are we going to talk about him again? You can't do this to yourself forever, babe. I'm worried about you ..." Ruthie admitted.

I hugged my legs to my chest, the same way I had in Austin's shower the first night I stayed at his place.

Just like that, he was gone. A ghost ship on my foggy horizon.

The lights in the studio were off.

It was time to leave.

"Why do we even come to yoga anymore? I'm not sure if this is still good for you, Ells. It seems to reopen old wounds. Wounds you won't talk about anymore."

Like always, Ruthie was right.

Rightly missing a key piece of the puzzle.

I smiled through the residual desire that coursed through me, knowing the truth.

That feeling, a feeling close to what only Austin could make me feel, was the *only* reason I kept coming back to Brielle's class.

Forty-Four

Austin

EIGHT MONTHS HAD PASSED ON Haroldeen Lane with no trace of my girl, aside from the belongings she'd left behind to remind me. I refused to mail them back to her. Her suitcase, scattered toiletries, and the sheets she'd slept on—the ones I hadn't changed since she'd left—were all I had to cushion the nine hundred fifty-two miles separating us.

We had so much unfinished business. There were so many things I needed to say. To explain to her.

But deep down, I knew that the only thing that stood a chance of helping her heal was the same thing I considered my worst enemy.

Time.

Elle's faded perfume might have softened, but the scent of apples still haunted me when I entered the guest room. The lost aroma kept me company as I sat on the edge of the unmade bed, reviewing the paperwork I'd put off signing for months.

Time was running out.

The anchor insignia embossed on the top of the document I held in my hands was a huge part of my identity. For ten years, it'd shaped me. It gave my life meaning and a path that nothing or no one else could. Serving in the United States Navy was the biggest honor of my life. But no honor came without sacrifice, and, boy, I'd sacrificed so much to get to where I was.

When Elle had disappeared again the day I took her to see Jesse, I had known she wasn't ready—not for me, what I needed to say, or even to understand what she truly wanted. Jesse had lost her by ignoring her needs and trying to control her future, so as much as my instincts told me to fight, to run after her and spill my truth, I knew she needed to come to that conclusion on her own.

I wouldn't allow my selfishness to disrupt such an important season of her life.

She had a tremendous year ahead between graduation and everything that would follow. The milestones she'd worked hard to achieve—the ones she'd gushed about in her letters—would soon become accolades on her wall. She deserved every moment of her success.

Of course, I didn't want to miss those highlights. I didn't want to ruin them for her either.

I couldn't.

"Standing Still" by Jewel played from the record player in the living room, an afterglow of our night together in front of the fire. The ballad fueled my delusion that Elle was simply in the next room, making lunch for us or jamming out to her favorite singer while I made the greatest decision of my career. Neither scenario was true.

Except for the one where she was back in Pensacola, without me.

Two options presented themselves in deep blue ink. A signature in the first spot would renew my contract with the Navy, increase my pay, and require an additional six years of dedication. Signing there would keep me in my current job, bring me closer to the twenty years of service mark, and ensure a lifetime of benefits when I eventually retired. It was an option many would die for—that many had died for.

I didn't take that lightly.

The second signature line offered something I hadn't known in a decade—*untethered freedom*. My contract expired in only two days, meaning I was free to leave the military as honorably as I had come into it, taking with me a lifetime's worth of experiences to be proud of.

The grandfather clock on the wall ticked on, aloof to the magnitude of the decision being made in its presence. A million hesitations bombarded my mind. Still, none were strong enough to deter me from making the choice that, truthfully, had already been made for some time.

I paused one last time before glancing out the window toward my woodshed.

Confidently, I clicked the top of my pen, placed the ballpoint tip onto the paper, and signed on the line that made me feel most alive.

Forty-Five

Elle

"You dirty little hooker!" Ruthie nipped before unleashing a playful smack to my thigh. Her voice desperately needed a volume button, but I'd lost that remote long ago. Not even the nasally announcer's voice blasting the score from the loudspeaker above us could match the octaves she could produce.

Another sip of sour beer elicited a purr from my lips that the group of guys sitting on the bleachers beside us couldn't ignore. Between Ruthie's vulgar language and my tipsy sounds of indulgence, the boys, who appeared to be freshmen based on their stiff postures and even stiffer gelled hairstyles, must've thought we were open for business.

"What?! I think number twenty-two is kind of hot. That's literally all I said! How in the world does that make me a hooker?" I asked.

Blush and hops heated my cheeks. I hated to admit it, but I was having a great time, standing and cheering for the home team. Coastal Pensacola's basketball team was the most impressive sports team it had—the only December games worth attending, in our opinion.

"Because I slept with number twenty-two sophomore year—that's why!" Ruthie declared.

"Oh my God, you're right! Shit, I didn't realize that was Henry the Hound. I'm so sorry!" I squealed.

We laughed, the kind that rocked you so hard that no sound came out. The kind only the realest of friends could concoct. Laughter erupted between us while our heads fell back and forward with amusement.

"You're lucky I love you because if anyone else called him hot, I'd punch them right in the titty!"

Ruthie reached for my left nipple, mimicking a crab with her ruby-red acrylic nails. I swatted her sexy claw away just in time.

"Only one titty? Why not both?"

I re-created her attempt, stretching to give both of hers a quick squeeze instead of just one. She caught my hands, redirecting them to my sides. Suddenly, I was a naughty student.

"*Both* titties are only reserved for people who truly screw up. Like Jesse. I'd give him the titty twister of a fucking lifetime."

I froze. *Why did she have to bring him up?*

"That asshole moved on quicker than Mary-Kate and Ashley could solve a damn mystery." She nodded disapprovingly, eyeing the bottom of her beer. "I swear, if I ever see him again, I will rip his balls off and hang them from my showerhead like euca-fucking-lyptuses," she said, adding two hilarious insults to my injury.

I downed the last half of my drink before any more could spill onto my tank top. Ruthie stared at me in equal parts awe and horror.

"Anywaaay …" She grabbed my arm and pulled us down onto the bleacher as the halftime bell blared. "Have you decided yet about that position Professor Oramae recommended you for?" Ruthie reached under her seat and retrieved the mostly spilled carton of popcorn she'd bought on our way in. She turned to face me, giving me as much attention as her buzzed, reddened eyes possibly could.

"Yeah, I don't know yet. I applied for it when Jesse was in boot camp. I really wanted to surprise him and tell him I'd landed a big-girl job in Chicago, but I don't know if it's a good fit anymore …"

Suddenly, I felt it. The invisible tide washing away my restraint. The pull toward him.

Toward Austin.

"Are you insane? You've literally been talking about it since you started your grad program. What better place to help people with addictions and trauma than a freaking VA hospital? You could make a real difference, working in a place like that."

She stuffed a modest palmful of popcorn into her mouth. I reached into her bag and followed suit, finding mostly kernels.

"I know. It just hits a little too close to home. The way things ended with Austin and everything. I'm not sure I can handle being back there. So close to him …" Chills climbed up my spine at his name. Saying it out loud reminded me he wasn't just a memory.

For a time, he had been real.

"I know you told me about him, but why do I feel like I'm missing some details, babe?"

"You're the only person who knows what happened. What else is there to tell?" I lied.

Ruthie's head tilted, her sassy squint overflowing with curiosity. She knew me well.

Too well.

"Did you happen to leave out the part about how you can't get him out of your head since you ghosted him? And that maybe you regret leaving before hearing him out? Because I know that without you saying a single word."

"That's the problem. I'm *trying* to get him out of my head, but he won't fucking go. He's like an indestructible, annoying rock," I sighed.

"A rock?" Her palm cradled her chin like she was evaluating me. "If you said *rock hard*, I might be on board. But just a rock? I'm having a hard time with the visual."

She smiled. We both knew sarcasm and jokes could never loosen his hold on me.

"I figured I'd get through graduation next weekend and then make a final decision. I have two weeks before Oramae needs an answer."

"Needs an answer on the rock, number twenty-two's cock, or the job offer?" She giggled.

"The job, Ruthie." I shook my head.

Nothing she said surprised me.

"Sorry." She straightened and cleared her throat, reentering serious bestie mode. "If you *do* take the job in Chicago though, it means it won't be so easy for us to spend time together like this anymore." My best friend's lips pursed downward, her face mimicking that of a begging puppy.

We needed each other.

If I moved away, our schedules wouldn't align as perfectly as they had for the last five years—a thought that pained me. But we often talked about how our lives would change one day. Careers, partners, and kids would come along. We knew it was inevitable. We'd also hoped maybe we had more time.

"Let's not waste a perfectly good night worrying about the future, okay? I promise you'll be the first to know when I decide." I hugged Ruthie the same way I had so many times before—genuinely and with the level of connection I felt only for her. "It's a huge decision, and I want to be in the right headspace when I make it."

Even tipsy, I was the levelheaded one of our duo. Our opposing magnetism attached us at the heart.

"I love you forever, Ellie Vanellie," Ruthie said adoringly.

Love—a powerful word that had deceived me too many times. I clung to my best friend, her presence like my life jacket as I threaded my arms around her.

She made me want to believe in it again.

Forty-Six

Austin

"Your estimated arrival time into Pensacola International Airport is eight thirty a.m., with an approximate flight duration of two hours and five minutes. We'll keep the overhead lighting dimmed until eight a.m. for your comfort. Prepare for weather in the fifties today, with no rain in the forecast for the rest of the week. Please sit back, relax, and enjoy your flight."

My knees jammed into the seat back in front of me, which was occupied by a poorly placed elderly man, sporting a floral Hawaiian shirt and drinking a Bloody Mary before the sun rose. The vacationer traveled alone, yet the fiery glances he darted my way whenever I adjusted my legs told me he would be a handful, no matter which beach bar he spent his holiday break in.

"Sorry," I offered.

He said nothing back. Instead, he answered my apology with a cold, northern stiff hand gesture that said it all for him.

Coach was hardly accommodating for people taller than six feet, even in the aisle seat. My compressed spine, indenting the seat back, proved it. Unfortunately, snagging an extra-legroom seat in the exit row hadn't been an option when I booked the flight three months ago. My plan to fly to Pensacola for Elle's graduation had changed since the last time we had seen each other. I only hoped that her reaction to me would too. When the aircraft reached its cruising altitude and leveled off, it hit me. Only a few more hours until I was in her territory.

I couldn't fucking wait.

Two hundred forty-four days had passed since my eyes had feasted on her. Since my mouth had had its first taste of her. Month after agonizing month, I allowed each day to crumble with no bids toward her. No reaching out, no surprise visits or mysterious letters.

The urges to beg her for forgiveness and cut our time apart short were relentless. I fought daily—downing whiskey almost nightly—to stop myself from catching a taxi ride to the airport and moving my body until it collided with hers. But I'd vowed to let her finish her graduate program and make plans for her future without my influence.

A promise to her and to myself.

As hard as it was to live without her, I *needed* her to go on without me. To give herself time to decide if the future she'd planned for herself had room for me.

I was determined to prove to her that it did.

An unsweetened bottle of iced tea stared at me from the tray table—a far cry from the syrupy delight Grandma Justine had effortlessly whipped up when I was young. Still, it provided a sliver of support that only a grandmother could provide. I sipped it, knowing she would be proud that I was going after the woman of my dreams.

I slid my carry-on bag out from under my seat and peeked inside to ensure—for the third time—that I hadn't forgotten anything. The gift I'd brought for Elle was a big part of my plan. I released a breath when I saw it was still there, neatly packed, where I'd left it.

The gift wasn't lavish by any means, but it brought the occasion to life. The one I hoped would pull her back into my orbit because if it didn't …

I wasn't sure what would be left of me.

Elle was smart enough not to let materialistic gifts sway her. She needed the truth and the admiration of a man who loved her for all she was.

That was in the bag too.

Unable to find stillness while being physically uncomfortable, I popped earbuds into my ears and closed my eyes, hoping that Elle would come to me in my dreams.

The only thing that found me was Mr. Grumpy Old Hawaiian Shirt and his pompous slurps of Bloody Mary.

SLEEP SWEET

Am I overdressed? I wondered, adjusting my silken tie as a humid draft followed me into the auditorium at Coastal Pensacola College.

The buzzing line of people before and behind me was the only thing containing my excitement, enveloping the energy that made it impossible for me to think clearly. The line crept forward slowly, painfully, as it diffused deeper into the space.

I'd march on forever if it gave me the opportunity to see her again.

The echoes of the growing crowd, the flags of distinction stretching across the back wall, and the line of cap-and-gown-donning professors settling into seats on the stage reminded me of graduation days back on base. Ironically, I imagined that I felt the same way Elle had when she arrived for Jesse's boot-camp graduation ceremony.

Will it end the same way for me today as it did for her? I shuddered, revisiting the pain that had overtaken her face twice.

Once when Jesse broke her.

The other time when I had—the first and last time I would ever let her down like that again.

I swatted my intrusive thought away as if it were a bloodthirsty mosquito, replacing it with the pride I felt for Elle and her accomplishments with every step closer to the main event. *To her.* Until starting my naval career as a recruiter, I'd never set foot on a college campus. Higher education had never been in the cards for me.

Nothing made me happier for Elle than knowing a good education was a part of her deck.

I gripped the knitted handles of the bag containing Elle's gift, pulling it into my chest when a voice greeted me.

"Last name of your graduate, sir?" chirped the young man ushering families to their designated seating areas.

His unkempt blond hair proved he'd overslept while the hickey purpling his neck revealed all I needed to know about college boys.

They were animals.

"Madelyn. Elle Madelyn," I replied, praying the rascal directing me didn't know my girl.

"Let's see here …" He dragged his pen over the list, fastened to the front of his clipboard, and paused on the name that would forever choke me. "She'll be seated in the graduate studies section, first two rows back from the stage, sir."

I glanced down at his list and noticed several names next to hers in red ink, under the column titled *Ticketed Guests*. Every name, apart from mine, sat beside a checked box.

"Can you tell me who else purchased guest tickets in her group?" I asked.

The way his smile lifted on one side told me he'd been asked the question before, probably for reasons much different than mine.

"Ah, yes. Don't need good old family politics dampening the joyous occasion," he hypothesized.

I let his comment slide, hoping he would spill the beans before the people waiting to be seated behind me got antsy.

"Let's see … looks like Kimber Madelyn, Tony Madelyn, Ruth Porter, Austin Carterson, and Preston Thompson reserved guest tickets. You're the last to check in, which means the rest of the group should be seated somewhere over … there." He motioned to the audience section, left of the stage, this time faster and less patient than the first.

Wait. The dress shoes I'd worked so hard to shine earlier reflected my troubled expression.

Who the fuck was Preston Thompson, and why hadn't I thought this seating situation all the way through? Would Elle's parents or Ruthie recognize me? I expected to recognize Ruthie because Elle had shown me several photos of them together on her phone when we were snowed in. Did Elle even have a picture of me to share with her best friend or her family when she inevitably turned to them, heartbroken over the lie I'd told? We hadn't taken any when we were together.

You're about to find out …

Determined, I unstuck my shoes from the floor and walked through my trepidation.

The day was about Elle after all.

Moments later, I approached her cheering section, knowing I was in the right place when a familiar profile stole my attention. Elle's mother was instantly recognizable. One arm draped over Ruthie's shoulders like she was her second-born child. The other dripped pure kindness as it waved to another family a few seats away.

Gold-tinted eyes, blonde hair a few shades darker but still in the same color family, and a smile identical to the one I loved bringing to life on Elle lit up her face. If Mrs. Madelyn was an aged reflection of her daughter, I imagined that her husband was a very happy man.

And he looked it.

He beamed proudly beside her with a clunky, outdated camera hanging from his neck. Mr. Madelyn fiddled with the controls, probably ensuring it was ready to capture his daughter as she walked across the stage.

"Ladies, please. I need to grab a test shot. Could you both stay still for *two* seconds? That's all I ask!" He laughed, shaking his head. Affection laced his request, which succeeded in holding the duo still long enough for him to snap the photo.

Never taking my eyes off of them, I found a seat directly behind Elle's family. Close enough to feel like I was a part of them, positioned strategically enough to remain anonymous if needed. Aside from the side-eye glance Ruthie sent me, they didn't seem to recognize me. I smiled at each of them from behind. They were the gateways into Elle's life. I hoped to get to know them one day.

To be accepted by them.

Maybe even to be loved by them.

And then I saw him, the boy from the guest list, whom I assumed to be Preston. His permanent, computer-generated-looking smirk and overly lip-balmed lips overflowed with mischief.

I'd worked with many young men in my career, allowing me the opportunity to develop a strong bullshit-o-meter. The damn thing rang off the hook as it silenced every sound around me.

Potential Jesse 2.0 was trouble.

My chest vibrated in its attempt to process who the hell he was. A new boyfriend? A cousin? A lab partner?

Glossy paper scraped against my skin as I rolled the commencement program between my thumb and pointer fingers. I leaned forward, turning my head to get a better listen into their conversation. There was no way that Elle had moved on to someone else so quickly. Our time apart was for her to heal. To live *how* she wanted and learn *what* she wanted.

Did I fuck up, allowing so much time to pass? I cursed myself.

"Oh, Kimber, if she's anything like you when she grows up, I'll be a happy man," Preston preached. But a preacher he was not.

Instead of inspiring anyone, he only elicited a stiffened upper lip from Mr. Madelyn.

Daddy Mady hadn't come to play.

I swallowed, forcing the chuckle desperate for release back down my throat. Elle's father and I would get along wonderfully. If he spotted bullshit the same way I did, maybe he would recognize how good I could be for his daughter—how perfectly our jagged angles fit together.

"Oh, Preston, if *he* or she is anything like you when they grow up, what the hell are we going to do with *two* of you? Having *one* of you hanging around, hitting on my wife, is bad enough. Imagine another boy coming around. *Christ.*" Mr. Madelyn's expression screamed annoyance.

"I'm so sorry, Mr. M. You know how my stepbrother can be. He's a player. Always has been, always will be. The news that Preston was becoming a father came as quite a shock to all of us. I have *noooo* idea how Olivia puts up with him."

Ruthie flung her arm across Preston's chest as if she were holding him back before kissing him on the cheek. Playfully, he swatted her away.

He's Ruthie's stepbrother.

Relief washed my panic into the crowd as my shoulders retreated into their sockets. A fuckboy turned expectant father—Elle had already been down that road before.

He wasn't her type.

Twenty minutes later, a swarm of students draped in caps and gowns flooded the main floor from multiple entry points. I stood, my short fingernails burrowing into my palms.

And then it happened.

No matter how tough I thought I was or how much life experience I had, the moment I spotted her left me second-guessing my need for oxygen.

Elle Madelyn was my goddamn oxygen.

Her head swiveled as she simultaneously walked and searched for her family. Her assured expression and matching posture let the crowd know she didn't need anyone to tell her how proud they were of her. She was proud of herself.

Confidence looked incredibly sexy on her.

For eight months, I'd hoped I'd be able to keep the blood from rushing to my dick when I saw her—at least until after the ceremony—but, good God, all I could picture was shredding her gown and splitting her open again. I needed to touch her again.

To taste her.

I stared at her, unable to look anywhere else. She was stunning, maybe even more so than I remembered. Her hair was longer, in a half-up, half-down style that showcased her slender, sun-kissed neck.

Shiny peach lip gloss coated her lips, the overhead lighting reflecting off her mouth. Even yards away, I could practically taste their sheen.

Down, boy, I begged. My tailored dress pants tightened at the thought.

Elle sat in her assigned seat before turning our direction. For a moment, her gaze found every other family in attendance, apart from her own. When she finally found the row of people supporting her, she squinted and waved cheerfully, absorbing the distance.

She paused.

Frantic, I sat and reached under my seat, fingering tissue paper deeper into the gift bag I'd slid underneath, in an attempt at staying hidden a bit longer. Elle didn't need to see me and panic before the ceremony even began. The moment was hers; she deserved to shine on her own merit while being free of me. A pill that never got easier to swallow. When I sat up, her body faced the front of the room. The stage and the aged, accolade-decorated woman approaching the podium held her attention.

The back of her head still consumed mine.

Thirty minutes later, holding back my applause as she accepted her degree was not an option when she strutted her incredible ass across the stage. Instead, I clapped and cheered her name while she received her achievement, confident my presence would wash into the sea of whistles and *woooo*s around me. Elle paused again, mid-stride this time.

Could she recognize my voice from so far away? Did she hear me? See me?

Her name felt therapeutic as it left my mouth. Her pace back to her seat in the center of the floor told me she hadn't seen me, but I halfway hoped she'd heard me.

Her family sure had.

"Are you here for Elle too?" Ruthie turned around and asked. The flirtatious tone of her voice revealed that there were no wrong answers.

Between the hunger in her eyes and the dark lipstick staining her lips, I knew immediately that she and Elle together would equal a kind of trouble I couldn't wait to see in action. Maybe she knew who I was after all.

"Yes, I am." I smiled, nodding.

"Who are you exactly?" Her curious gaze studied mine.

"Of course. How rude of me," I said. I reached forward and shook Ruthie's hand. Her deep grip surprised me. "I'm an old friend of Elle's," I added.

"Really? How nice of you to attend today!" Kimber exclaimed, turning around in her seat. When Ruthie let go of my hand, she reached for it with both of hers, shaking mine genuinely.

Elle's mother traded glances with her husband. Validation that they didn't know who I was.

"You have a name, son?" Mr. Madelyn asked.

"Austin Carterson, sir. It's a pleasure to meet you. All of you."

I firmly shook her father's hand.

His stare lingered on my face before looking me up and down. "I'm Tony, Elle's father," he added.

"It's wonderful to meet you, Austin. How do you know our daughter?" Elle's mother flipped her lengthy, straight hair over one of her shoulders. Many of the facial features now centered on me were shared with Elle, the timeless kind. Like the shape of her eyes and her naturally flushed cheeks.

"Yeah, how *do* you know our Elle?" Ruthie echoed.

"We were, *uhhh* … pen pals," I concocted.

Tony's puckered lips revealed he needed more convincing.

"You know, through one of those programs where college students send holiday cards and letters of support to service members to cheer them up. We became friends when I served in the Navy, and I wanted to surprise her today. I know she's been through a lot this year. I couldn't miss it," I added.

"Aww, that's *sooo* sweet! Funny, she never mentioned you." Ruthie brought her fingers to her chin and stroked mischievously while examining me. "Come to think of it, I would have *loved* a pen pal like you!" Ruthie gushed. She bit her bottom lip excitedly and bounced in place.

She knew.

"Maybe she wanted to keep us a secret in case she ever needed me. Our connection has always been unspoken in that way," I divulged, planting more seeds in Little Ms. Nosy's mind.

"Yeah, I can tell just by seeing you in person why her pull to you would be so strong." Ruthie smirked.

My chin dipped to her stiff middle finger, which lay flat against her thigh. Clearly, it was positioned there just for me. I smiled and looked directly into her eyes, respectfully acknowledging her cryptic message.

Yep, she definitely knew.

Small talk with Elle's family grew as the remaining students of the graduating class walked across the stage, one by one. While I enjoyed it, feeling more immersed in Elle's world than ever before, the time separating me from her stretched on like it was keeping us apart by design. Maybe, for a moment, it was. However, time was no match for the moment that the ceremony finally concluded.

The moment Elle and I came face-to-face in front of her family and friends.

Forty-Seven

Elle

Gripping my leather-bound degree, I sauntered through the post-graduation chaos until I found my parents, Ruthie, and her stepbrother, Preston. Cheers and claps erupted from my crew when I approached, filling my soul.

Thankful was not a strong enough word to describe what I felt for them.

When my parents embraced me, they didn't speak—they didn't have to. The joy uniting us grounded me quicker than words could. They were proud.

I'd never been prouder of myself for giving them that.

Ruthie and Preston pressed yellow roses into my arms, followed by a delightfully suffocating three-way hug.

"Congratulations to the smartest bitch in the room!" Ruthie caressed the fabric sashes and threaded cords decorating my collar.

Honor Society, magna cum laude—each honor represented a piece of my hard work and dedication. For the first time in months, I felt like myself, accomplishing everything I'd set out to.

Well, *almost everything*.

No matter how hard I'd tried, I couldn't erase the man made of Elle magnets and orgasms from my memory. His boldness, his body, his tattoos, the way he'd cooled me down like summer rain on asphalt. Austin was beyond memorable. He was exceptionally unforgettable.

"Come, honey. Toss your cap into the air and give me a cute little pose. I want to get a video so I can show off my incredibly brilliant offspring," my mother directed.

She was good on social media, better than Ruthie and me combined.

Was it slightly embarrassing at times? Yes. Did I do it anyway? Also, yes. Because if it were my daughter graduating, I would want to capture the moment and share it every way I could.

After kicking my right leg to the side, I held it bent and smiled like I'd just graduated with a degree in game-show-host-ology. I flung my cap a few feet above my head, only for my dad to grab it when it came back down.

"For the memory box," he said, pressing it against his chest and staring solemnly at me.

I rubbed his shoulder and nodded, knowing the day meant as much to him as it did to me.

"My turn," he added. "I always get the best pictures."

Ruthie and I embraced before posing for endless shots on my dad's beloved camera. She kissed my cheek, leaving her signature lipstick stain behind on my skin.

"Your friend was looking for you earlier. He sat behind us, and we chatted quite a bit during the ceremony. Nice guy," my dad reported.

I froze.

"Yeah, he's something else, babe," Ruthie said, the enthusiasm in her voice infecting my every pore. Her sharp gaze bored into me.

"My friend?" I sputtered.

Each person encircling me smirked as the walls of the auditorium narrowed. Jesse wasn't back for more, was he? The reactions surrounding me wouldn't be so ... off-kilter if that were the case. Besides, they'd all met my ex; he was old news. Even my dad had sounded genuine when he mentioned my "friend." That alone told me it wasn't Jesse.

But it couldn't be Austin.

"Said he was an old pen pal from some military charity project. Good-looking dude," Preston added.

I looked at Ruthie desperately, knowing her expression would reveal more than anyone else's. We were fluent in *best friend*, often practicing the unspoken language when we wanted to communicate in groups without anyone else realizing it.

I grabbed both of her hands and stared at her, silently begging her eyes to speak to mine. Instead of answering their call, they remained still, locked on something behind me.

The moment he touched my shoulder, I knew.

His wintry scent.

The hands that wandered my body every time I closed my eyes and imagined my happy place in yoga class. *Every time I touched myself.*

His energy had its own identity, and it stood right behind me. A jolt swam through me before my neck swiveled and my body collided with one composed of steel and heat.

His.

Instead of a naval uniform, Austin's body filled out a dark gray suit and deep blue tie. The fabric—pasted over his thighs, shoulders, and neck—barely concealed the splendor of his statuesque build. His two-toned watch glimmered in the overhead lighting, reflecting the magnitude of his oversize hands. I knew what those hands could do. No longer was he trapped in my desires.

He was standing right in front of me.

"Congratulations, Elle." Austin's silky voice was as medicinal as I remembered. He smiled down at me like a ray of sunshine, cutting through the storm clouds surrounding our last encounter.

"Uhhh … wha-what are you doing here? When did you get here? How did you …" I spewed. The fragmented questions dissipated as they left my lips.

"I couldn't miss this," Austin said. His voice didn't sway, the words as solid and sturdy as he was.

He stepped closer suddenly. Dizziness drizzled my thoughts like hot fudge. I was happy, pissed, angry, overwhelmed, and a dozen other emotions my mental-state sundae bowl couldn't accommodate.

I stepped back.

What was he doing here after all the time that had passed? He had flown to Pensacola and introduced himself to my family without my knowledge, just to watch me graduate and leave? I wasn't going to let him destroy me all over again after I'd barely made it out alive the first time around. I couldn't.

"I can't believe you're here …" I released.

"In the flesh," he replied.

Sure, I was pissed at him. It didn't change the fact that I could listen to his voice forever and never tire of it.

"And what mighty fine flesh it is, if I do say so myself," Ruthie added.

She'd sat with me while I cried about Austin on multiple occasions and rescued me from my yoga-induced la-la-land fantasies more than once, so why was she so quick to forgive him?

He has that effect on women, I thought. *Not me. Not anymore.*

"A little notice would have been nice." I straightened, regaining the composure he'd stolen the moment I saw him. "Not everything revolves around the one and only Chief Austin Carterson."

"Well, I'm not so sure about that," my mother interjected, scanning him like a barcode reader from every angle.

She, too, appeared enamored, based on the giant ear-to-ear grin plastered across her face. Both she and Ruthie were in for a stern lecture by the end of the day.

Were they *that* blinded by him? I couldn't blame them.

Austin's suit didn't help my case.

"You're right. I should have told you I was coming. But I was in town for work, and I wanted to be here. I'm proud of you. I needed you to know that."

Pain masked Austin's perfect features. The strength I remembered remained, yet new, darkened shadows sat above his cheeks. Guilt struck my anger, softening it.

"I hope you'll join us for a celebratory dinner this evening. I'm sure the restaurant could accommodate one more on our reservation. We'd love to hear more about your time in the service. Plus, they make the best chicken Parmesan in town," my father suggested. He placed a hand on Austin's shoulder, positioning himself as his silent second.

Why on earth was he so inviting toward Austin? I must've missed a few things during their introductions because—*oh, that's right*—I was busy graduating.

"As much as I appreciate the extremely kind offer, Mr. Madelyn, I wouldn't want to intrude. I only wanted to congratulate Elle and give her this."

Austin lifted a gift bag from the floor beside him and placed its knitted handles into my hand. The bag's contrasting emerald and silver coloring reminded me of the snowflake-kissed trees surrounding his house, the ones I'd admired from his kitchen window when we did the dishes together.

The ones I'd barely noticed when he led me to his woodshed and chose me as his frozen dessert.

"Open it later, when you get home," he urged. "I don't want it to distract you from your celebration."

He let go, leaving the gift in my possession and the warmth from his fingertips lingering on my palm. His touch could have burned a hole in my skin, and I still would have accepted it. I didn't want to need his touch, but it felt like I still lived for it.

"Why can't she open it now? Is it some *top-secret* pen-pals-only thing?" Ruthie chimed in. Mischief and sarcasm saturated her questions.

She knew exactly who he was; we'd found a photo of him online when she begged me to look him up. Only one was posted on the recruitment website, but it was enough.

"Something like that." Austin nodded her way before immediately redirecting his stare back to me. His desperate smile planted a forest of aches deep in my chest.

"I'll save it for later then," I muttered cooly. Perhaps a thank-you would have been the right thing to offer. Instead, I sharpened my verbal weapons to defend myself in case he tried to break me open again.

"It was a pleasure meeting all of you. Maybe one day, we can get to know each other better over a proper meal," he suggested warmly.

Austin's mouth was more distracting than my best friend's, mimicking a panting dog behind his head.

"Honey, that sounds lovely. I'll get your number from Elle, and we can arrange something the next time you're in town," Mom chirped.

My mother could try all she wanted, but would soon realize it was impossible to get his number from me because I didn't have it myself.

Unease seeped into my mind at the thought, knocking my confidence. He'd never even given me his phone number. How could I have ever let him have such a hold on me?

The crowd surrounding us seemed to fade. He and I were back at the top of the Ferris wheel for a moment, and like then, Austin's torment was unmistakable. His facade remained calm and strong from the outside, but I knew him well enough to know his insides were a blazing inferno, just like mine. The way his smile didn't fully expand when he leaned in to hug me goodbye proved it. There was a reason I'd avoided our first goodbye—I had known it would be impossible to follow through with.

This one felt no different.

"One last thing," Austin offered. His magnetic voice met my ear as he leaned closer and whispered his last words. "I hope you can find it in your heart to forgive me because I'm beyond in love with you."

I flatlined, unable to move or respond.

He kissed my cheek and disappeared into the crowd while my family stared at me, waiting for answers.

Another auditorium, another graduation, another heartbreak.

I squeezed the handles of the gift bag in my hand and died inside all over again.

After arriving home from graduation dinner, emptiness filled my bedroom. I sat on the floor and lost a staring contest with the mysterious bag before me. Both Ruthie and my mother had begged me to open it at dinner, but there was no way I could allow them to influence whatever decisions lay inside. I'd promised Ruthie a tell-all as soon as I was ready.

Was *I* even ready for whatever was in the bag?

If I'd learned anything about my emotions in the last year, it was that closure was a necessary evil. As much as I'd tried forgetting about Austin, refusing a final shot at closure wasn't doing me any favors. No, Austin hadn't been fair to me, but I could still be fair to myself.

How could I follow my heart if half of it was still missing?

Silver knitted handles hung from both sides of the impressive packaging. Finally, I pulled it closer and untied the bow, widening the opening. Like a claw machine, I felt around for my prize and discovered four bundles, composed of letters, and a small box, topped with a snow-white bow. My heart fluttered intensely as I laid out the contents.

Immediately, I recognized the first bundle of letters as the ones I'd exchanged with Jesse. I hadn't seen his handwriting in almost a year.

"He made copies," I whispered.

They meant something to him.

My eyes welled with tears, a sting tickling them from their sockets. The letters, now separated into piles, were labeled one through four. Each had a large yellow piece of stationery attached.

Puzzled, I reached for stack number one. My nose scrunched. The twine supporting the bundle separated, falling apart in my hands with one light tug. Austin's handwriting graced the back of the yellow square on top.

The letters in this stack are from Jesse.

I met you at Coastal Pensacola College the same day you met him.

The difference between him and me is that I never forgot you.

When I cleaned out Jesse's bunk and found these, I couldn't stop myself from writing back …

Fuck.

My vision blurred as another clue was added to the unsolved mystery that was Chief Austin Carterson. Desperate for more, I grabbed the second pile of letters, labeled number two, and read the note attached to the top. Every letter in the stack was typed. And then it hit me. He'd typed them so I wouldn't notice his handwriting …

I shouldn't have read the letters I'd found, but I did.

I shouldn't have looked at the pictures you'd sent, but I did.

I'd pictured your face a thousand times, and out of nowhere, it appeared in my world.

I couldn't let your heart shatter as you waited for more letters.

If I never wrote back, you'd be waiting forever.

I had to ... and I'm sorry.

My mind swirled with too many thoughts, making it impossible to focus on any of them. A cocktail of anger, defeat, and empathy swam through my bloodstream.

For the first time in my life, I wasn't sure how to feel. My sudden departure from Illinois did nothing but muddy my reality of the situation. Self-sabotage at its finest.

Austin had cleaned out Jesse's bunk after catching him with Rita. He'd found the letters, read them, and written back to me to save me the heartbreak. *Okay*, but none of that explained why he hadn't communicated that Jesse wouldn't be at his graduation. Austin had *wanted* me to come, knowing I would find out in person. Knowing I would have nowhere else to turn. *That* hurt my soul.

Bundle number three, which turned out to be only a neatly folded sheet of parchment paper, revealed another truth. I flattened it, allowing Austin's handwritten words to find me.

Roses are red, hydrangeas are blue.

For eight months, their presence reminded me of you.

I know I fucked up. I'm so sorry, Elle.

But how could I ignore the way that I fell?

Call it coincidence, call it fate.

Perhaps I told you the truth too late.

But if by chance, perhaps it's not,

I'll be waiting for my final shot.

But this one won't be built on lies.

Instead, you'll know peace when you close your eyes.

Now, close your amber and think of my green.

I'll wait for you forever at the house on Haroldeen.

"Oh my God," I cried.

My lungs searched for relief as they experienced a breathlessness I'd only ever felt once before—when Austin emptied them in his woodshed. Aimlessly, my fingers traced the thin straps of my graduation dress as his prose infected me like dark magic.

I shook like a vibrator, digesting the power of the page in my hands, before trading it for the fourth and final truth—another note. The one that spoke the loudest. Affixed to the bottom sat what looked to be several dozen sealed envelopes. I brought the whole pile closer and began reading.

One last thing ...

I knew my best attempt at a poem wouldn't be enough. So, I decided to write to you in our time apart.

These envelopes contain all the conversations I wished we could have had.

Anytime I felt the urge to talk to you, I wrote.

Anytime I thought of you or had something exciting to share, I wrote.

I want you to take your time, without the pressure of promises or me standing in front of you, and read them.

Learn about me, my struggles, my strengths. Get to know me, the real me, in the same way I got to know you.

Fall for me the same way I fell for you, Elle.

I know this is a lot, and if you're not ready, you don't have to let me back in.

All I ask is that you let my words in before deciding if this is really the end.

Words are powerful. Let mine prove to you that we're meant to be.

I could hardly fucking breathe. The only thing I could do was sob.

"Elle, are you okay in there? I hear tears! Please, let me in right now!" Ruthie's voice crept under my door. She knocked repeatedly.

I needed her.

"I'm ... I'm fine ... *I think*. You can come in!"

Not a second elapsed before Ruthie busted through my doorway. She struggled to catch her breath.

"Were you listening at the door?"

"No, of course not. What kind of lunatic would do something like that?"

Ruthie looked at everything but me before sinking beside me. I chuckled through my falling tears.

"Oh my God, what's the matter? Whose ass do I need to beat this time?" My best friend pulled me in, surrounding me with compassion that only she could offer.

"I'm ... fine," I urged, sniffling.

"Yeah, that's not gonna work this time, Ells. Talk to me. Did you open the present?" She flipped the gift bag upside down, ensuring no contents remained.

"I opened some of it. Not the box though. Not yet."

Before I could finish my thought, Ruthie was already reading Austin's notes.

"Oh my God!" Ruthie shouted.

She shot up and continued, frantically piecing together the puzzle that was Austin. I couldn't find the energy to stop her. When she finished his final confession, she sat down cross-legged and faced me. Realization found her wide grin as she fanned the envelopes containing Austin's words like a poker hand.

"If all of this"—she scanned the piles of effort now surrounding us—"isn't the most romantic thing I've ever seen, I don't know what is!"

"I know. It's *something* ..." I shrugged, still in shock.

"Sure, he shouldn't have done any of it to begin with. He should never have kept that big of a secret from you. But shit, babe, this is huge. Almost as huge as he is!"

"Stop. Be serious. I need to think for a second," I said. Pausing, I brought my hands to my forehead before running them through my hair to the back of my head.

"No, no thinking required. You need to take a deep breath, put these new letters on your nightstand to binge tonight, and open *that* immediately!" Ruthie squealed.

I looked over at the immaculately wrapped gift box she pointed at. It taunted me.

"Here, I'll help you." Ruthie plucked the bow from the lid, removed the top, and placed the box, open-faced, in my lap.

A flash caught my attention.

Inside lay a necklace and pendant—the silver snowflake charm glimmered like glass. Austin's creative use of snow was something I could never forget. His gift proved he couldn't either. I wanted to smile, but my jaw remained half open.

"Hello? Earth to Elle. That is gorgeous! What do you think it means?!" Ruthie stared into the box, admiring its contents before interrogating my demeanor. She looked at the necklace and back at me.

"I think it means I fucked up, Ruths," I said, staring directly into my racing thoughts.

Austin's body made him unforgettable. His rank made him untouchable. His distance made him unreachable. But his thoughtfulness, the way he had admitted to picking up my pieces before they ever had a chance to touch the ground, turned him into someone I wanted back in my life.

Someone *undeniable*.

For the first time since accepting the counseling position in Chicago, I felt like the tides were finally back on my side.

And I knew, even before reading whatever new truths Austin's letters would reveal, exactly where I was supposed to drop my anchor.

Forty-Eight

Austin

Dirty dishes overcrowded my sink on New Year's Eve—a week and a half after attending Elle's graduation ceremony. The existing pile was so impressive that when I placed yet another on top, the stack tumbled. *Clink.* A muddy substance splattered the faucet, along with my need to keep my kitchen neat and orderly.

"Damn it!" I growled, sucking a drop of blood from the fresh slice along my thumb. I allowed water from the faucet to rinse it, too annoyed to grab a Band-Aid.

It was time to get my shit together.

When I gave up on dishes and walked to the bathroom, the signs of depression I'd been trained to recognize in my recruits sprouted like weeds all around me. The piles of laundry, my unmade bed, and the rage boiling over silently inside of me. Hell, I practically lived in the woodshed now. My emotional deprivation tank, of sorts.

But I needed a goddamn break.

A break from being alone with thoughts that continued to suffocate me. Earning Elle's trust again in Pensacola had been my goal. I sighed shakily, recounting how I'd sorely missed my target.

What else could I have done?

I'd shown up for her, spilled my truth, given her time and space to process, and told her to come to me when she was ready. Unfortunately, emptiness was the only thing that had followed me home. She now had my phone number, which I'd specifically left in one of the dozens of new letters I'd written to her.

The phone never rang.

Will she ever come back to me? I thought five minutes later, gripping the back of my neck with one hand, adjusting the shower faucet with the other.

Trails of sweat streamed down my body as the tiles beneath me filled with leftover wood scraps and grime. For me, showers had a way of cleansing more than just the body after a long day.

They felt like the only warmth left in my life.

Chief Carterson would never let another human being take such a toll on him. If Elle wanted me, she'd come. If not, I could let her memory haunt me forever, but I couldn't become a miserable shell of the man I knew was still inside. That wasn't me. That wouldn't be who she needed if she ever came back either.

Should I hold on to something that never truly belonged to me? The depressing thought drained me faster than the metal grate chugging water under my feet.

When the water temperature cooled to an uncomfortable level, I turned it off and stepped out onto the rug, ignoring the stale towel hanging lifelessly nearby. Its musty scent disgusted me without even having to touch it. I cursed the material, reminding myself to wash it later.

Laters were becoming increasingly common in my life.

How many more *laters* could I possibly withstand?

Still naked and drenched, I attempted to dry my hair with a washcloth, leaving spots behind on the mirror with every pass around my head. The wet bullets joined the crew of white stains that already covered half of my reflection. I swatted them away through the foggy haze, blurring the view of myself I wasn't sure I could stomach looking back at.

While I brushed my teeth, the hair that was far outside Navy regulations, which I had sported for a decade, bullied me. My fade had grown messy. Frantic and unkempt.

"Add it to the list, asshole," I mumbled.

Laundry, haircut, dishes. My annoyance grew as I considered the time it would take to accomplish each task.

Time I only wanted to spend with one person.

A single clean pair of boxers remained in my dresser drawer. They clung to my damp thighs as I rolled them on.

Unmade in the middle of my bedroom, the bed invited me in. I yawned on cue, revealing a man in desperate need of rest.

Sleep Sweet

Rest that my new life screamed at me to find.
The rest I'd avoided so that Elle couldn't find me in my dreams.
Rest that never came.

Forty-Nine

Elle

HAROLDEEN LANE GREETED ME LIKE an old friend as my taxi driver descended the familiar road. As it was the last time I had seen it, Austin's house and the surrounding grass were blanketed with snowfall. The front windows were illuminated by an interior glow that reflected off the frost covering them like silver-stained glass.

Blue hydrangeas still lined the porch.

The flowers that reminded him of me ...

This time, they danced with every cool gust of wind that tickled them. The scene was every bit as magical as it was inviting. Excitement strangled my heart.

"Thanks for the ride, sir." I handed the driver my fare before he popped the trunk and retrieved my overstuffed suitcase and duffel bag—my only belongings.

"No problem, darlin'. How long are you planning on stayin'? You want to schedule a pickup?" he offered.

"Actually, no. I won't be going home anytime soon. I just accepted a job in Chicago," I replied. Icy breath clouded the space between us. I brushed my palms together in a sad attempt to warm them up.

Would I ever get used to the cold?

"Wow. Big-city girl, huh? Enjoy then. And welcome." The black-haired gentleman, who could have starred in an old-school Mafia flick, climbed back into the driver's seat and sped away. Slick ice was no match for the chains on his tires.

"Time to start my new life." I spoke into the chill, hopeful that the decisions that had brought me back were the right ones.

My new job started on Monday, which meant Austin and I had almost a week together before I was due to move into my new apartment fifteen minutes away. With no return ticket holding me back, I was finally ready to face the invisible tether I'd avoided for far too long.

The one anchoring me to Austin.

If jitters were countable, I'd say a thousand swarmed my body when I stomped the snow from my boots and stopped on Austin's doorstep.

I looked around. The house was exactly how I remembered it, aside from the new structure now standing next to its infamous woodshed and the hand-carved sign hanging from its peak. *The Chief's Woodshed* was legible from the road, making me wonder if Austin had taken his hobby to the next level in my absence.

The planks below my heels creaked when I inched forward. Would my arrival precede me?

"Here we go," I released, counting backward from five. Firmly, I knocked on the door. I couldn't wait to see him, to surprise the hell out of him.

To forgive him in person.

Knock, knock.

Second attempt, and still no answer.

The Ol' Green Goddess was parked in its usual spot. It was after working hours; surely, he was home, *right?*

I jiggled the handle, and the door swung open. Did that mean I should enter? I took it as a sign and walked inside.

The house, overflowing with comfort the last time I'd been in it, was frigid and dark. Its once-tidy interior was riddled with laundry piles and empty liquor bottles. One lamp was switched on in the living room.

What the hell?

I asked myself what could have happened in Austin's world from graduation to now to cause the type of chain reaction I was staring at. Realization narrowed my throat when I realized precisely what had caused the bomb to drop.

Me.

Suddenly, a soft hum of running water met my ears. Austin was showering. The last thing I wanted to do was scare him. If he thought I was an intruder, there was no telling what kind of wrath I'd find myself in the middle of. He had been trained to counter potential threats after all.

I hung my coat in his entryway, positioned my luggage next to the front door, and spent the next few minutes alone, loading the dishwasher. Quickly, I wiped his kitchen counters down and then sat at his table, where I awaited my fate. My knees, practically attached to mini trampolines, bobbed against the underside of the table.

I should have called and told him I was coming, I thought, chewing at the corner of my manicure.

Too late.

The sound of running water disappeared. I heard Austin curse. After a few silent moments, his footsteps asserted themselves down the hallway, one by one, as they crawled toward me. I clenched the table and stabilized my breathing like I'd learned to in yoga. If I were in boat pose, the bitch was about to rock.

Much like he did when I imagined my safe place, Austin emerged—his body bare, aside from the tight boxers stretching against his waistline. He dripped wet.

I swore, he turned into ice when he looked up and noticed me. I watched in awe as his chiseled chest rose and fell, glistening.

"Happy New Year's Eve, Austin."

"Elle?" he breathed. His eyes narrowed. One nostril flared bigger than the other, like a vampire catching a whiff of fresh virgin blood.

Austin's repeated blinks and broken exhale told me that in his mind, I was a ghost. I made my living, breathing presence known as I rose from the dead and crept toward him. My hands trembled, though I begged them to remain still.

"I didn't mean to surprise you," I said, his magnetism drawing me forward. "But you surprised me at graduation, so I felt it was only fair." I shrugged innocently. "I knocked a few times, and it was freezing, so ... I didn't think you'd mind if I let myself in. The front door was unlocked, and ..."

"You can walk into this house anytime you want," Austin cut in. His response was firm and serious. Intimidating. "It's nothing without you. It's been nothing since the day you walked out that door ..."

Peppery pricks tickled my arms. His statement was a novel, confirming everything I wanted to hear again.

"Tell me about the suitcases," he demanded. He pointed toward the luggage clogging his entry. No other part of him moved while he awaited my answer.

"I accepted a counseling position in Chicago. I live here now." I glanced at my imaginary wristwatch before continuing, "As of two hours ago, when my flight landed actually. I thought maybe I could stay here for the weekend. My apartment will be ready in a day or two, and my new job starts Monday."

"You … you live here now? In Chicago? Which is less than an hour from me." His tongue spread like sweet jam across his lips. "I don't understand. Help me understand what's happening right now," he begged.

I said nothing.

"Can I please touch you?"

Slowly, I nodded. My eyes beamed toward him like bright southern stars, lighting his path through the room.

I noticed the ridges in his arms pulse as he approached me and cautiously pulled my hands into his. A shadow crept into his infectious grin.

"I'm not going anywhere," I whispered, inhaling him deeply.

Austin tilted my chin up before I could breathe, his line of sight melting into mine. His firm touch remained glued to my jaw, ensuring I couldn't look away.

Multiple shades of green reflected in the gaze that reminded me of the northern lights, easily capturing my full attention. "Elle, before I do what comes next, I need you to tell me every single thought that's lived in your pretty little mind for the past eight months because being here without you, constantly thinking about you, has been a fucking nightmare." His tone grew deeper. Deadlier. "And if you wake me up from that hell, I'll never go back to sleep. Before that happens, I need to know *exactly* what brought you back here." His confession was as carnal as the tension building between us.

I let the moment consume me.

"No matter how hard I tried not to, I've thought about you every day since I left," I admitted. *Have I stopped breathing?* I couldn't tell while we stared into each other. "I never should have gone before giving you a chance to explain. I was hurt and confused, pissed even. I'd thought I was falling for Jesse in those letters, pouring myself and my future into the man I thought he could be. But reading them again, the old ones and the new, I saw how different you both were and how good your words made me feel. How strong and genuine of a man you are, even if it takes breaking some rules to prove it." I paused before adding, "I didn't fall for Jesse. I fell for you."

Immediately, his thick biceps stiffened around me, cloaking me before he sank to his knees and pulled me into his lap.

"I forgive you, Austin. For everything. The letters you wrote me in our time apart ... they were beautiful. Reading them felt like I was getting to know the real you. I'm finally ready to see what we can be ..." I spoke against his arm. My eyelashes brushed his skin.

"I'm so sorry I didn't tell you," he said with regret. Red patches spread like wildfire across his chest.

Embarrassed Austin was a version of him I hadn't yet experienced. It was vulnerable and scorching hot.

"I understand why you did it."

"You do?" Austin sat back, positioning himself where he could see my face while still holding on to me.

"Well ... sort of." I shrugged. "The letters helped with that. They showed me even more ways we fit together. Our personalities, the wants for our lives. Reading them felt like talking to a best friend, one I'd known for my entire existence." I swallowed before saying, "But, maybe ..."

"But maybe what?" Austin's expression fell, stuck somewhere between relief and worry.

"Maybe you can help me understand it better, Chief ..."

The weight of my suggestion sank me deeper into his embrace. He shifted slightly.

"And you're sure about this? About us? Because I can't lose you again ..." His eyes clamped shut, as if the memory of our time apart pained him.

It hurt me too.

"I'm sure," I said confidently. "I'm sure I'm crazy enough to love you, Austin."

Fifty

Austin

THE WAIT WAS OVER. My future no longer presented itself in black and gray. Instead, it was colored by the endless ways Elle ignited my soul.

Hand in hand, we walked into the room where it had all begun. No words could prove how I felt. No more apologies or gifts. I needed to *show* her how happy she made me. Her return and confession in the kitchen had been enough to free me from my restraints.

Elle Madelyn was finally mine.

My girl scanned the guest room like a broken bobblehead doll, her forehead scrunching at the realization that her belongings remained scattered where she'd left them. Untouched.

"I never put your things away in case you decided to come back one day," I admitted.

"Have you even washed the sheets since I left?" Her grin as she admired the unmade bed was stolen straight from *Mona Lisa*.

Was I obsessed? Yes. Did I care anymore if she knew it? No.

"Of course not. It was my reminder that you existed and weren't just a fever dream."

I released her hand, not because I wanted to, but so I could look at her better when she slowed. She stopped before reaching the bed.

"That's not creepy at *allll*," she said. Her last word stretched longer than the rest.

I chuckled.

"Men in love do terrible things. You're lucky that's all I did."

"Are there ... other things you wish you had done, Chief?" She stepped closer, challenging me.

The word *Chief* hissed as it left her lips and sank its teeth into my dick with a venomous bite.

My Navy days might have been behind me, but she could call me Chief for the rest of my damn life. The impact of the word spread through my groin. I shut the door behind us before returning to her.

"Why don't you get on the bed and let me show you?"

My request barely touched the air before I grabbed what was mine by both shoulders and sat her sternly on the edge of the mattress. Elle bit down and softly sucked one corner of her bottom lip.

I couldn't look away.

She was even more cosmic now that she finally saw me for who I really was—hers.

"If I ask nicely, will you take off your clothes?" I continued, needy. I'd beg if I had to. Adrenaline spread like lava through my veins.

She was a masterpiece in high-waisted jeans and a skintight vanilla sweater that blended seamlessly with her chest and neck. I noticed her French manicure too—my perfectly polished beauty.

"Isn't that your job? What happened to the Austin from the woodshed? He'd never ask nicely." She beamed.

Her thumb rose and drew a line from my cheek to the corner of my mouth. She deserved to see the parts of me I'd kept hidden under aliases of professionalism and gentleness the last time I saw her.

Her wish was my command.

"It's time for you to prove you're not going to take off on me again. So, I'll say it a little less nicely this time. Take. Off. Your. Fucking. Clothes. Before. I. Shred. Them."

"Or what? Is Big Bad Chief Carterson gonna get the surveillance camera hooked up and expose me to all my secret admirers?" she sassed.

Oh, she'd poked the bear.

"Mmm."

My angel had a dark side that was equal parts inviting and hypnotic. My eyes closed. My boxers tightened. Every inch of me begged for release.

Silky honey hair was the only thing remaining on her bare shoulders after she obeyed my command. I stepped back to admire the girl who had stolen my heart piece by piece. Elle quickly shimmied her pants off as if she were allergic to every thread.

"Good girl. Finally listening to the man who has known what's good for you this whole time. If only you'd listened sooner, we could have avoided all our lonely nights."

I couldn't help pausing to admire her. Her tits were perfect in every sense of the word, even more so with the snowflake pendant and delicate chain stopping short of her breasts. I made a mental note to buy her more jewelry because seeing her wear something I'd picked out made my dick pulse.

Throb.

Her nipples hardened under the cold air—my new favorite part of living in Illinois. My trance remained intact until Elle dragged her white lace panties down her legs, fracturing my attention.

She was pure magic.

"If you *actually* knew what was good for me, you'd shut your mouth and kiss me..." She scooted higher onto the bed, purposefully putting an additional foot of distance between us.

Her doe-eyed gaze never left mine. Our time apart had strengthened her resolve. I loved it.

I fixated on the glossiest lips I'd ever seen, knowing they'd taste even sweeter than they looked.

They did.

"Yummy," I growled lightly into the skin next to her mouth. The flavor of her cotton-candy lip gloss brought me back to the Navy Pier. Slowly, I straddled her and pulled my lips away, less than an inch from hers, pausing before barely tasting them again.

And again. And again. And again.

Until it became fatal for both of us to hold back any longer.

My cock hardened.

"I think I've proven that I know the difference between what's good for you and bad for you, haven't I?" I whispered.

"Not recently," she panted.

The good-girl facade came naturally to her, but her heavy, lustful expression told me she was ready to be something other than innocent. Goose bumps crawled up her stomach and arms when I traced the heart-shaped freckle below her collarbone with my tongue.

She sighed, loving it.

"Do you trust me?"

Her brow arched. "I'm here, aren't I?" Without hesitation, she released the words into my atmosphere, filling my brain with the trust she'd found in me again.

Her sweet, feminine scent multiplied my cravings as she stared at me.

I imagined her touching herself to thoughts of my mouth on her, my cock in her, and my memory flowing through her since the last time she had been in my arms. Shock waves pummeled my stomach at the thought.

"Last time I walked away for five minutes, you vanished," I stated. I gently placed her hands above her head onto the mattress, then continued, "This time, I have a plan." My warning wasn't faux; it was focused. I grabbed the roll of black paracord sitting on my nightstand.

When I couldn't sleep, I often spent the time sharpening the rope-tying techniques I taught my recruits. Square knots, clove hitches—I could tie hundreds of variations of nautical knots with my eyes closed.

"Do I have your permission to tie you to the bed so you can't run away again?" I asked ever so politely.

Elle's face ignited. "You have my permission to do whatever you want to me ..." she moaned feather-light, shifting her bare hips—the ones calling out for me.

My teeth met, and my lips parted in answer. I hovered, holding most of my weight in my legs as I brought her hands to the bedposts and secured them one by one. I'd never hurt her, but it sure was fun, proving to myself that she was mine in a real way. No more lies separated us.

"Handy stuff, this paracord, huh?" I sounded calm, but the view from above my girl suffocated me.

Her back kissed the sheets, and she winced, the stiff cord lightly nipping her wrists. The knots weren't tight, but they were rigid enough to create some friction. To gently mark her as mine.

"Should I stop?" I stroked her cheek, unwilling to cause her anything but pleasure.

"Please don't ..." she begged.

I heard it in her heartbeat, the way her lean stomach rose and fell with the same desire pummeling mine. She needed me as badly as I needed her.

I ran both hands down her arms, pulling them away just before finding her neck. Bowing to her, I ducked my head and licked, savoring the taste of her salted candy skin. Her back muscles faded deeper into the bed, accepting their fate as I continued my invasion.

"That feels incredible. You're not allowed to stop," she ordered, breathy.

I paused, skimming her body until it reached her face.

"Oh, I don't plan to. *Ever*, Elle. You're mine."

The bedposts quivered, jolting with every little nip I administered to her flawless skin. She moaned again when I approached her wide hips.

They were my favorite gateway drugs.

"Any last words before I eat you for dinner, dessert, and a midnight snack?" I asked.

"Austin, please ... I ..."

The cat had her tongue, but my tongue was about to catch that tasty little cat.

One thigh rested between my heated cheek and tattooed arm. I pulled her other leg toward me, resting it opposite the other. It was more than enough to send me over the edge. We were from two different worlds, but those differences had built us. Differences had no power when the tides were in control.

No doubt remained that they had been exactly what brought her back to me.

I planted a kiss into the crease separating her thigh from the depths of her and paused, delaying the touch a few seconds too long. I placed a second kiss, this time closer to heaven. One final swipe of my tongue grazed the last centimeter separating my taste buds from her clit.

"I need you ... now," she whined.

The sound struck me deep in my core.

I whispered into her, "Finally."

Finally, she needed me like I needed her.

Desperately.

I broke the distance between us, and my tongue dived into her like rain meeting the ocean, neither of us able to distinguish what was her and what was me. Her pussy and my mouth were a single cresting, jumbled wave.

I let it pull me under.

"You taste so ... fucking ... sweet." I nipped, every word separated by a flattened flick of my ravenous, starved tongue.

There wasn't much I loved more than making out with the swollen, salivating parts of Elle spread open before me. No matter how much of her dripped down my throat or my chin, it would never be enough to quench my insatiable thirst for her.

I quickened, allowing her shivers to guide my pace and my movements wildly left and right.

"Come on, baby. I need more of you. Show me how much you missed me." I spoke into my microphone.

The sentence vibrated her legs on impact. Her steady moans and the erratic tremble of her thighs told me she was close. But I didn't need her close.

I needed her so far past the edge that she'd never forget whose mouth she had been made for.

"*Ahhh*, yes ..." she cried out.

Finally, she crumbled around me. Her thighs tightened around my temples while I savored her release.

My smile dissolved into her. I took great pleasure in the satisfaction I brought her. Not only did she deserve it, but it turned me on in ways that receiving pleasure of my own never could. My gorgeous girl reeled, radiating from every inch of her overwhelmed body. Slowly, her breathing steadied as she joined me back on earth.

"Untie me," she urged, attempting to sit up quicker than I'd anticipated. She couldn't though, her restraints keeping her in place.

"But I'm not quite done with you yet. I ..." I spread my palm and fingers wide against her stomach, halting her.

"I'm serious. Untie me," she ordered.

Oh no, had I gone too far? I obliged immediately, unwilling to push her past her limits. The paracord securing her unraveled, falling onto the corners of the bed as soon as I untied the knots.

With her freedom came a sudden, devious grin. She eagerly motioned to reverse our positions and climbed my body, mounting it like it was hers.

Without a doubt, it was.

Relief overtook me. No longer the rag doll being thrown around, my girl became the puppeteer.

I was more than happy to be her puppet.

"I love you," she whispered, nestling her nose into my neck, her legs draping my sides.

"I loved you first."

I wrapped my arms around her waist, feeling like a completely new man since her return to Haroldeen Lane.

The best night of my life was just getting started, and all I could think about was the time I'd spent wishing she were mine.

But I didn't have to anymore because, finally, she was.

Fifty-One

Elle

"Cream, my love?" Austin chirped when I entered the kitchen.

Delighted, I nodded. Coffee sounded therapeutic. The happiness draped across his face as he issued a splash of creamer into my mug and approached me with it was nothing short of serene.

"I could get used to this," I confessed, admiring the solo sex show before me, wearing nothing but sweat socks and a black apron loosely knotted above his ass cheeks.

Is this really my life now? I thought after he handed me my coffee with a wink.

The girl's girl in me wanted to snap a photo for Ruthie, but the view was so spectacular that it kept me from sharing it with anyone.

The way he looked at me with hope in his eyes invigorated me.

How he'd waited for me patiently for months impressed me.

But the way Austin's little gestures made me feel seen for every bit of who I was told me I'd made the right decision. Yes, that level of attention would take time to get used to, but I smiled, realizing it would be time well spent as I settled into my new job, life, and apartment—an apartment that would sit empty if Austin didn't stop making me feel so darn good.

My eyes glazed over his body as if it were a doughnut, tempting me to take a bite. Every crest, every bulge, every scratch of ink tortured me with temptation.

He was a literal masterpiece.

"I'm going to start calling you The Thickening because you seriously have the most incredible ass I have ever seen," I said nervously.

He cackled, the sound warming my compliment and soul.

"Did you notice anything ... different about me last night?" Austin asked. His shoulders shrank, and he itched his head.

"In what way?" I shot him a look of concern.

What had I missed? It wasn't like I'd forgotten our anniversary or something.

"Like, for example, perhaps somewhere in this area ..." Austin's index finger outlined the space on his right side, semi-concealed by his apron.

I studied his skin from where I stood, still unsure of what he was getting at.

"Why don't you undo these apron ties and come find out?"

He set our mugs down on the countertop and scooted his bare butt in my direction. Along with being devastatingly hot, he was also adorable—a combination deadly enough to lay any woman to rest.

I plucked one end of the apron ties and pulled, loosening the fabric only secured by the loop hugging the back of his neck. When I lifted the front of the apron to reveal whatever he was getting at, a new vertically placed image, covering several inches of the side of his ribs, appeared.

"Oh my gosh, what the hell did you do?!" I gasped.

My hand sprang toward my face to conceal the shock that dipped my jaw toward the floor. The doughnut I planned to devour had a new sprinkle.

A permanent one.

"Whatever are you talking about, my love?"

There was a reason he wasn't making eye contact—and I knew exactly what that reason was the moment I saw it.

"When did you decide to add ... *that* to your collection?" I lowered further and touched his side, leaning in for a better look. He took the apron from my grip and pulled it over his head, removing it fully. "Wait, Austin ... is that—holy shit ... you didn't ..."

"Oh, but I did," he replied deviously.

I'd always wondered what it would feel like to be with someone obsessed with me. Now I knew how it felt.

Intoxicated, I stared at the fresh tattoo carved into Austin's side.

Reminiscent of a pose that long-lost lovers might strike after finding each other at the end of a hard-fought war, a man dipped a woman back and leaned in for a kiss. The inspiration behind the ink felt familiar. The woman kissing the man had blonde hair about my length and a body type like mine. A short sundress flowed around her legs. The man she kissed wore a Navy dress uniform while he clasped a stack of envelopes in the hand that wrapped the woman's waist—*our letters*.

If swooning were an Olympic sport, I'd win gold.

If surprising me with bold, romantic gestures were, he would.

"I don't even know what to say. It's … incredible. When did you do this?" My heart fluttered.

"When you kept me waiting for far too long …" he said.

"You knew I'd come back, didn't you?" I assumed.

He nodded, grabbing my arm and pulling me into him. His lower back rested against the countertop. I kissed him as if I needed him—because I did.

"I forced myself to give you all the time you needed to find your way back because I knew if you ever did, I wouldn't be able to let go."

Tingles spread like softened butter down my limbs with every word he spoke. He had known I'd be back—he had that much faith in our connection. It was a level of confidence I'd kill for.

"Do you like it?" he asked, playfully nudging my arm.

"What, the tattoo or the obsessie-possessie confession?" I giggled.

His lips parted slightly as he reached for my steaming mug of coffee and brought it to my lips, inviting me to take a sip. So, I did, not realizing how sexy having a man pour something warm and sweet into my mouth could be.

"Hmm, both?" He continued to tempt me with his satiated grin. It looked delectable, plastered across his stubble-lined face.

It was nice, not having a reason to avoid looking at him.

"As sexy as your honesty is, I must return it to you." I stepped back. "I think we can both agree that honesty is best, going forward. Right? The tattoo is a big gesture …" I admitted.

Watching his chin drop and his ego clean the floor crushed me.

"But I still fucking love it," I added.

Being sassy with Austin was fun; the wash of relief that cleansed his expression and rewarded me made it even more enjoyable.

"See, I do know you. I knew you'd love it!" Austin lifted me onto the counter, threading my legs around his waist.

"Okay, secret lover, is there anything you *don't* know about me?"

"I'm sure some things remain undiscovered. Good thing I have time to figure them out."

He had an answer for everything. Thankfully, so did I.

"I move into my new apartment in a few days, so you'll have to make your discoveries quickly."

"Oh, I have a sneaking suspicion you won't be spending much time there." Austin confidently stared down the bridge of his nose, knowing he was right. "I *do* have some things to tell you before then though …"

He slid a chair out from the edge of his kitchen table with his foot, carried me to it, and sat me down. I laughed before he lowered into the seat across from me.

"Eight months is a long time." He paused.

The way his hand lay flat on the table, palm up, waiting for me to grab it, told me all I needed to know. I placed my trust in his hand and gripped it.

"In that time, we've both had to make big decisions. I thought making them without the other's influence would be best. Just in case …" he said.

Sadness blanketed his remark, confusing me. I nodded supportively anyway.

What is he getting at?

"I made two huge decisions in that time." Another pause. "One of them being … I got out of the Navy. Permanently."

"Oh my God. What?! Why?"

"I loved my time serving. The Navy gave me a purpose that nothing else could. It will always be a major part of my life. One I'll never forget. It's an accomplishment I will always be proud of. It also brought me you."

My fingers tightened around his. Not only did I respect his decision, but I craved a deeper understanding of it.

"But it always held me back from other things I wanted to accomplish in my life …" He trailed off. Austin brought his free hand to the back side of mine, both his hands consuming my dainty one. "For years, I tried to find someone worth pursuing a relationship with. And I knew the moment you landed in my life that I wanted to see what that would feel like. For the first time, you gave me that feeling. I had to try with you. Step one was making you mine. Step two is making you happy and giving you the life you deserve, one with someone who wants to be the best he can be for you ... which brings me to the second big decision I made ..."

Was this what it felt like to be with someone who cared as much about your future as they did theirs? It had to be ... because how could it feel any better than his words did? I stared into my future with renewed faith and a contentedness held on with Austin-certified adhesive.

"And what's the second decision you made, Chief?" My neck tilted, and my concentration zeroed in on his mouth.

"Well ... I've decided to give the woodworking thing a real shot. It's not official yet, but I know I'm good at it. And I know that I love it. I trademarked the name The Chief's Woodshed, and I've been selling firewood throughout the winter to carry me while working on furniture and sculptures in my free time. I've got a big meeting next week with Trelis Hotels about a possible commission for their new lodge near the base. I want to see where it takes me."

"Wow, that's incredible, Austin. I can't think of anything more you! I want to see everything you've been working on. I'm sure your pieces are as spectacular as you are ..."

"It's a big change, lonely at times," he sighed before smiling widely. "But not anymore ..."

Austin tugged at my hands, showering me with a complimentary gush of praise. I knew exactly what he meant. I felt it too.

"Not anymore," I agreed. My jaw expanded, accommodating my toothy grin.

I rose from the table, circled, and sank into my man's lap like I'd found the start of my forever. Without anxiety or doubts holding me back, I realized I finally had.

My arms wrapped around his neck when I brought my mouth to his, savoring his truth as it swept me away. If the way he looked at me between each gentle suck and pause told me anything I didn't already know, it was that because of him, I was sure of three things.

I am calm, I am safe, and we are finally together.

Austin Carterson was mine. All mine.

Fifty-Two

Austin

Three Months Later

Our story isn't perfect, but *it's perfect for us*, I thought, hitting snooze on the alarm clock on my nightstand like I hadn't already been awake for hours.

I looked over at Elle, whose constant smile, even when she slept, told me that relaxation had followed her into her dreams. Three months had passed since she had come back to me. Admiring her never got old.

Sure, I was up, but my day didn't start before she touched me. She stirred, her leg resting over mine. Our sheets tightened with her soft movements.

"Morning, babe. Did you sleep well?" A fake yawn left my lips, my attempt to counter the anticipation of the day ahead.

"I slept sweet, if that's what you meant." She beamed.

A feeling of knowing hugged my heart like a mitten. I loved it when Elle pulled words from our letters into the real world. It meant she'd come to love them as much as I had.

"Shit, does that say seven? I've got a session at eight fifteen! I gotta go, like now!" Panic stole her calm.

She stood far too quickly and rushed around the room, struggling to compose herself.

"What can I do?" I offered, slightly guilty that my schedule was shaping up to be less demanding than hers.

It was okay though; every ounce of stress she felt would leave her in the next few hours when she learned what I had in store. There was so much to do to set my plan into motion. The longtime, award-winning poker face I'd earned in my downtime with the recruits served me well.

"A coffee to go would be amazing. Can't taint our weekend by starting a Friday morning without caffeine." One leg at a time, Elle hopped into her dress pants—a tantalizing view I looked forward to drooling over for the rest of my days. "Are your clients still coming over for dinner tonight?" she asked.

Even while scrambling to get her shit together, she still found time to remember mine. Her half-naked body continued gathering clothing from multiple drawers simultaneously, like a breathtaking, disarranged tornado.

She still blew me the fuck away.

"Yeah, they are. I tried to cancel, but they insisted on meeting with me while they were in town," I lied. I'd sworn I'd never lie to her again, but this time was the exception. I knew she'd agree.

"No worries. I only have four sessions today. I'll bring a change of clothes and my makeup bag to freshen up after lunch. They'll never know I came straight from work," she said.

I knew she only had four sessions scheduled for the day because I'd discussed them in detail with her boss, who promised to give her an extra-long afternoon break so she'd have plenty of time to change and feel refreshed before the big surprise.

Twenty minutes later, my girl hurried through the house with a to-go coffee in hand. She kissed my lips tenderly and ran out the door I held open for her, never forgetting the meaningful gesture, no matter how busy she was.

"See you later, Chief. Can't wait to meet your new clients tonight and tell them how gifted you are with your hands ..." She winked.

"Oh, I'm counting on it. You're good for business." It was true.

With Elle's help, I was already championing a hobby group for disabled veterans at the hospital and working on my latest top-secret commission.

One she would see when the time was right.

Leaning into a post on my front porch, I waved and said, "I love you."

"I love you more." Elle blew me another kiss before hopping in the front seat of my Jeep.

I hated seeing her go, but loved watching her climb into my car. The Ol' Green Goddess never looked sexier than with my dream girl in the driver's seat.

The engine sprang to life, leaving me closer than ever to the most important day of my life.

God, my grandparents would have been proud. They'd have loved her like they'd loved me.

Like they'd loved each other.

Fifty-Three

Elle

NO, MY OFFICE DIDN'T HAVE a corner window or a view of the city. But I had my own freaking office.

I couldn't be happier.

"Ms. Madelyn, you look gorgeous, as always. Hot date tonight?" my boss, Dr. Isabella DeRossi, complimented me before sitting on the therapy couch across from my desk.

Since I'd started, she'd proven to be a real girl's girl, showing me around the hospital and providing critical support when needed. As the department's lead psychiatrist, what she said went. Her availability, presence, and positive attitude had motivated me more than she probably realized. I envied the way she led a team.

"Austin has some new clients meeting us for dinner tonight, so I'm trying to make a good first impression. He really deserves this opportunity. I'm excited for him." Pride possessed my posture. I meant every word.

Dr. DeRossi's short jet-black hair sat perfectly angled just below her chin. Her stunning cream suit reminded me that on a lengthy list of words one could use to describe her, fashionista sat close to the top.

"The department loves the work he's done here. He seems like a great guy. I'm happy for you two. And talk about a gorgeous couple ... I mean, *wow*." Her hands came together, clasping in front of her chest.

She meant it.

"Thank you, Doctor. We both very much enjoy our time here." A rosy hue, matching my freshly applied lipstick, flushed my cheeks. "I've actually been enjoying *everything* Illinois has to offer, if you know what I mean …"

I chuckled, feeling more comfortable with her than I probably should have. Her laughs met mine. Ruthie would smack me if she saw me chatting and laughing with another female.

"Only one more session, and you'll be on your way," she chirped, wide-eyed. Isabella stood before continuing, "Enjoy your weekend. I'll let your next appointment know you're ready for them."

Before I could thank her, she left the room and gently closed the door. I brushed the breast of my button-up top, ensuring it was wrinkle-free.

A candle flickered on the corner of my desk, adding to the relaxing ambiance of my office.

"So you'll never forget the smell of home," Ruthie had told me when she gifted me the coconut-breeze-scented candle the day I left Pensacola. "Or the taste of it," she'd added, stuffing a healthy piece of her famous strawberry Danish into my mouth.

God, I missed her.

Minutes later, a knock on the door signaled it was go time. One more hour, and I'd be in my man's arms. I stood from my chair, ready to greet the next person who entered. The ritual I'd learned in grad school was how I began every appointment—to always rise to the occasion of helping someone heal.

"What the …" I froze, my next client not the one I'd anticipated. "Ruthie? Oh my God, Mom! Dad?!" Shocked, I dived around my desk and into the arms of my favorite people—the embraces as loving as they were unexpected.

Ruthie spun me around, stealing my attention and pinning my arms to my sides tighter than I'd have expected she could. My mother never let go of my hand, gripping it behind me.

"Surprise, bitch! Ellie Vanellie and Ruths are back at it again!" Ruthie yelped.

Tears rolled down my face, dampening my makeup. Who cared though?

I'd never been happier.

"We missed you so much, my baby," my mother said lovingly as she made her way behind Ruthie to see me better.

Sleep Sweet

"I missed you all too, Mama Goose," I whimpered, squeezing her hand while still tangled in my best friend's arms.

"Move it, Ruthie. I think dear old Daddio deserves the next hug. My little girl made it! I mean, look at this office." My dad scanned the room in a way that tripled my pride. "You did it, honey. Your mother and I couldn't be prouder."

Like I was a pinball, my biggest fans passed me around, their happiness holding me upright while they took turns wiping the liquid love that continued to melt my eyeliner.

"I can't believe this. You're actually here. When did you all arrive? Where's everyone staying?" I stepped back, taking them all in.

Three months was the longest I'd been away from my parents or Ruthie since we'd met—our endearing reunion proved it. I craned my neck around the room, hoping Austin would appear. He'd had something to do with the surprise—I was sure of it.

That was when I saw him.

Our eyes fused, calming my nerves instantly. That was, until he stepped fully into my view, wearing an outfit that would bring any woman to her knees—a classic, tailored black suit.

As if he were parting the cerulean sea, Austin approached me in slow motion and walked through the center of my family like he was already part of it.

I had a feeling that he would be someday soon.

Out of the corner of my eye, I watched my dad hand Austin a small box, his attempt at nonchalance sorely missing the mark. I was glad because my father's involvement in whatever was happening meant the world to me. It meant my family supported us.

Everything had happened so quickly for Austin and me—our beginning, our separation, and our reunion.

The moment he sank to one knee before me was no different.

"Oh my God …" I whispered.

He lifted his head and poured life into my soul, the one forever anchored to his.

My hand trembled when he grasped it and began, "I have no doubt I loved you in a past life." Confidence carried his meaningful words. "I want to love you until we move on from this one so I can find you all over again in the next because getting to you was the adventure of a lifetime."

We smiled in unison, entertaining the irony.

"I can't think of anything more meant to be than us, and I'll spend forever proving that to you." He beamed. "There was no better way for me to ask you this than surrounded by the people who built you. I'm obsessed with you and with us. And I need to know …" Austin swung the small box my dad had handed to him to the front of his body, took back his hand, and split it in two, presenting a ring so uniquely beautiful that it had to be vintage.

The oval diamond, resting upon a yellow-gold setting, was entwined with intricate vines of small emerald stones. Its gleaming center, surrounded by little drops of green, stole my breath.

"This was my grandmother's ring. She would have loved you so much. They both would have," Austin released. A lone tear fell from my future's right eye.

Of all the things we'd been through, seeing him cry wasn't one of them. Apparently, one Austin tear equaled fifty of my own because mine multiplied the moment I noticed his.

"Elle Madelyn … my dream girl … my pen pal … my angel, my world, will you marry me?"

I paused, just long enough to allow the moment to sear into my memory.

"Of course I'll marry you," I answered without a second thought.

Austin slid the ring onto my finger, lifted my heels from the floor, and swung me around. He gripped my waist tightly, reminding me it wasn't the first time his strength had taken me higher. My legs wrapped around his waist, and I inhaled my peace.

A string of sniffles, claps, and congratulations surrounded us. My family gathered around Austin and me as we kissed, lost in each other.

"How the hell did you pull this off?" I whispered into his ear.

"You're in for a lifetime of surprises, I'm afraid. I hope you're ready …"

I melted into his neck with a satisfied smile.

There were things about Austin and me that I would always wonder about—questions even he couldn't answer, although I'd never asked. Because the answers didn't matter; it only mattered that we'd ended up exactly where we were meant to be.

Together.

Would we still have found each other if my letters to Jesse had never reached him? If Austin had never written back to me or waited for me to show up on graduation day? Would I have accepted the position in Chicago and met him in passing at work or at a nearby coffee shop? Would we have matched on a dating site or bumped into each other while he was in Pensacola for work or a weekend away?

No matter how we had been brought together or who'd had a hand in ensuring our paths crossed, one thing was for sure: as soon as I'd stopped fighting the tides, they'd pulled me to the place I was meant to be—anchored to the most incredible person I'd ever met.

The man I could spend endless lifetimes loving.

Who would love me with equal parts intention and dedication because we both knew the rewards outweighed the effort.

My future husband, Austin *fucking* Carterson.

Bonus Letter

March 2012

CPO CARTERSON

CONFIDENTIAL COMMUNICATIONS

Dear Mr. Tony Madelyn,

I am writing to share information that I believe would greatly benefit you. I do not have children of my own, but if I did, I would want to be well informed if their health and/or safety were in jeopardy. I have reason to believe that your daughter, Elle, is in danger of settling into a future with the wrong man—a man far below the kind she deserves.

Ships can't travel in the direction they're destined for if they're anchored in the wrong location, and Elle is currently tied to a man who is disrespecting her beyond belief.

Recruit Jesse Jenkins joined my division in February and was recently caught on surveillance performing sexual acts with a female recruit in a storage locker. Not only is coed mingling against policy, but it is unacceptable behavior for a man of his fortune. Fortune so good that he somehow had the privilege of being with your daughter.

Recruit Jenkins has been removed from the boot camp training program and will remain in a holding division until his disciplinary review is complete and further action is determined. It could be weeks or months; I have no set date yet.

I was responsible for cleaning out Jesse's bunk and personal belongings, and in doing so, I came across the letters he had exchanged with Elle—letters that your daughter had poured her heart and soul into as she counted down the days until Recruit Jenkins's graduation ceremony.

Her letters display a level of dedication that I'm sure you are incredibly proud of. As I explained, Jesse will not attend his graduation ceremony on March 31st, but I know your daughter has already planned to fly to Illinois and stay for the weekend.

If Elle's letters indicate the type of person she is and the kind of family she comes from, the brand of broken trust she will experience when she arrives will be earth-shattering.

She deserves so much more.

With this being said, I do not want to start on a lie with you, so I will tell you the truth before making my request—I have been writing letters back to your daughter, in Jesse's name, since he was caught.

Sir, I must apologize ahead of time, but I could not allow the flow of letters to her to stop and break the spirit of such a pure soul. Reading through their letters was an invasion of privacy, but it was also incredibly eye-opening to learn that people like your daughter existed. People with drive and ambition, loyalty and grace, humor and intelligence.

I feel drawn to her in ways I can't explain.

With your permission, I'd like to explain this situation to Elle in person and show her video evidence of Jesse's wrongdoings so she can move on with her life and never look back.

I assure you that I have her best interests at heart and will do everything I can to soften the blow of her heartbreak, offering her support in any way possible.

Surprisingly, I met Elle at Coastal Pensacola College several years back. I believe she will feel comfortable with me, having met me before.

Maybe I'm not the man for her. But there's a chance fate has brought us together in this unusual way to teach us something. I will never push your daughter into a relationship; I know she will need time to heal. My only goal is to prove to Elle that good men still exist in the world so she can keep her heart open to the right man when the time is right for her.

I would never do any of this without your permission.

Please call me at the number listed below so that I can answer any questions you may have. I would love the opportunity to get to know you as well. I want to ensure that you feel comfortable with my role in this situation.

One day, I hope we can show Elle this letter together and reflect on our beginning. Until then, I'd like your permission to help Elle the same way she has helped me—by ensuring that no matter which direction the winds take her, she anchors herself exactly where she deserves to be.

I am greatly looking forward to speaking with you and perhaps meeting you someday.

All my best,

Austin

Acknowledgments

TO MY HUSBAND, YOU INSPIRED the hell out of me the entire way through, just like you always do. The best plot-hole-pointer-outer, brainstorm partner, and my best friend. *Our* letters were just the beginning of our story. I'll forever look back at them with happy tears and gratitude, knowing where they led us. My greatest adventure will always be you. I love you beyond words.

Rebecca and Jett, the ultimate hype team. I told you about my "little hobby" three years before *Sleep Sweet* was written, and you both smiled quietly, *confidently*. Together, you've shown me, and everyone around you, what true love looks like. *Dedication* is the word that comes to mind when I think of the love you have for each other. Thank you both for encouraging me to pursue this story and the ones that I hope will come after it. Your support means more to me than you'll ever know.

G-Babe, what can I say? You're my role model for more reasons than I can count. Anytime I was anxious about this project, I called you. Anytime I needed to know if something was awesome or lame, I called the coolest person I knew—*you*. Maybe you don't know it, but YOU helped me finish this book. Sometimes, I'm not sure you realize how special you are. Let me tell you, you're effing incredible. I'm endlessly thankful that we were paired up together all those years ago. Thank you for being you. I love you so much.

L.A. Martin, my beautiful, dark poet, the first soul to ever read a page of Austin and Elle's journey. I cannot thank you enough for the energy you surrounded me with while I very, very slowly wrote this story. Chapter by chapter, you assured me that these characters were good enough. That *I* was good enough. I hope you know how amazing you are. If you're 18+ and enjoy angsty, dark poetry full of trigger warnings, check out @l.a.martinwrites on Instagram.

Marni, your words and presence are a gift to the world. I can only hope to share the support, genuineness, knowledge, kindness, and encouragement you've shown me with someone else one day. You taught me that words have the power to change someone's life, as yours have truly changed mine. You also taught me that I can't eat Greek food when I'm nervous because *how* did I not finish those delicious meatballs that day?! They were amazing, but your company was better. All I can say is, THANK YOU FOR EVERYTHING!

Rachel Rowlands, you are absolutely wonderful! I am thankful that, somehow, our paths crossed halfway around the world. You've taught me so much. You know *just* how to say things that need to be said while leaving room for creativity and growth. One day, I hope we can meet for coffee and chat in person—perhaps at the Cat Café?

Jovana Shirley, thank you for guiding me in ways I didn't know I needed. I am *honored* to have worked with you and appreciate your professionalism, kindness, and endless knowledge. You're amazing!

Andy Payne, you took a million thoughts and created something beautiful. Thank you for accommodating my ideas and never making me feel crazy.

Pamela, Elizabeth, and Em—you ladies are simply the best! Thank you for taking the time to read this book and provide feedback. I am honored that you three were involved in this process, and I'll never forget it!

E.V. Richards, positivity is not always easy to find these days. Thank you for your support, bookish memes, and encouragement. You helped me feel less alone. I appreciate you and can't wait to finally meet for a long-awaited iced coffee!

To my readers, THANK YOU for taking the time to read my book. If you read *Sleep Sweet*, it means you took a chance on me. I appreciate your support!!! There are dozens of times I thought about never releasing Austin and Elle into the world, but then I imagined them finding readers who would love them as much as I do. Thank you for encouraging me to do something completely out of my comfort zone without even knowing it.

About the Author

ERICA EASTON WRITES STEAMY ROMANCES featuring morally gray heroes and tempting twists. She is the proud wife of a United States Navy veteran, which allows her to bring an authentic perspective to her military storylines. When she isn't reading or writing, she spends her time making memories with her friends and family and dreaming up her next love story.

She resides in sunny Southwest Florida and has degrees in psychology and health science, two fields that fuel her love of writing about emotions, desires, and the fictional human experience.

Erica loves to connect with her readers!

www.ericaeaston.com

Instagram: @hotpantsreadsromance

www.ingramcontent.com/pod-product-compliance
Ingram Content Group UK Ltd.
Pitfield, Milton Keynes, MK11 3LW, UK
UKHW042003230426
12048UKWH00009B/517